# CONFESSIONS
## — OF A —
# TRAVELOHOLIC
## || TO TRAVEL IS TO EVOLVE ||

## COL ASHISH RAISINGHANI

BlueRose
Publishers

First Published in May 2019

**ISBN:** 978-93-5347-375-4
**Price: INR** 449/-

BLUE ROSE PUBLISHERS
www.bluerosepublishers.com
info@bluerosepublishers.com
+91 8882 898 898

Cover Design:
Deepak Lal

Typographic Design:
Sonia Suyal

Distributed by: Blue Rose, Amazon, Flipkart, Shopclues

*Dedicated to*

**My Beloved Daughter Arianna**

*"We Travel not to Escape Life, But for Life not to Escape Us"*

AMITABH BACHCHAN

**March 25, 2019**

### REVIEW

Reading a travelogue is like traveling in itself. You open the pages and someone you've never met takes you far away. The book can become a companion for you, by bridging the gap between a person's inner self and a city's soul. It beautifully captures for you  the unmoored life of a traveler, guiding you to enjoy the essence and true character of a place, helping you to be flexible in your travel plans, be open to experiences, accept challenges and be ready for change because you will not be the same person on the other side of your journey.  This  book for the traveler, knows where it's at. The emotions are honest, non-melodramatic and non-superficial.

In an age of consumer travel where people think experience is something they can buy, this book with its travel tips, insights and information from years of traveling, bringing alive the everyday life of each place visited,  has enough  stories and tips to make you want to get on the road for as long as you can handle it.

**Amitabh Bachchan**

Col. Ashish Raisinghani
Engineer Branch
HQ South Western Command
Pin. 908 456
C/o. 56 APO
Email: archies_home@rediffmail.com

# Preface

*"Travel is the only thing you buy that makes you Richer"*

I am from the Armed Forces since last more than twenty years and my profession give me lot of opportunities to travel and see new places. However, I have been travelling much before I joined the Army and have received this 'Travel Bug' from my parents who themselves are avid travellers. So, the travelling commenced since I was a kid, first with my parents, then on my own or with friends and now with my family, as this Travel Bug has now got infused in my wife and my three year old daughter as well. I love to see new places, meet new people & learn everything about that place, my area of expertise being Trip Planning & Budget Travel. I don't prefer organized tours & package trips, as I feel the true essence of travelling lies in experiencing that place with the locals, living & eating like locals. I have covered almost the entire India, and a lot of places abroad but my quest has not ended, in fact my hunger for travel keep increasing with each trip.

My travel experiences are of varying nature, which includes solo backpacking trips as well as backpacking trips with friends and family, road trips both by four wheeler as well as challenging bike rides, family holidays of all kinds with my wife, elderly parents and even with my small daughter. We have been travelling as a family now both within India and abroad, in fact, my daughter has already visited almost ten different countries in her first three years which included backpacking trip to Europe when she was 15 months old and bike trip to Bhutan when she was just 6 months old. I have been penning down my own travel experiences in form of Travelogues since last more than 15 years now. These travelogues cover not only my own trip experience in detail, but also give an insight about the place along with few practical tips for fellow travellers to plan their trip to the same region or place. I have compiled thirteen of these personal travel experiences in this Travel Book.

In my opinion travelling is an art in itself which everybody does it differently, but one common aspect remains in case of travel of any kind, and that is the fact that it's a continuous learning process from each other's experiences. The most experienced traveller would also look for some kind of advice or suggestion from fellow travellers or from travel guide books, before planning a new trip. There is no dearth of travel material or guidance available today with internet being a powerful tool and travel websites in plenty, still there is always a different kind of assurance which you get from personal 'first-hand' travel experiences of fellow travellers. Being a hard-core self-travel planner myself, this is one aspect I have also felt always while planning for any of my trips both within the country or abroad. Travel blogging is a very common thing these days but these travel blogs are restricted to being either very brief in giving information about a place or a trip, or they cover only few specific aspects at any given point of time. So, this calls for investing additional precious time to search for travel blogs of varied kinds for one single trip, and then extracting important aspects from all those blogs to plan your own trip effectively. This is where my book scores over the rest, as each of the travelogues included in the book not only gives out a very personalized experience of a real traveller, it also gives out details of the destination and also lists out few important practical tips for better assimilation and realistic travel planning – all of this compiled together in every chapter of the book.

Travel writing has come to me as an influence of subscribing to many travel magazines such as Lonely Planet, Outlook Traveller, Travel Plus etc all these years, wherein I have been highly impressed by all the travel writers who write for these magazines. My travelogues follow the same path as these articles in the magazines, however adding a personal touch and valuable travel tips, thereby making them a comprehensive travel information document about any region or location. The book is an interesting read, as the Thirteen Travelogues included in this book are of varied nature and written in a manner that any reader would be able to relate to the travelogue. I have shared these travelogues with few of my family members and I have been conveyed that when they were reading the travelogue, it was like they were 'living the trip' along with my experiences. So go ahead and 'Live these Trips' along with me as I bring to you, my personal travel experiences...from my bachelor trips to family trips...from challenging bike rides to backpacking trips with a baby...and from trekking expeditions to exploring exotic foreign locales...it's all there in these **'Confessions of a Traveloholic'** !!!

# Introduction

*"Tourists visit – Travellers explore"*

This line actually brings out the true essence of travelling and also sums up my entire book **'Confessions of a Traveloholic'**. It also brings out the very important difference between being a Traveller and a Tourist, which has been aptly brought out by Paul Theroux in his quote - *"Tourists don't know where they've been, Travellers don't know where they're going."* Each of the thirteen travelogues in the book brings out how tourists usually opt for conventional hassle-free organized package tours, while travellers will plan their own trips which would not only take more effort and time, but will also bring lot of uncertainty in their travel plans. But this uncertainty in your travel plan is what gives you the true happiness of exploring a place and being a traveller in the actual sense.

**"Confessions of a Traveloholic"** is a compilation of Thirteen Travelogues within the frame of a Travel Book which I want to share with rest of the world. The aim of publishing the book is to share my experiences with like-minded people and fellow travellers. As mentioned before that I have been an avid traveller since a very young age and have always believed in planning my own trips, and that is where going through travel experiences of others have always assisted me in making my own trip much better & easier. I had started penning down my travel experiences initially only as a personal record and to share with few close family and friends. However, when I got positive feedbacks from the family and friends who commented that these travelogues not only motivated them to travel but also assisted them in planning their trips, I decided to compile all these travel experiences of mine in one single book.

The travelogues in this book covers my personal travel experiences during a long span of period of almost twenty years, the first being of way back in 1998 and the last being as recent as 2018. This in itself brings out the variety of travel and types of trips I have made in all these years, starting as a bachelor and then travelling with my wife or my parents, and finally with my small daughter. The book is also extremely useful for the varied kinds of trips it covers in each of its chapters – ranging from difficult adventurous solo trips to comfortable family road trips, from unknown Indian destinations to exotic foreign locales, from challenging bike rides to backpacking trips with a baby and from camping-cum-trekking experiences to unconventional budget trips with friends. The book also contains few photographic illustrations compiled together from all travelogues and placed in the centre of the book, to actually give the reader feel of the place, as also relate to the text when they read it. The chapters are of varying lengths and the word limits range from about 2000 to more than 10000 for some of the travelogues. These travel experiences also contain few very useful and practical tips for readers which would actually assist them in planning their own trips. The chapters are deliberately called 'Travelogues' and have been placed in chronological order of occurrence year ranging between 1998 and 2018. You will also notice a change in vocabulary as also the choice of words being used as you progress ahead from first chapter, and would also notice a progressive increase in the word count of travelogues. This is mainly due to the fact that I started penning down my travel experiences more than fifteen years ago and have been continuously trying to improve upon my writing skills, at the same time gaining confidence in increasing the length of each travelogue with time.

The **First Travelogue** is from my Army training days in Indian Military Academy and is closest to my heart, as it has been a 'life-changing' experience for me. This was not only my first exposure to hard-core adventure activity of attempting to scale a 24,000 feet mountain peak, but also because of being in a near-death situation so early in my age, and hence became a life-defining moment for me. The writing in this travelogue is straight from my heart and will be very basic in terms of choice of words and writing style, but this is one travelogue which still gives goose-bumps to me and my family every time we read it – even after 20 years of the occurrence of the incident.

My life's first experience of a self-driven road trip forms part of my **Second Travelogue**, wherein two young Lieutenants of Indian Army took off in an 1986 model Maruti 800 car, in a region which was unexplored and untouched at that time – the 'Dev Bhoomi' of Himachal Pradesh. The trip was not only unique for its two travel companions using the old 'war-horse' transport, but also because of the fact that it was an unplanned and spontaneous road trip with no pre-planned travel agenda, no pre-arranged stay options and no pre-decided destinations in mind. This trip can also be recorded in golden words for Maruti Suzuki Car Company, as its first original Japanese engine Maruti 800 launched in India was taken all the way to Tibet border, where most of rugged vehicles also fail to reach.

The first of many foreign backpacking trips to follow is the **Third Travelogue** of the book, and it also saw slight promotion in the rank as this time three Captains took off on a backpacking trip to Europe on a shoe-string budget trip. We covered eight countries in eighteen days in the heart of mainstream Europe and the entire trip was planned on our own with extensive use of Eurail and Youth Hostels. It was kind of novelty for Europeans to see few Indian backpackers on this type of rugged budget trip in Europe roughing it out, as way back in 2005 it was not a common thing for an Indian traveller. The bonding created between three of us is still holding strong, mainly due to the ups and downs we went through during this 'Bachelor Europe Backpacking Trip' – living our 'Zindagi Na Milegi Dobara' moments more than ten years before the cult movie was released.

The **Fourth Travelogue** is again a very special trip for me as this was the first foreign trip with my new 'travel companion' – my wife. The trip was to the most commonly known and maybe the most economical foreign destination for any Indian traveller – South East Asia. In spite of taking my wife for her first abroad trip and being newly married, I still was brave enough to stick to my signature style of 'Budget Travel' and could complete a ten days Singapore – Malaysia trip at an unbelievable budget for a couple. It just required some smart planning and advance preparations, and mind it, this was much before Air Asia had any presence in India.

In the **Fifth Travelogue** I am covering a region which I consider not only the most picturesque mountainous destination in India but in the entire world (And I say this convincingly after visiting Swiss Alps, Scottish Highlands, Canadian Rockies and Southern Alps of New Zealand). This was my third visit to Ladakh (with all three being of different kinds – first one on bike with a batch mate, second one was a family trip, and this time on a rugged Scorpio with wife) and I must say that each time Ladakh offered me something more and something different. So, take this wonderful road journey with me into some of the remotest parts of this 'Heaven on earth' in this travelogue.

The **Sixth Travelogue** took me on a long family holiday to a country which can be described as a complete vacation destination for tourists of all ages and types – Canada. This was also the first time when our entire close family was together on a holiday, and we made the most out of it by covering this extremely beautiful country completely by road. Canada boasts of a vibrant eastern coast, highly picturesque central Rocky region and unique western coast. Our month and a half long journey comprised of covering the complete breadth of Canada and was highlighted by smooth roads, serene countryside, economical local stays at lovely Bed & Breakfast, wild & beautiful Rocky Mountains and pristine coastal towns. Canada is truly a travel destination where even 45 days seemed less and there was so much more to see.

I have been a big fan of Rocky & Mayur show – Highway on my Plate, and my **Seventh Travelogue** was something done in the HOMP style. It was an official posting from Pune to Bathinda for me, but I turned the movement part into a road trip across four states (and a Union Territory) exploring the highway Dhabas & local cuisines along the route. The eventful journey took us through the states of Maharashtra, Gujarat, Rajasthan and Punjab with a stopover at Daman, wherein we travelled without any fixed places to stay or any fixed places to eat. HOMP book was our Bible for the journey and it didn't disappoint us at all, giving us the culinary experience of local delicacies which you can't get in any top notch hotel or restaurant in any of the metro cities.

My next trip took me back to my bachelor days as I collaborated with one of my backpacking Europe trip co-traveller after a span of eight years and this time we decided to cover the country which got left out during our previous sojourn – United Kingdom. My **Eighth Travelogue** brings out a three week long backpacking trip with a friend in which we covered almost the entire UK, including Scotland, Wales, England and North Ireland. The main focus of this trip was to keep it under the folds of 'Budget Travel', as we were venturing into one of the costliest regions and the Pound-Rupee ratios was touching an all-time high during that time. But with precise planning and meticulous advance preparation, correct mix of road-rail-self driven transport and choosing economical Youth Hostels, we could get the perfect trip well within our budget.

The **Ninth Travelogue** is an interesting read for all those traveller parents who think that their travel days are over on arrival of a baby in their lives. I got the chance to go on an extremely challenging but a beautiful Bike Ride in the 'Land of Happy Dragon' – Bhutan, with few lovely bikers from various parts of the country. I grabbed the opportunity with both hands and also did the 'unthinkable', of taking my family along in a rented four-wheeler which included my six-month old daughter (while I carried on with others on bike). Read about the manner in which a toddler braved the adverse weather & road conditions along with rugged bikers as we covered the complete length of Bhutan, entering from the western side and exiting from the eastern side of this highly picturesque country.

The trip to Bhutan opened doors for me to expose my small daughter to more travel and my **Tenth Travelogue** gives you a detailed insight of how to go 'Backpacking with a Baby' in a foreign country. After lot of deliberations we homed on to Scandinavian region as our backpacking destination to be done with our 15-month old daughter. This was an absolutely fresh turf for me to play on and something I had never done during my entire travelling life. But both me & my wife took it head-on and did a three week long budget backpacking trip with our baby in Scandinavia & Europe. The trip turned out to be one of the most memorable ones for us, as we three bonded with each like never before during this trip and our baby took it as if she was a born-traveller. This particular travelogue will give you numerous practical tips and ideas of how to go about taking a backpacking trip anywhere with your little one, and not let anything come between you & your travel dreams.

In the **Eleventh Travelogue**, I am covering a Bike Ride which is considered to be one of the best biking trips in the world and to be any super-biker's dream ride – The North Thailand Superbike Ride. Being a hard-core Royal Enfield guy myself, it was a new challenge for me to go 'Vroom' on 500/650/800/1000 cc super bikes and that too on challenging mountainous terrain of North Thailand. This travelogue would open up a brand new horizon for all bikers to actually go on the road with me for this six day trip through my words. I have deliberately written this travelogue in a different manner, covering important aspects of prior preparations, route conditions, day-wise itinerary and then going over each day's ride in detail.

My **Twelfth Travelogue** covers another delightful trip which would be music to the ears of young parents with small kids, as we embarked on a full-fledged Camping-cum-Trekking trip with our two-year old daughter. This trip was unique in many ways due to the fact that one, it was completely planned on our own (and not going with any camping package tour company) and two, it was not in any mainstream hill destination. We chose Parvati Valley in Himachal for carrying out camping & trekking with our small child, and picked up couple of Himachali homestays apart from the camping site as our abode for experiencing the true essence of being in wilderness with your loved ones. Do read this travelogue to remove all misnomers about 'roughing it out' with a child, as I bring out the facts how my 'travel-groomed' daughter just loved this experience.

The last and **Thirteenth Travelogue** would take you on a mesmerising journey 'down under' to one of the most picturesque island countries in the world – New Zealand. This is the most recent and last of the family foreign trips done by me in the year 2018 itself, and with conviction I can call New Zealand as one of the best countries I have visited till now. We again went there as a family with my daughter being almost three-year old and covered quite a bit of New Zealand in about twenty five days. The South Island road trip was the highlight of the trip and the travelogue brings out nicely why NZ is called as the 'Adventure Hub of the World' and how there's something for everybody here. Another very important aspect which makes this travel destination more attractive for Indian tourist is the fact that our driving license is valid here and driving is exceptionally easy and comfortable means of exploring this wonderful country.

**'Confessions of a Traveloholic'** is my first attempt at writing a book and I can convincingly say that it would definitely live up to its title, as these thirteen travelogues are more of personal journeys of mine rather than being structured travel articles. The title of the book comprises of two important words and is true to the meaning of both these words. All the above travelogues bring out my travel experiences which were hidden somewhere in my heart and the 'Travel Tips' I have inserted in between are very practical and realistic in nature, so these are more of my 'Travel Confessions' than anything else. Finally, I am absolutely sure that after going through all the travelogues, you will understand that somebody who is passionate about travelling will do so in any condition, any situation and with anybody – be it solo, with a friend, with family or even with a 6-month old baby. Yes, I am a 'Traveloholic' and I accept it !!!

I leave you now to go on and read the book with a small but very relevant quote from Mark Twain...

> *"Twenty years from now you will be more disappointed by*
> *the things you didn't do than by the ones you did do.*
>
> *So, throw off the bowlines, sail away from the safe*
> *harbour...Catch the trade winds in your sails...*
>
> *Explore – Dream – Discover...!!!"*

**Happy Reading**

# Contents

# Kedardome

## A Thrilling Experience

### The Beginning

There are some incidents, which an individual cannot forget throughout his life. These incidents may be funny, sorrowful or thrilling. There is one experience, which I cannot forget throughout my life. When a person joins the Armed forces, he knows that he has to face death anytime in his life. But in my case I had the experience in my training days itself.

It all started in my second term Indian Military Academy Dehradun. The Academy was planning to take an expedition to KEDARDOME PEAK, one of the highest peaks in Garhwal hills. The team consisted of 4 Officers, 36 Gentlemen Cadets (GCs) and 2 Nursing Assistants. We started from the academy and after a few halts reached Gangotri By road. We started off our journey on foot after Gangotri and reached Gaumukh which was our base camp. From here started a long and patient journey of acclimatisation, ferrying of stores and training. Long glacier walks, mountain climbing and forming small teams were the highlights of next few days. We used to get some respite in all this by meeting few foreign country climbers (especially of the fairer sex) and in-between get amused by "Tapovan Baba". We reached the next camp at the base of KedarDome after few days of ferrying stores and moving in bits.

### The Climb

At this camp our team was divided into three groups I was in first group consisting of 10 GCs and 1 Nursing Assistant headed by Capt Banerjee. The duration of the climb from the base to the summit was 12 hours so we decided to split into two parts. We planned to climb the summit camp already established by the Sherpa who was our local guide. We planned to spend the night there and climb next morning. The peak was just a four hour climb from summit camp so we could easily get back to the base camp. The 3 groups would reach the summit on the 10th, 11th, and 12th of June respectively and we planned to start back on 13th morning.

It promised to be a clear crisp morning on 9th of June, but promises are often broken. Full of enthusiasm to achieve our aim, we had a light breakfast. However, our group was reduced to nine Gentlemen Cadets, as GC Ranjit Jha who happened to be my buddy pair, had developed snow blindness. Any way we started moving at 0700 hrs and after a few halts en route reached the summit camp at 1400 hrs. Gradually the weather began deteriorating. By the time we reached summit camp it started to snow. The Sherpa received our party with hot tea, and by the time we finished pitching our tents it started snowing heavily. I ended up with GC Thapa and GC Manhas, the only two first termers in our team in a conical tent in the centre of the camp. Our plan to reach the summit next morning had to be scuttled due to heavy snowing throughout the night and next whole day. As for food we had to make do with chocolates and biscuits only. Next whole day went in sticking to our tents, only to move out after every few hours to clear the snow around our tents.

## The Avalanche

Capt Banerjee decided that if snow stopped by 10th evening we would attempt to scale the summit on 11th morning otherwise we would have to move back. But we were blissfully unaware about what the night had in store for us. We slipped into our sleeping bags at 2000 hrs and were talking to each other. We could hear snow thundering down. At 2300 hrs we heard another Avalanche cascading down, we were half –asleep. Then suddenly there was a loud thump and then silence. Something was wrong our tent had apparently shrunk to the size of football and our noses were almost touching the tent. We realized that we were totally buried in the snow. Any movement was impossible since our hands and legs were zipped up in the sleeping bags. Thapa and Manhas confirmed that they were in the same state as I was. In our dazed state we tried our best to break the sleeping bag zipper but couldn't. We tried to shout for help but lack of oxygen didn't allow us. All we could hear was the crunch of footsteps on the cover of snow over us. So we could make out that our tent was invisible from outside. Slowly and painfully oxygen supply was depleting and we were being choked near to death. I was even imagining the scene at my home front – white bed sheets on the floor, a garland around and my photograph and everyone crying their hearts out. With these horrifying thoughts, I started to lose consciousness and blacked-out.

Just when I was ready to meet the 'Maker' my sleeping bag was dragged out with me inside as if an invisible giant hand was pulling me from hands of Death. I gulped in huge amounts of life giving air not believing I was still alive. Looking around me I found that Thapa and Manhas were also alive and kicking, may be not kicking but certainly alive and breathing. This was our experience in the tent. What exactly happened outside was told to us later. When the Avalanche hit the summit camp all our tents were buried under snow and only the Sherpa was able to come out who cut open the tents. We thanked God looking over us and turned to never ending task of every living thing –Survival. We gathered up whatever we could trace and wore whatever we could find.

## The Survival

The Sherpa told us that there was a danger of more avalanches coming down so we had to move out fast from that site and place. We started our journey back to base camp at midnight in the heavy snow blizzard, zero visibility and complete white out. The Sherpa led us to a place, which he thought was safe from avalanches. He was not able to trace the path back because of invisibility and we decided to wait there till morning. We spent five hours digging fox-holes, singing songs and encouraging each other to remain alive.

At 0600 hrs next morning we started again with Sherpa leading the way and beating the snow to make way for us. The visibility was still zero and the snowstorm was getting bad to worse. After about 2 hours of continuous snow beating the Sherpa got really exhausted and asked Capt Banerjee to send for replacement. Then we decided to do the snow beating for 50 steps in rotation. We walked for about 12 hours in knee to thigh deep snow and knew that we were lost. The common effects of mountain sickness, frost bites and hallucinations started to creep in everybody's mind and body. After about 12 hours of continuous trekking, our Nursing Assistant Naik Sharma gave up and told us that he can't go any further. So Capt Banerjee chose a big boulder as the landmark and decided to wait near it along with two more GCs. He told us to find the base camp and send rescue party as fast as we could. On seeing the condition of the Nursing Assistant, we literally started running in search of base camp and traced it out at about 1930 hrs. We immediately sent the rescue party in the direction of big boulder. But unfortunately Naik Sharma could not wait that long and we lost him.

## The Conclusion

At the base camp we were given hot soup and noodles and our wet clothes & shoes were changed. All of us were suffering from frost bites, chill blains and snow blindness by then. GC Manhas was suffering from serious frostbite in one of his feet. Even when I got up next morning I was not able to stand up, as my left foot had suffered low degree frost bite. We were lucky that the weather cleared for few hours the next day and the helicopters could come. We were evacuated from the base camp and were brought to Military Hospital Dehradun.

After that one more attempt was made to reach the summit by the second group but they were unable to reach even half way to the summit camp because of bad weather. So the expedition to Kedardome was called off. After these 19 hours of togetherness, the ten of us shared a special chord of bondage. The time which we spent together fighting against all odds and walking not on physical strength but only on will power - the will to survive and hope to reach the base camp. The loss of our nursing assistant who was such a josh type man was unfortunate.

*"This is one incident I cannot forget throughout my life."*

**# Refer Page - 151 for Photographs of Travelogue - 1**

# Kinnaur

## God's Own Land

### The Hills Came Calling

Pristine mountain-valleys and amazing flora & fauna is typical to Himachal Pradesh and has always been casting a mysterious charm on the wandering travellers who religiously try to find new and fresh locales to explore. Such was also the malady affecting us & thus after some enthusiastic over-packing of rucksacks, me & my course mate Shailender Arya met up at Chandigarh for our next foray in the mountains. Our launch pad to the mountains was my sturdy looking Maruti 800 with a huge sticker on the rear screen: "Don't follow me, I am already lost". The car was stacked up with fruit juice packs, potato wafers, Bacardi-the principal component of our improvised roving bar, and last but not the least some petrol cans.

We had decided to explore the Kinnaur region of Himachal Pradesh, the Dev-Bhumi or the land of the Gods. It is considered to be a remote geographical entity, nestled in apple & almond orchards & a paradise of unparalleled beauty as well as a region where the Indo-Tibet cultures have seamlessly blended over the times. Disturbing neither the tribals nor the trouts, we merely longed for some untouched trekking trails and photograph our way through the ubiquitous charms of the mountain valley.

### The Mainstream Destinations

Our first halt was Chail, a small tranquil town enveloped among drifting clouds & tall pine trees. Chail is a small town with a total population of 1000 persons or so, reads the board in the main and only market; and is thankfully devoid of honking auto-rickshaws competing to ferry the tourists back to the hotels. The twin claims to fame of Chail are the Maharaja's Palace, built by the erstwhile Maharaja of Patiala with a sneer desire to construct his palace on a hill higher than neighbouring Shimla, and a cricket ground which is the highest in the world. We got lucky when we got a palatial suite in MES Inspection Bungalow, thanks mainly to a surprised staff officer at Station HQs who got smitten by the fact that two "youngsters" are on a driving trail in his region on leave. The next day we caught up with the NH-22 at Kufri & then drove towards Narkanda, a roadside town offering a breath taking view of the Hatu peak. From Narkanda we started to disagree with the road map & steered for a village called Thanedhar on a chinar-lined road. Nestled between acres of sloping apple orchards, this village was a perfect getaway for the made-for-each-other-who-are-you honeymooning couples. We stumbled upon a gem of a place there, a dream resort called the Orchid Retreat. It was an old wooden house tastefully redone in a contemporary style with elegant wood-work offering only books, birds and serene views for company. This property was later on taken over by Banjara Group.

The following day we resumed our drive on the highway along with the mighty Satluj, only to take the diversion near Karcham to move on a narrow winding road which steadily climbed up along the gushing Baspa River while giving chills & thrills of driving along steep mountain cliffs, and into the Sangla valley. At times, the road (so called) was so narrow that you got to actually reverse quite a bit to make way for the opposite traffic. The Sangla valley is our very own Himalayan Shangri-La, adequately distanced from Delhi or Chandigarh to ward off hordes of weekend tourists who descend on Shimla and Musoorie with blaring music in their cars and accompanied by spoilt brats with their typical funny attire. This valley is lush-green, apple, almond & peach trees dot the countryside, snow-covered peaks stand guard all around & the bubbly Baspa meanders through the valley before it tumbles down to join the might brown torrent of the Satluj.

> **Tip**
>
> *It's advisable to check the weather status always while taking this stretch of the route. Adequate spares for the vehicle needs to be catered for, especially if you have an old war-horse like Maruti 800. Carry basic eatables and enough water in the car, for any unforeseen circumstances.*

### Off the Beaten Track

The next few days went past in a joyous trance, exploring the valley & observing the gentle & unhurried pace of life which goes on unnoticed amid the bounties of nature. One day we trekked up to the Sangla meadows, a lovely meadow surrounding a lake situated high in the mountains. Since the local folks had never known about our Internet-generated research, the word 'Sangla Meadows' drew completely blank looks on their faces. But our school time skills in dumb-charades came to our rescue and on being presented with a vivid and adequately animated description of a high lake surrounded by pasture land. *'Kande'* became our day's mantra as we made our way up asking shepherds for the route towards *kande* which simply means 'pasture land' in Kinnauri.

It was a fairly steep climb through a dense deodar & juniper forest & offered breath taking glimpses of the entire Sangla valley juxtaposed with the majestic Kinner Kailash which hovered protectively in the background. The tree-line gradually receded after a few hours of climb and gave way to a moss-covered mountainside interspersed with small exotic flowering plants. Our trek culminated at the lake which was formed by a large number of small snow-fed streams. From the Sangla Meadows a trek further leads to a mountain-pass which can be negotiated in summer months with adequate gear and protective clothing.

We trudged back to Sangla village to our favourite hangout — a modest roof-top restaurant run by a perennially-smiling Kinnauri boy in his late teens who never missed an opportunity to practice his broken English. His menu-card was a delight. It read 'soop' for soup, the chicken dishes were priced cheaper than most of the vegetarian dishes, beans were followed by coffee as the next item, which was followed by momos in a native 'just-learned' sequence, and one could relax by sipping salt-tea which may be ordered by 'cattles' (kettles). We sat down one evening in his restaurant and drafted a new menu-card with sincere attempts to divide the menu under various high sounding headings like 'From Kinnauri Kitchen' and 'Sangla Special'. We were touched by his concern for us; he was always ready at unearthly hours with packed breakfast and lunch for our treks, and invariably sent a boy to guide us to the outskirts till we homed on to the correct trail among dozens of trails which wind up near any settlement. In a way, we might have been quite an interesting sight in the village, roaming in boots which were more suited for high-altitude warfare than for trekking, and always loaded with enough equipment to "launch" into a trek at the shortest notice.

## Testing the Old War Horse – Maruti 800

Our last foray in this picturesque valley was Chitkul, the last Indian village situated on the old Hindustan-Tibet trade route. We kick started the journey in the morning very enthusiastically with our car splashing across the small streams on causeways with great élan. But alas as the day progressed & the ice melted, every causeway become increasingly difficult to negotiate & finally we were forced to abandon our Green 'Monster' on the roadside and take a walk to the next village, Rakchem. At Rakchem, we were assured that the car is as safe on the road as in a locked garage because car-lifting was unheard of since the roads creeped in the valley. We continued our journey in a hired jeep on a four-wheel drive moving towards Chitkul on a narrow precipitous gravel-road passing over full-fledged streams and slush pools. Chitkul is a tiny village consisting of few huts put together in a Tibetan style, a handful of cobble-stoned sloping alleys running amid the clustered hutments. In close vicinity flows the Baspa River streaking the valley like a fine line of molten silver. The trees are few and scarce and the villagers celebrate both the Hindu and Buddhist festivals with equal gusto and fervour — a symphony of religions nurtured by the mighty Himalayas.

In the bygone days of the silk-route, Chitkul was a significant trading outpost on the Hindustan-Tibet trade route through which the trade of salt, sugar and spices flourished. Interestingly, the Indian Army also calls this area 'Sugar Sector' in its parlance, probably a name carried forward from the era of predominant trading in sugar. A further amusing interpretation came from an aging ex-porter in Sangla village who confidentially conjectured that this name has been derived from the presence of *Chinee log* (Chinese people) across the border and motivated us to join the ITBP.

Though Chitkul appears to be absolutely inaccessible, a number of long-distance treks emanate from here, some to the remote border posts manned by ITBP personnel and a prominent six days trek to Harsil over the Lamkhaga Pass which thus joins the two fabled abodes of the divine as well as the two hill states of Himachal and Uttaranchal. An enterprising villager had ventured to open a hotel in Chitkul that season, which actually was a two-room extension of his house and the 'refurnishing' of the goat-shed as a 'designer lobby'. The occupancy rate in the inaugural season was amazing courtesy two Germans, his first-ever guests, who could not leave the place for days because of heavy landslides. Perhaps we do have a thing or two to learn here and can shut down our airports in metros for a record-breaking season after the foreign tourists fill up!

We returned from Chitkul to find the car absolutely safe. In fact, some Good Samaritan had placed stones around the car to warn any incoming vehicles. We also came across a motivated group of pilgrims on a holy trek aiming to encircle the Kinner Kailash following a route called the *parikrama*. There are numerous other attractions nearby. Reckong Po and Kalpa valley are just a few hours' drive from Sangla; and subsequently one may continue the tribal odyssey towards Nako to finally join the Leh-Manali road after completing the circuit.

---

### *Tip*

*The Sangla valley is extremely picturesque and must be explored at leisure. A number of treks emanate from here having difficulty levels ranging from easy to moderate. It's better to check from the locals. Stay arrangements in Sangla & Chitkul are basic home stays which are the right way to stay for such a trip.*

---

### Time to Bid Adieu

Sangla is a nature's auditorium screening its very own *son et lumiere* shows wherein you cosy up to the campfire on the banks of the *Baspa* and reflect about life while the valley reverberates to the rhythmic sounds of flowing water and the subtle play of moonlight on the peaks produces an unending array of surreal images. The next day we bid adieu to Sangla valley & drove back the same way, spending a day en route at Sarahan, a serene hill-station famous for its Bhimkali temple. Fresh with memories of Sangla we spent our time en route playing country music & placing bets on the end-results of the photographs. We parted ways at Delhi, flying back to the scorching sands in deserts & exploding shells on the Line of Control. But there is always another day, another time & another destination waiting to be discovered.

# Refer Page - 152 for Photographs of Travelogue - 2

# Bachelor Backpacking Europe Trip

## On Shoe-String Budget

### How it All Started

Think of it this way: if there was one place you could visit before you die where would it be? I put the question to myself & couldn't decide. I asked around & then asked some more, until I came up with the answer. Life's too short for such an ultimatum. I want the holidays of several lifetimes, and I want them all in this world, not the next. It is during the Degree course at College of Military Engg, Pune I realized that probably it is the last time when many of us like-minded course mates, hard-core bachelors will be together.....as bachelors. So, along with two of my close friends & course mates – Madhu Nair & Amartej Singh, I decided to plan a "lifetime holiday" during our term break between two semesters. And, what better place than.... Europe. Somebody asked me, "Why Europe?"

Europe is a chameleon; its colours change rapidly. One day you can be on the cobbled streets of a medieval city, the next atop a snow-capped peak. Nowhere else greets you with such a swift succession of different languages & menu changes. Europe's appeal lies not just in an influential, often bloody past & a largely peaceful present, but also in its mix of culture & nature. Da Vinci & Picasso masterpieces aren't far from the countryside or popular beaches. Whether you dream of experiencing the romance of Paris, blazing own trails in the Alps or downing a few beers in Germany; this multifaceted continent can satisfy all your tastes.

So, after extensive planning & preparations (being true Army Engineers) extending over a period of 2 to 3 months, with the help of information from internet, various travel books, tour pamphlets & of course, the "bible for each traveller" – The Lonely Planet, we were ready to 'explore' Europe. Not to forget, winning a hard-fought & 'almost lost' battle for procuring Schengen Visa – this is the visa required for travelling to most of the countries in Europe (details of this 'visa-battle' cannot be disclosed as it contains some confidential stuff to). We did our planning on a complete "shoe-string" budget by taking the least expensive flight, obtaining a 15-day EURAIL Pass & booking accommodation at various Youth Hostels all over Europe. As good Army Officers, we divided the responsibilities of the trip equally – I was chosen the official 'map-reader & guide' of the trip, Amartej being an ace photographer, took the task of capturing our trip in his camera & Madhu being physically strongest among us, took the responsibility of helping with the load during our 'exploring-walks' in all the cities.

> ### *Tip*
>
> *A backpacking trip in early 2000s was not a common thing in India and required extensive planning and pre-booking. Eurail and Youth Hostels are the best way to ensure a 'shoe-string budget' trip to Europe.*

## Historical Italian Journey

On 12th of June 2005, we took our flight from Bombay to Rome via Moscow. Shortly before take-off I glimpsed the pincers of city of Bombay. Soon we were scudding over a pink bed of sunrise clouds, so pretty that the pilot must have chosen his flight path just for fun. But he obviously knew his way, because eight hours of flying time & six hours of somnambular stroll through Moscow airport (straight from the Hollywood movie "The Terminal"), we were descending to another sunset on a very different land – Rome. It was half past eight in the night & to our surprise, the sun had just set & the headlights of cars were far from required. So, here we were, finally, the first of our destinations in Europe – Italy.

Rare is the traveller who isn't smitten by Italy. Everyone loves the Italians – their quirky outspoken zest for life, and their gorgeous country & rich culture. A country of ancient history, artistic splendour, divine food & wine, and a romantic olive-grove dappled landscape, Italy hits the heart & soul fast. Natural & historic beauties aside, modern Italy is exceptionally vibrant & simmers with a unique passion. When it comes to sightseeing, that old saying – *"Roma, non basta una vita"* (Rome, a lifetime is not enough) – couldn't be more true. Next day, with some local guidance about the public transport, we visited Vatican City – the world's smallest country. In 1929, Mussolini, under the Lateran Treaty, gave the pope full sovereignty over Vatican City. Christendom's most famous church, St Peter's Basilica, stands on the location where St Peter was buried. The interiors of the Basilica cannot be defined in words.

Exploring Rome is like peeling the skin of an onion, as the city reveals layer after layer of an ancient & multi-cultured history. Rome's 2500-plus years of history have produced a veritable archive, from the remnants of ancient Rome to the artistic splendours of the Renaissance & baroque period. We explored the city of Rome by peeling all the layers, traveling either by the underground metro or by walking - be it Rome's best-known monument – the Colosseum or the well-preserved Pantheon or the Trevi Fountain, famous for grant of wish by throwing a coin in it. And, as true budget-travellers, we survived on slices of oven-hot pizza or panini (an Italian sandwich) with beer. Whether you have a day or a month, Rome will swallow you whole, charm you to pieces, and then leave you craving for more.

## The French Kiss

The same night we took the Eurail – a Trenitalia train – for Nice, the famous French Riviera beach. The train took a beautiful coastal route to reach the border-city of France next morning. The largest country in Western Europe, France stretches from the rolling hills of the north to the seemingly endless beaches of the south; from the wild coastline of Brittany to the icy crags of the Alps. It retains a confident culture with a strong sense of identity & a rich treasure house of arts. The capital of the French Riviera, Nice is coined as the playground of the rich, famous & tanned, with Cannes, Monaco & Monte Carlo just a coin's throw away. We spent the entire day at the beautiful Riviera Beach with crystal-clear blue water. Fond memories of the famous serial – "Riviera" – were revisited. Here we discovered the importance of two very special 'products of globalization', which took care of our survival throughout our Europe trip – McDonalds & European Supermarket.

Next day we were in France's *"bijou extraordinaire"* (extraordinary jewel) – Paris. Paris remains the benchmark for beauty, culture & class the world over. Even the most cynical traveller can't help but be charmed by its magnificent avenues & cosy café life, its unparalleled arts scene & energetic but composed pace. Paris boasts of one of the best underground metro networks in the world. The extensive metro & RER (local trains) network helped us commute in Paris with great ease & we started to feel like locals there. For two days we toured Paris' tourist attractions, but they just didn't cease to finish. There's the famous cathedral of Notre Dame, the Grand Palace, Champs Elysees – world's most fashionable & stylish street, which radiates from Arch de Triomphe – a national icon. The paintings, sculptures & artefacts on display in one of the world's largest collection in Louvre Museum are mesmerizing. Not to forget the most widely celebrated work of art hanging on its wall – da Vinci's *Mona Lisa*. I was slightly shocked that Paris' most famous landmark turned out to be my favourite as well. I am talking about the gigantic architectural wonder of the world – Eiffel Tower. When we reached the third level (top level) of this amazing piece of steel architect, we were totally spellbound by the view from top. Paris by night is a different city altogether. While one night we watched the world-famous Lido Show & strolled on Champs Elysees, the other night we took the dinner-cruise on River Seine.

> ### *Tip*
>
> *The magical catch to a budget backpacking trip is 'Eat like locals, Stay like locals & Travel like locals'. The golden rule of cutting cost is to look for local street side eateries and search for best deal on public transport (Both these options are available in plenty anywhere in Europe).*

## Europe's Magic Centres

Next morning we took one of the best & fastest trains in Europe – the Thalys – and reached Brussels, the capital of Belgium. Brussels is a calm, quiet &

secretive city. It's imposing 15th century central market square, Grand Place, tops the itinerary of sightseeing here. Of course, a visit to Brussels cannot be completed without visiting its national symbol – the Manneken Pis Fountain. Our Youth Hostel was beautifully located & we had a nice evening in its pub – the Backpackers Bar.

Next day we were in Amsterdam – Europe's 'Magic Centre'. 'God created the world but the Dutch created the Netherlands' – it's an old saying. The Netherlands isn't the most budget-conscious option, but transport is efficient & well priced, the nightlife is pumping & the Dutch are most hospitable. Amsterdam is perfect for travellers, with enough sensory delights to keep even the shortest attention spans occupied: take your pick from 17th century architecture, canals, galleries, museums – and notorious sleaze. As soon as we reached Amsterdam, we took a 7-hour day tour which took us around the picturesque Dutch countryside – lush green farms, enormous variety of windmills, green timbered houses, fishing villages and a visit to a wooden shoe making factory, a cheese farm & a diamond factory. In the night, we visited the 'infamous' Red Light District of Amsterdam. It's bewildering; you'll find tourists of all stripes gawping at the blatant display of sexual currency.

## The German Experience

We spent the next two days in the powerhouse of central Europe – Germany. It is an accessible, popular & fascinating tourist destination. For backpackers in particular, the central location, excellent transport & hostel infrastructures, and plentiful supplies of cheap beer, strong cocktails & cutting-edge music make this an essential port of call on any European trip. Our first halt in Germany was Cologne. The justly famous cathedral – Kolner Dom – dominates the cityscape, but it's also worth visiting this lovely city for its interesting museums & vibrant nightlife. Beer in Cologne reigns supreme. The city has more than 20 local breweries, all producing a variety called *Kolsch*. So after exploring the old town, streets & museums of Cologne the whole day, we settled down on a riverside café for beer & sausage.

Next day morning, we took the train which passed through the 'fairy-tale-famous' Black Forest – home of the cuckoo clocks. Our journey terminated at a charming town on the Necker River – Heidelberg. Its magnificent castle & medieval town are irresistible draw cards for most travellers. We spent the rest of the day exploring the imposing red-sandstone castle, strolling by the riverbank & enjoying the weather, before we caught the night-train to Austria.

### *Tip*

*Extensive utilization of your Eurail pass will not only fetch you the best of scenic views, but also give you that needed rest and recoup to gear up for your next city exploration. Look for scenic route trains and take an 'unplanned' journey.*

## Austrian Architectural Wonders

Austria is not just Arnold Schwarzenegger's homeland, but it also attracts many visitors, who are either wooed by the historic treasures of the former Habsburg Empire or by the sounds of Mozart & Strauss or by sparkling mountain vistas of Alps. Our first halt in Austria was Vienna – an architecturally rich city packed with galleries & museums. We were totally amused by the stunning architecture in almost every building of Vienna – be it St Stephens Cathedral, the Imperial Palace, the Museum Quarter, the City Hall or Schloss Schonbrunn. Our journey in Austria continued from Vienna to Innsbruck. Innsbruck lies in the valley of River Inn, scenically squeezed between the northern chain of the Alps & the Tuxer mountain range to the south. The first thing we did on reaching Innsbruck was to visit Swarovski Crystal Palace, which consists of crystal-encrusted caves under a lush green 'giant-fountain'. The evening was spent simply wandering around narrow, covered streets of Innsbruck's old town & soaking up the atmosphere. We caught the night train to reach Zurich next morning.

## The Swiss Sojourn

The next day we were in the "Crown of Europe" – Switzerland. Chocolate, cheese & clocks; strait-laced bankers, big business & neutrality – the terms associated with this small, fiercely independent nation are likely implanted before you arrive. But beyond the stereotypes, you'll encounter boundless adventure opportunities & some of the most exquisite natural beauty on the continent. Mountains & lakes, tinkling cowbells & alpine villages – this is a land of such breath taking beauty it defies description. Our first excursion was to Europe's largest waterfalls – Rhein Falls, before we reached the photogenic city of Lucerne. That day we explored the town a little, checked out few landmarks like Chapel Bridge & the Lion Monument and spent the evening by Lake Luzern. Next day morning we were off to the most-visited place in Switzerland – Mt Titlis. It is the fastest reachable glacier connected by cable cars in three stages, including the world's first revolving cable car – "Rotair". In the evening we caught the "Golden Pass Panoramic Train" to Interlaken which gives one of the best Swiss-countryside views.

Flanked by the stunning Lakes Thun & Brienz is ever-popular Interlaken – a great base for exploring the delights of the Jungfrau region. Our Youth Hostel was beautifully situated on the lakeside. Next morning we caught the 'cogwheel train' to Jungfraujoch, or 'Top of Europe' – as they like to call it. At 3500m, it is the highest railway station in Europe, attracting half a million visitors a year. The scenic beauty on the way is postcard-worthy, with lush green meadows merging with snow-capped mountains, flower trails, mountain streams and picturesque lakes. On top, as luck favoured us, we got clear weather for couple of hours & the view was indisputably spectacular. We came back to Interlaken with some fond memories of the Aletsch Glacier, the Ice Palace with some awesome ice-sculptures & snow-games of Jungfraujoch. We said goodbye to Switzerland that night & left for Venice by train.

> ### *Tip*
>
> *Both Austria & Switzerland have so much to offer for a tourist – choose your areas of interests carefully, as many of the 'sightseeing' options may get repetitive in nature. For example, most of the Swiss snow mountain peaks offer similar views & activities.*

## Other Italian Delights

Unlike other cities where the railway station opens into the seedier part of downtown, replete with automobile fumes, litter & touts, Venice reveals herself in her full glory as soon as you enter the city. A city that's sinking at an alarming rate of two & a half inches per decade has no time to be coy. Come. See. Fall in love. And fall in love you will. Everybody does, Venice really is very, very charming. A confusing array of narrow alleys which suddenly open up into little squares which in turn lead into narrower alleys.....so on & so forth. Getting lost is inevitable, so enjoy! And following you faithfully along your delightful journey is the silvery green Grand Canal, which divides the city into its main six sections.

Once checking into our apartment in a narrow alley, we took up, what is the key to discovering Venice – walking. After doing alternate rounds of exploring & getting lost for some time, we reached Piazza San Marco, the biggest square in Venice. Described by Napoleon as "Europe's Drawing Room", the piazza is fronted by St Mark's Basilica & lined by several *cafes* & *ristorantes*. Post lunch, we utilized the public transport of Venice – the *vaporetti* (water bus) to visit the neighbouring islands of Murano – home of Venetian glass, and Burano – a sleepy fishing village, renowned for its lace & colourful houses. The evenings in Venice are picture-perfect for a romantic rendezvous with your significant other. But three of us had no such inclination towards each other, so we preferred to hit the sack.

Next day morning we took the train to Pisa - its iconic tower is among Italy's most recognizable sights. Pisans claim their 'Field of Miracles' is among the world's most beautiful squares. The manicured lawns provide a gorgeous backdrop for the cathedral, baptistery & bell tower – all leaning. We spent the afternoon being mesmerized by the Leaning Tower of Pisa, before returning back to Rome. Here, our European circuit was complete after 16 days of hectic, but unforgettable travelling. From Rome, we made a day-trip to Naples – 'the Mumbai of Italy'. Stunningly situated on the Bay of Naples & lorded over by Mt Vesuvius, Naples is gorgeous, edgy, raucous, overwhelming & above all fun. But it was not much fun for us. While returning from there, the train was delayed & by the time we reached Rome, all public transport had stopped. We spent that night at the platform-benches. It was good to be acclimatized back to our own country's systems.

> ### Tip
>
> *The ideal way to explore any European city is by walking. This would not only give you the feel of the place, but will also be friendly on pocket. Most of the main touristy areas in any European city are within walking distance and lets you explore the 'real' city / town.*

## All Good Things Must End

On 30th of June 2005, after 18 wonderful days in Europe, we caught the flight back to India. It was a mixed feeling of both happiness & sadness. On one end, I was feeling sad to leave this multifaceted continent with fond memories, but on other end I was glad & excited to reach back *apna desh*, as I was already missing *dal-chawal......* I felt that odd sense of discovery that only travel brings: I felt, in the way you can't sitting at home & reading a book or watching television, the wonder of experiencing the place yourself. At its best, Europe can be compared to a great meal – varied, surprising, plentiful yet leaving you with a sense of wanting more. Like a long & complicated meal, not every taste of Europe sits well on your tongue, and like some dishes, some experiences are an acquired taste – some you hate but they come back & knock on the window-pane of your memory, asking to be let in long after you thought you'd got rid of them.

# Refer Page - 153 for Photographs of Travelogue - 3

# South-East Asia

## Indian Traveller's Backyard

### Planning the First 'Married' Foreign Trip

"You have travelled to all Foreign Locales alone as a Bachelor, and with me you are only traveling within country!"... "The only place out of country (literally) I have been is Andamans!"... "We have been married for a year now, and only traveling within India!"....These were few of many statements I have been hearing from my 'better half' since last one year, from the time we got married. Not that I have lost my zeal and enthusiasm for my passion of seeing new places, meeting new places and traveling abroad, it's just that as a bachelor, cost of travel can be manipulated and can be cut down drastically. I am not saying this because it means only sustaining one person, that is obviously part reason, but the main reason is that as a bachelor, one can plan & travel in the most budget costing possible. However, with a lady one has to do much more planning for any kind of trip, especially for a trip abroad.

But not withstanding these facts, I finally decided to give a taste of my extensive Budget Travel Planning skills on "Shoe-String Budget" to my wife. The least cost effective option for this kind of 'Dangerous Experiment' with minimum risk factor turned out to be South East Asia. When we think of South East Asia, it's an enormous task to decide on exactly which countries to cover and which ones to be left out. After careful research on the subject, we decided on two countries very different from each other in all aspects – Singapore and Malaysia. Both these places emerged clear winners to host our budget gourmets. They are in our backyards (access is economical and convenient), first World (but cut-price), easy to navigate (using punctual and thrifty Metro System) and the accommodation was surprisingly reasonable (not to mention a friend's place in Singapore).

The planning aspects commenced about two months in advance. In the beginning was the Budget, and the Budget was with God, and then the Budget was itself God. Finally, the Budget smiled from the corner of its mouth, giving out the verdict that my wife & I would positively go for our first *'phoren'* holiday. But this was no easy task, after all, our frugal budget (no more than 70 – 80 K all inclusive for a ten day trip for both of us) would make backpackers blush. Mission Impossible? No way. We could do it, and we didn't even have to rob a bank. Months in advance, we searched on the internet till our fingers were sore and we scoured travel magazines (special mention for Outlook Traveller) till our eyes started paining. We selected and rejected repeatedly – all kinds of Package Deals offered to us by various Tour & Travel agencies. It may not be everyone's cup of tea, but we swore to cut down on all possible unnecessary expenditure. And so emerged the flesh made word : The Itinerary. And may I emphasize, a very detailed & exhaustive itinerary, down to the last 'crab claw'. So when we packed our bags, we left our worries behind and soaked in loads of extra energies to have a trip of our lifetime. And then we were off, on a whim and a prayer, aboard the cheapest flight available (Tiger Airways...anyone heard about it?) that could be taken without hijacking.

---

### Tip

*If taken well in advance, Tiger Airways offer two-way tickets to Singapore for as low as 10,000 INR per person.*

---

## Singapore – The Lion City

Our first destination was "Uniquely Singapore". What makes this unique tourism tagline appropriate for this sunny island? It is a city, capital, state and nation, all encapsulated into a little red dot within Asia. For visitors, Singapore is an extraordinary destination with a constant sense of renewal, always something new to see, to buy, to taste, to experience. Apart from the world-class malls, iconic architect like Esplanade, Singapore has also shed its staid image and now boasts a swinging nightlife. But behind the city's gleaming face still beats a traditional heart, which is evident within ethnic enclaves such as Chinatown and Little India.

On board Tiger Airways plane out from India, a honeymooning Jain couple struggled with the problem of food, we just wondered what's going to happen when they reach the lands of people who eat almost 'anything that moves'. When we finally landed at Changi Airport of Singapore, we thought we are within the main city itself, the Airport is like a mini-city, with shopping plaza, food courts, gardens & landscapes, and even small amusement park within this world-class Airport. And we heard that the Expressway from Airport to City is itself a temporary runway for emergencies with a "movable" divider. Now that's what I call 'Technology'!

The first views of this Lion City were truly amazing. The streets are as clean as they say, the buildings as glitzy, the MRT as smooth, and the reckless chewing of gums and littering is indeed subject to fines. Singapore's ultra-efficient MRT system (Metro) is simple and user-friendly for even a blind man to reach his destination. We were as blind and lost when we reached there, never even imagined that within a day, we will be traveling with such ease as locals here. We reached our destination with relative ease – to a warm welcome by my old classmate Sarita and her husband Sachin.

**Tip**

*Take the "EasiCash MRT Pass" rather than buying individual tickets. It works out more convenient and more economical.*

Next day morning we decided to do what is already familiar to a couple of generations of Indians - Go Shopping! True to the Indian tradition, Deenaz had packed light to avoid paying excess baggage on return. This country has something for everyone – almost everything on your list. Orchard Road is the shopping Mecca – a promenade lined by huge and sophisticated malls, for the 'high-end shoppers'. Each Mall is a destination in itself, comprising of World's best brands like Chanel, Versace, Dior, Luis Vuitton etc. with well-stocked Food Courts to satisfy your taste-buds as well. Malls like Wisma Atria, Ngee Ann City and Tangs are sort of monuments in Singapore, where one can spend an entire day (and fortune). But smartly enough, we stuck to Window Shopping and Photography here and moved on to our next destination, but not before we had savoured on some authentic Singapore cuisine like Hainanese Chicken Rice and Satays at one of the Food Courts.

## The Essentials of Singapore

Our next destination on that day was the Singapore Zoo and the World famous Night Safari. If your vision of a zoo involves feeding animals in prison-style cages, then come here to change your mind. Here, the entire ecosystems have been recreated and one can watch over 150 species of mammals, birds and reptiles in their natural habitats. The Zoo's highlights include up, close and personal encounters with few of the most ferocious and endangered animals like White Tiger, African Lion, Giraffe and Komodo dragon. The interactive sessions with birds, orangutans and sea lions are not to be missed. Once Deenaz had got fed up of Zoo (as I was taking more pictures of animals than her) and after breaking her shoes (after walking and soaking in rain), we headed for the Night Safari which is right next door.

The wildly popular 'Night Safari' has won the Singapore Tourism Board's Leisure Attraction of the Year award a number of times. We were greeted by a Tribal Performance of Fire & Arrows. It's truly an amazing experience, whether you are following various Walking Trails (which actually takes you through open forest in pitch darkness) or you board the tram (with live commentary on board) from which you can watch the nocturnal life of animals. The experience of walking the "Leopard Trail" or going through the "Free Bats Dome" where bats will comb your hair is unforgettable. Then, to finish off they have "Creatures of the Night" show with live performances by dangerous night creatures.

> **Tip**
>
> *If you are fond of four-legged and the feathery ones, buy Three-in-One ticket for Zoo, Night Safari and Jurong Bird Park. Individual tickets would cost more. Also check out 'Family Passes' for all three sightseeing options.*

The next morning we were ready to discover Singapore City with vigour & enthusiasm. The number of people who visit Singapore each year is double the population of the island. We wanted to know just what these people come here to see. And what better way to soak up the atmosphere, than to walk around the city and use the local transport. The Singapore Metro will give you opportunity to enjoy the best of Local Fashion, which is very upmarket and everybody is trying to compete with each other in 'looking their best'. As Deenaz says, "Wear everything good here, as you've got to look super and gorgeous all the time".

We started our walking tour from the Singapore River which pulsates through the bustling city, with the glittering skyline on one side and all the 'Heritage Buildings' on the other. After going through the endless restaurants stretch across Boat Quay, we plunged a bit in the History of Singapore before getting awe struck by the magnificent Fullerton Hotel and Cavenaugh Bridge. After I bored Deenaz with lots of Heritage buildings like Victoria Theatre, Supreme Court, Parliament House, Asian Civilizations Museum, St Andrew's Cathedral, we headed for the most recognizable symbol of Singapore – "Merlion" the half-lion half-fish icon. It was the most photographed site with Merlion on one side and Esplanade-Theatres on the Bay (a larger-than-life recreation of the local Durian fruit) on the other. On our way, we had an exciting rendezvous with a ten foot long, 25 kgs of Indian Python (Deenaz will tell you in detail about this encounter).

After refreshing ourselves at Star Bucks Coffee, we headed for the shopper's paradise of Singapore – Bugis Street. This is one crazy place with almost everything on offer at great bargains. Deenaz freaked out here checking the variety of clothes, handbags, shoes, accessories, the most fashionable party and casual wear, one can find at the prices based on your haggling skills. This place was full of Hawker Street Food, the incredible variety of good food at reasonable prices is the biggest attraction. After satisfying our taste buds on Satays, Char Kway Teow and Hokkien Mee, we topped it up with fresh fruits on ice.

> **Tip**
>
> *Bugis Street is the right place to Shop, rather than Orchard Road which is good for 'window shopping' only. Bugis would offer you all the variety of shopping with competitive rates depending on your bargaining skills.*

We were told by somebody that no self-respecting tourist leaves Singapore without visiting the Sentosa Island. And, we had our self-respect to hold, so we caught the next metro to Vivo City, the newest and biggest Mall of Singapore.

This is the start point for Sentosa Express which travels over the sea to reach Sentosa Island in just 15 minutes. After we had our fill of ogling at the Star Cruise ship (anchored in the harbour just beyond Vivo), we caught the express to Sentosa. All is fun on Sentosa – the Malay word for tranquillity. Choose from an assortment of sights and activities : Butterfly Park & Insect Kingdom, Dolphin Lagoon, 4D Magix, Tiger Sky Tower or the lifetime experience of Underwater World. This island is for walking, taking the Sentosa bus or tram or the exciting Luge and Skyride for the more adventurous types. The experience of touching and feeding deadly Sting-Rays and having a ferocious Hawk perched on your arm are truly amazing. After touching the Southernmost tip of Asia and enjoying Tiger Beer at one of many shacks (Bora Bora) on beautiful beaches, we headed for newest and best attraction of Sentosa – "Songs of the Sea" – an amazing Light-Water-Fire extravaganza.

> ## *Tip*
>
> *There is no requirement of taking any 'package' of Sentosa Island. It is more convenient and flexible to cover this wonderful island on your own – doing things of your liking and skipping what you don't prefer.*

If Songs of the Sea was amazing, so was the sight waiting for us on return – Singapore coastline and skyline by night. The sight of Singapore River with Boat Quay and Clarke Quay was something to save for later. Clarke Quay may have been an ugly row of riverside warehouses once, but it's the hub for Nightlife today, with clubs, bars and breweries at a stretch. Don't miss the 'Hooters Pub' here, especially for the guys...the South-eastern waitresses here are 'hardly dressed'. Our perfect day came to an end with the iconic Chilli Crab at Boat Quay, a romantic dinner by the river-side.

## Malaysia – Truly Asia

Next morning we were off to our next destination – Malaysia. Instead of going through agony of custom check/immigration formalities/travel between city and airport, we took the efficient and faster means of communication to Kuala Lumpur – a Luxury Bus. And, luxury was what we got on board – comfortable push-back seats, fully AC, LCD screens in front of each seat with headphones to enjoy movies etc. Within five hours of viewing Intel billboards and regimented rows of date palms, we reached Kuala Lumpur from Singapore, which includes quick exit/entry formalities on the national border.

> ## *Tip*
>
> *Bus Travel is the fastest, cheapest and most convenient means of transport between Singapore and KL. Easy online bookings are available for One-Third the price of air fare and the transit at the border is much easier.*

Here we were, after the too clean, too organized, too preserved Singapore, into one big melting pot of cultures – Malaysia. It has sparkling seas and pristine beaches, sprawling mountain ranges and mysterious caves, jungles, lakes and lagoons, the frenzy of sightseeing and shopping, and the 'playground' for rich and poor alike. Touring the country is cheap, safe, hassle-free and convenient. Kuala Lumpur - Malaysia's bustling, lively, somewhat manic capital combines big-city energy with laid back little pockets. KL boasts of having the best of all worlds – a vibrant street life, a very busy nightlife, fabulous food, skyscrapers, mosques, and museums, all in one city. With a little of 'Delhite' haggling skills, I managed to get hold of a taxi to reach our hotel – Hotel Radius International (booked on our own from internet). It was located right next to Bukit Bintang – the most hip and happening street in KL. From our tidy rooms, we enjoyed perfect views of the mammoth 88-storey Petronas Twin Towers and mesmerizing Menara KL Tower.

Without wasting much time in settling down (much to the annoyance of Deenaz) we commenced our "City-Tour" on our own, using user-friendly city-maps and 'highly-confusing' Metro system of KL. After a small fiasco in KL Metro (a repeat of Aamir-Preity scene of DCH), we started our KL tour with Masjid Jamek, which is the most famous and oldest mosque of Malaysia, with beautiful white dome. The great thing about KL is the way in which absolutely contradictory things co-exist in close proximity. Masjid Jamek is in the heart of the bustling city surrounded by high-rises. Go around the mosque, and you reach the famous Merdaka Square, or the Freedom Square – the site of Malaysian Declaration of Independence. The square showcases some fine architecture, including a 100-year old fountain and the tallest flagpole in the world.

After submerging ourselves into Malaysian history in scorching sun, we headed for fully air conditioned Central Market – KL's answer to Bombay's Crawford Market. This is the right place for 'collectibles' for home and an excellent (and dirt cheap) Food Court. We freaked out on Curry Laksa, Nasi Kandar, Nasi Goreng stalls, and authentic Nonya cuisine. My memory may be weak, but my taste buds will always remember these names. Just two lanes away from here lies (in)famous Chinatown. In spite of the only Chinatown having a Hindu Temple (along with two Chinese temples), religion should be the last thing on mind as you walk through Petaling Street, an arcaded pirate market which sells just about everything – from convincing designer watch knockoffs to shoes to branded clothes to DVDs to perfumes – 'designer' goods at non-designer prices. This is one frenetic Sarojini Nagar stretch of manic shopping, where you need great bargaining skills. That night we went club-hopping near Bukit Bintang to have a taste of KL's nightlife, followed by another landmark place in KL – Jalan Alor. This is the most famous street for Hawker Food - from Nasi Goreng to Hokkien mee to even Frog dishes. We dug our teeth into BBQ Stingrays, fried Chicken wings, fried squids and hokkien mee. I wanted to have a go at Chilli Frog, but had to choose between "the dish" and "the wife" !!!

---

**Tip**

*Do all Shopping from either Central Market or Chinatown. There is scope for heavy bargaining at Chinatown.*

---

Any trip to KL cannot be complete without gazing your heart out at the magnificent Petronas Twin Towers, which look like two sharp needles thrust up from a thimble base. At a stupefying 1483 feet, this is KL's single-most recognizable feature. The sky-bridge connecting the two towers offers sprawling views of the city. But for that we preferred the Menara Tower, KL's strikingly beautiful TV tower which is the highest in Asia. It boasts of varied kind of activities here for all ages, with the viewing deck on top offering breath taking views of KL, including Petronas Towers. KL at night is an entirely different city by night when the KL cityscape lights up and the two "jewels" of KL look simply gorgeous. While Menara Tower looks like a giant red-and-blue disco ball shimmering away in the sky, Twin Towers are beyond any kind of description. We never imagined that this was going to be our most memorable Valentine's Day ever, as we reached the Twin Towers at night. The sight was astonishing, something which stays in your memories for a long long time, as you don't get enough of this spectacular sight. Taking your pictures with the Petronas in backdrop is a tricky thing, for which one has to actually lay down on the ground to ensure the 'tips' of the towers come in the photographs.

When we returned to Bukit Bintang, with never-forgetting memories of our Valentine's Eve under the Twin Towers, we were due for a pleasant surprise. They don't call this street 'The Night-Street' for nothing. Being a Saturday night, and Valentine's Day, this place had converted itself as one-big-party. Rock shows, impromptu break dance competitions at street corners, couples walking with flowers and other gifts, it looked like the whole world had closed in on this small stretch of road. We gave ourselves up in this atmosphere filled with "Love in Air", hopped from one roadside café to the other – all playing beautiful 'Love-Songs', and returned back to our Hotel after a romantic dinner.

---

**Tip**

*Take Hotel close to Bukit Bintang. This buzzing and happening street is a paradise for all Nightlife – lovers. Also with Jalan Alor close by, you can enjoy Malaysian street food as well.*

---

Our next destination was Genting Highlands – a city shining upon a hill, a favourite family destination for all ages. This hill resort is a one-stop shop for fun of all kinds. Imagine, our own Shimla or Mussoorie - now convert all of it into one huge covered entertainment complex on top of a hill. A complex of interconnected malls, video game arcades, casinos, hotels and theme parks. A complex where you can walk or take escalators for miles without ever coming out in open. We took the Go Genting Express Bus, followed by Genting Skyway

(One of the longest distances we have been in a Cable Car) to take us right till our hotel doorstep. The next 24 Hours were spent in unlimited fun and frolic – taking really scary theme park rides, do sky-diving inside Skyventure, experiencing the amusing world of Ripley's Believe it or Not, artificial indoor ice-slopes and also trying out hand at gambling on slot-machines.

> ### *Tip*
>
> *All Inclusive pass for Outdoor Theme park is a must, Indoor Theme park rides can be given a skip. Stay of one night is better than a day-trip.*

### The Paradise Island of Langkawi

After the exhilarating experience of Genting, we caught the Air Asia flight to an entirely contrasting locale – Langkawi, a laidback island with white sand beach fronting calm lagoons, where you can buy really cheap, really good 'Duty-Free' items to enjoy them on the beaches itself. The first sight of Langkawi from the aircraft was mesmerising, and we knew that we have chosen the right place as our last destination. The Holiday Villa Resort which was our home for next 2 days, was a 4-star beachfront resort with deckchairs under the palm trees perfect for stretching and snoozing on. After settling down in a well-equipped room with beautiful ocean views, we hit the beach just in time for the sunset. The orange sun sprinkled silver on the punchy ocean before slipping behind a tree island in the distance. The beaches here are long, lovely stretches of white sand, and a sea that comes warmly to your ankles and thanks you for coming to meet it. Walking is the best way to soak up the island-town atmosphere, with beachwear shops, small supermarkets, seafood restaurants/shacks and souvenir shops.

> ### *Tip*
>
> *Air Asia is the best and the cheapest way to travel within Malaysia (with air tickets as cheap as 900 INR per person one-way during that time).*

The next morning we took an 'Island Hopping Tour' (one of many tours to choose from) which took us in a super-speed boat to a number of islands, where we could see the rainforests and fabulous caves, take a dip in fresh water lake, experience the 'Eagle-feeding' up, close & in person, and not to forget getting left on an uninhabited island for a look at the kind of beauty the absence of man helps preserve. Water was so crystal clear and unbelievably blue, that you don't need to go for snorkelling to observe corals and underwater life. With memories to cherish for life, we returned to our resort to plunge in its pool with a bar within the pool.

Langkawi is a duty-free island, so shopping comes next to lying on the beach on the priority list. We also made the most of it and indulged in two of our favourite things – Shopping and Eating. This place has got some of the best seafood cuisine (like Lonely Planet recommends Lighthouse Restaurant) to offer, which one should not miss. A romantic dinner on one of many beach-front restaurants is a must on your itinerary. With heavy hearts (of not able to stay more), we boarded our Air Asia flight next morning from the Langkawi Airport, one of the most hassle-free airports I have seen.

> ### Tip
>
> *Entire Langkawi Island is duty-free and ZON duty-free Mall at Pantai Cenang is the best and biggest place for shopping. It's a one-stop destination for all kinds of shopping.*

After landing in KL, we caught the luxury-coach and returned to Singapore, for one last day of our trip. This last day was worth the wait, as we visited the recipient of several awards – Jurong Bird Park. The 20 hectares of recreated tropical gardens play host to some 8000 birds of over 600 species, many of them endangered. First, we attended the 'All Star Birdshow'. Next, we watched the 'Penguin Parade' and 'Birds of Prey Show'. Specializing in tropical birds, this place has number of Aviaries including Waterfall Aviary which is home to some very lucky African birds who are free to fly around their own 100 feet high waterfall. The favourite attraction here is the Lory Loft aviary, named for the parrot species that are its primary inhabitants. These impossibly coloured creatures are very friendly and are truly a snapshot-taker's delight. We terminated our trip at a place which no Indian tourist miss out in Singapore – Mustafa Centre in Little India. This place is heaven for shoppers, what started as a tiny store has grown into two huge departmental stores which sell almost everything possible, and prices don't get much better than this!

> ### Tip
>
> *Do the Electronics shopping from Mustafa Centre in Singapore, but be careful of the 'fake' genuine items sold there.*

With heavy hearts and unforgettable memories, we bid adieu to two very different, but unique in their own ways, countries – "Uniquely Singapore" and "Malaysia – Truly Asia". While one is designer-shopping haven, other is bargain-hunter's paradise. While one is cosmopolitan metropolis, other is historic melting pot. While one is antiseptically efficient, other is vibrantly chaotic. Both these countries are like multi-layered countries – each with a character and flavour of its own. When it was time to say goodbye, our exhaustive itinerary had given birth to a strange intimacy. Surely, this was a trip to remember for lifetime, and we boarded our Tiger Airways flight back to India with a promise in eyes of coming back for more.

**# Refer Page - 154 for Photographs of Travelogue - 4**

# Ladakh

## Heaven on Earth

### An Insight of Paradise

For centuries people have congregated in the bazaars of Leh. First came the traders from the plains and central Asia. Then came the Great Gamers, transgressers on the roof of the world. And finally travellers from all over the world. Ladakh - if not India's most visited destination, is certainly, most photographed destination. It's known for its stunning landscapes, lakes, and monasteries. It also happens to be a cold, harsh desert where temperatures remain below freezing for eight months of the year. But at 3000 metres above sea-level, it's not the air that will leave you breathless, it's the land beyond the Himalayas, where the azure heaven embraces the ochre earth in eternal bliss, and that will leave you mesmerised.

Ladakh is known for its unparalleled natural beauty which is pristine and ethereal, the vivid ambers, blues and whites and browns of Ladakh are magical and timeless. Here the nature mesmerizes you with its calmness and peace; the magnificent Himalaya makes it as one of the most sought after adventure destinations with numerous trekking opportunities. The Buddhist culture and lovely people make another reason why every traveller wishes to visit Ladakh at least once in his/her lifetime. It's a place I have always wanted to explore, and blazing a trail whenever possible, and that's exactly what I keep doing – again and again.

So, even after two previous trips to this fascinating destination (one of which was an adventurous Bike Trip on a scarlet Machiasmo, with my 'partner-in-crime' – Shailender Arya), here I was again in Ladakh – this time with Deenaz, and this time in a different 'Sawaari' – the Mighty Scorpio. I might think and believe that I have "Been there, done that" in Ladakh, but even this third trip had definitely much more in store for me. This time I wanted to stretch the limits of exploring this mesmerizing jewel of Indian tourism, this time I wanted to touch those locales that have not been imagined by anybody else and those areas which do not figure in any kind of tour operator's itinerary or in any travel magazine. But the harsh, inhospitable, high-altitude desert of Ladakh taxes the brain with its rarefied air. The laws of nature apply here like no other place & in order to 'not be a gamma in the land of lama', its best to acclimatise well before hitting the road in this region.

Leh is a pretty easy place to get comfortable in, with crystal clear air and the dazzling light, the imposing Leh Palace and the hills crowned with Buddhist shrines. But compared to what's on offer elsewhere in Ladakh, Leh's attractions are pretty average, which is perfect because it gives out time to settle down with the atmosphere and gain strength to take on the serious stuff. We spent our first couple of days walking around Leh town, starting with the Hall of Fame to the main bazaar. Women in headscarves and maroon *"gongchas"* – the traditional dress of Ladakh – sell dry fruits on the pavements. Bearded Muslims alternate with prayer wheel-spinning Buddhists, with the same sun-blackened faces, all selling the same thing. As we wondered down the narrow alleys of the market, there was a strange temptation to go native. In that true local spirit, we checked out one of the Tibetan Café for lunch with some authentic Thukpa, Tsampa & Kothey Momos, and these can be ideally drowned with a glass of *'Chang'* or a cup of *'Gur Gur'* tea. We spent the next day exploring Spituk monastery which was overlooking our guest room, and later spent the evening checking the internal lanes & bye-lanes of Old Fort area filled with world cuisine and typical European atmosphere.

---

### Tip

*Getting acclimatised for Ladakh trip is extremely important, especially if you are arriving by air. Keep at least 2-3 days initially resting and being within Leh town.*

---

### Eastern Ladakh – Untouched Beauty

After the required amount of acclimatisation, we armed ourselves in the sturdy black Scorpio leaving behind Leh town to glide into the relatively remote recesses of Ladakh. As we cruised on smooth BRO roads traversing the Indus Valley, lines of white-washed 'Chortens' slipped by like ghosts, and ancient forts and monasteries loomed overhead. Our first destinations were the twin-monasteries of Thiksey & Hemis. Hemis is the best known, richest & largest monastery in Ladakh, and is also unique as it's built not atop a hill but on its flank, probably to keep its location secret and its riches safe. Thiksey is a bit smaller than Hemis but more impressive, rising tier by tier on an open crag next to the Indus. As we ascended the steps following the deep guttural sounds of Buddhist chanting, we came across a lama swaying back & forth in frenetic prayer. *"Juley"* was the most commonly word used all along as we approached the terrace from where the views are superlative.

As we crossed Karu and along with it, the 'touristy' crowd taking the usual circuit of Chang La & Pangong Tso, we entered the Chumathang region. River Indus followed us like a shadow all along and the habitation started to vanish, as sheer, stark beauty of a high-altitude desert started to appear more clearly. It was like a high definition television set where shadow & light and heightened colour made a beautiful contrast, washing the land in shades of gold & ochre, pristine blue & green, purple & red – you think of the most unusual mountain colour & you would find it on this part of Ladakh. Considering it's a shamelessly naked terrain with hardly a tree in sight, these myriad colours of Ladakh almost seem like an anomaly. We drove at a leisurely pace till Upshi with 'haunting' Tibetan chanting gracing our Scorpio music system, with more stops & halts to soak in the true Ladakh atmosphere, till we reached our abode for that night – a lovely cottage converted as an Army guest room, right on the banks of Indus & with a view to die for. For all my friends from the Forces, I would strongly recommend at least a night halt here.

After a quick breakfast next morning at a dear friend's lovely house in Upshi, we braved our Scorpio on the 'non-existent' road of Tso Moriri. Leaving the main road at Mahe, we crossed the Mahe Bridge to come on the Tso Moriri jeep track where terrain is bereft of any permanent settlements because of its uninhabitable, hostile & harsh nature. The route was a bumpy ride but the breath-taking scenery was more than making up for it, as the mountains at one stage turned to burgundy as dense as an inkblot, before finally transforming into rolling hills. The small lake of Kyagar Tso appears in front of you as a disc of water beneath a mountain tiger striped with snow and the road looks like going into the lake. Skirting the lake with some distant views of *'kiang'* or the wild ass & some yak, we entered a shallow valley before descending to hit the gorgeous Tso Moriri, a 20 km stretch of saltwater encircled by golden hills & two of the highest mountains in Ladakh. A short way down the track which snaked along the side of the lake, tiny village of Korzok came into sight, with Korzok Gompa standing above it and a line of chortens. We checked into a beautiful tented retreat in the solitary confines of this postcard-perfect lake, and the tents were warm & comfortable. Our evening was spent interacting with few Changpa tribe women & children about their culture & lifestyle here in the wilderness. At night there were more stars than sky while the mountains around the lake looked surreal in the moonlight, their snow-capped rims glowing silver. It was a night to remember staying on the banks in a tent of this 15500 ft high lake.

After a night of fitful high-altitude sleep in the tent, and Maggi noodles for dinner, a golden dawn woke me up, as I walked along the lake and spotted black-necked cranes & ruddy shelducks to its far bank along with a lone golden eagle perched on a rocky outcrop. Before leaving this amazing water body I wanted to explore a bit more, so we made our own path over the vast flats around the lake, making sure to avoid the marshy patches. The Scorpio danced over the sands, and then suddenly two Kiang (Tibetan wild ass) appeared, running alongside us. Suddenly everything seemed to be happening in slow motion – the sand flying from their hooves as they galloped with all four legs in the air, their grunts – and then they veered off just as suddenly as they had appeared, leaving us stunned by what we'd just seen. As we made our way back to civilisation, little did we realise that we are actually headed to more wilderness as we proceeded to one of the remotest & one of the most beautiful parts of Ladakh – Rezang La & Tsaka La region, travelling closest to Indo-China border to hit Chushul from the other side. This route offered us absolute silence, just the sound of wind blowing through our windows and absolutely stunning Ladakh landscape, which was changing every few kms – from "beautiful" to "amazing" to "breath-taking"....and finally to "Oh My God" !!! The mountains were apricot, plum, champagne, sometimes crinkled with veins of snow. In between, a frozen stream threaded its way through the sandy bed – the colour of 'fried egg'. As we bumped our way on more boulders than road to arrive at Chushul late evening, we cozied up into our lovely Army guest room with 'Bukhaari'.

> ### Tip
>
> *This off-the-beaten track of Chumathang valley and approaching Chushul from the Eastern side requires special permits due to security reasons, but it's worth taking the effort due to its unexplored scenic beauty.*

## Pangong Tso from a Different Perspective

Next day we were excited to attempt a route not usually done by many – doing Pangong Tso from the other side, it was literally like hitting Pangong from Chinese side. We braved our trusted Scorpio yet again to get on roads which were getting from bad to worse, but the ever-changing Ladakh landscape kept us going on & on. It was a bright sunny day and the valley was glorious in the sunshine, but the wind ripped at our ears whenever we stepped out of the car. Pangong announced itself as a triangle of silver at the end of a geological rainbow. Gone was the harshness of the valley road, as serried peaks shimmered above the water, subtly shifting colour & shape. Pangong Tso lies like a giant snake, 130 km long, oblivious of international boundaries, about one-third of it in India & another quarter lies in the disputed Aksai Chin region. We hit Pangong near Merak village and travelled all along this pristine lake for 40 kms of lake road which is normally inaccessible to public. We took our Scorpio down to lake side & almost finished our camera memory with so many photos, each frame was like a calendar picture. As we crossed Spangmik, the last village open for public, we could see what the climax of "3 Idiots" has done to this beautiful lake. A train of vehicles were lined up on the sand projection in the lake where Kareena rode her scooter, trying to get their pictures captured at that spot – they have even opened a '3 Idiots Food Stall'....how pathetic !!! We refused to form part of this madness and instead carried on our journey after a nice lake-side lunch all the way to Tangste witnessing lemon & chestnut horses and yaks grazing on greenish-yellow moss carpeting the streambeds. At Tangste, we checked into another cosy Army guest room with board saying 'World's highest guest room complex'.

After five days of being on the move we were itching to get back to Leh for a much-deserved short break, before taking off to a different axis. We started after a hearty breakfast and started our ascend towards Chang La, one of the toughest passes of Ladakh region. The Scorpio started winding up the mountain as slabs of winter-hardened snow lay by the road, grey like granite and gradually snow began to creep across the road, first in blackened patches, then in fresh white. After skidding & slithering last few kms, we crested Changla with a sign truly reading out the characteristic of this pass – "Mighty Changla" . From here it was all downhill, the descent was steep & dusty, down scree & boulder-strewn mountains. We did couple of short halts on the way – first at Shey Palace & Gompa to see its fabulous old murals & Sakyamuni Buddha, and then at the original Tibetan settlement of Choglamsar. After the long & dusty journey, Leh beckoned like a shimmering jewel, an oasis of good food & comfort. A long hot shower was quick to dispel the tiredness but the mind was lost to the beautiful highs of the road just travelled, which I rewound in the form of a slideshow of photos.

The next day was spent taking a much-needed break & rest from past five days of madness, with few short drives to some of the monasteries in close vicinity of Leh town. Our exploration started with Stok Gompa & palace which like all other monasteries had a central courtyard with a prayer flag pole in centre. We strolled through the interiors of this historic Gompa & found our way up to the terrace, from where you get some of the best views of entire Leh town along with Indus valley. We also found our way up the winding road to the imposing Ladakh Shanti Stupa which has a unique peaceful atmosphere to it. But the pleasures of Leh are not confined to visiting of monuments and sites only. For locals and visitors alike, a stroll along the main bazaar, observing the varied crowd and looking into the curio shops is an engaging experience in itself. Soon it was time for dinner & we got into Pumpernickel, one of the best bets for western cuisine & German bakery kind of stuff.

---

**Tip**

*Ladakh region has numerous palaces and monasteries to explore which needs to be covered at leisure, as each of them have so much history and so much artistry to offer. Also, if possible, visit Ladakh during Sindhu Festival in July – it's a lifetime experience.*

---

### The 'Touristy' Part of Ladakh

Next day early morning we commenced our journey on the most commonly taken route in Ladakh – towards Nubra valley via Khardung La. The climb starts via the Tsemo Gompa road that veers over small villages, and it slowly leaves the vast spread of Leh valley behind as you cross the massive 'Khardung Frog' carved out of a single rock that sits on the road side. As we ascended on this treacherous road, suddenly a small blue lake appeared on our right, filling the valley almost to the brim and its water looked absolutely still. Snow-laden peaks stood reflected in it with crystal clear certainty, it's an ethereal landscape to experience. I was filled with a sense of awe & wonder in the midst of powerful nature forces which can crush me without effort but chose not to. First in patches & soon in broken lines, the road became edged with snow, glowing in the morning sunlight. At a point, I got a panoramic view of what lies ahead, snow-laden mountains spread out all around as far as the eye can see.

The road appeared as a thin line hugging the mountain ahead of us, winding on & on towards what I presume must be Khardung La. From this distance, the majestic peak stood tall, like a monarch wearing a crown of white. The highest motorable road in the world attracts most visitors to Ladakh, even if it is just for a photo-stop at its famous milestone.

As we descended on to the northern side of Khardung La towards Nubra valley, the road becomes hazardous, boulders of various sizes sit strewn all over the path & there is water everywhere. The road turned into a skiddy yak track cratered by fallen boulders. We took a snack break of hot Maggi noodles & omelette at Khalsar village before the vast expanse of Nubra valley appeared on the horizon. It spread itself languidly across the Nubra River which was split into many channels by islands of striking white mud. The beautiful valleys of Nubra & Shyok, with their grassy meadows & varieties of fruit orchards, almost flaunt their beauty to a generally arid Ladakh. The freakish white sand dunes of Nubra are home to double-humped Bactrian camels found near Hunder which maybe are the only reminder of the ancient trade-route. On the way we visited Diskit Gompa situated on a rocky spur above the village with a commanding view. The 100 foot high Maitreya Buddha statue was scheduled to be inaugurated by his holiness Dalai Lama a couple of days after our visit. A young monk volunteered to show us till the temple inside which still guards the wrinkled head and hand of a Mongol demon. We soon checked into the lovely guest room of Border Roads, and had an amazing evening at Dr Norden's Organic Retreat – this is one place nobody should miss, it's like an oasis in the desert.

> ## *Tip*
>
> *Nubra valley axis is much more than the customary photo stop on top of Khardung La and the double-humped camel ride. This cold desert has some beautiful homestays which is the right way to get the feel of the region and interact with locals.*

### Touching the Highest Battlefield in the World

Next day we explored this beautiful valley to the complete extent, as we drove our Scorpio on both the axes – one which follows Shyok River towards Thoise & Turtuk, and the other axis which follows Nubra River all the way to Siachen Base Camp. As we crossed the bridge over to Siachen axis, the first halt was Panamik village famous for its hot springs, this is the last village for tourists, and as we went ahead on this, the road turns & twists along the river, repeating a landscape that consisted of dashes of green, a vast palette of browns, and the occasional blue of the river. Gradually, the road became a roller-coaster as it began to undulate as if it were a wave in the ocean, as we approached the suspension bridge which is the gateway to World's Highest Battlefield – Siachen. It was an overwhelming feel when we walked into the war memorial of Siachen with apt words written on its arch gate – "When you go home, tell them of us and say, For your tomorrow we gave our today" !!! Deenaz was stunned when she experienced the true meaning of words such as 'belief' & 'faith' which is so common to us Army guys, when we visited the "OP Baba Shrine". This is built in honour of the soldier named Om Prakash who single-handedly braved an enemy attack on Siachen Glacier. It is a firm belief of all the troops in Siachen that OP Baba is a guardian deity who protects them from both nature fury & the enemy. Such is the faith of troops that a formal report is given to OP Baba before & on completion of every military mission. We were fortunate to witness one of those rituals as OP Baba was served lunch in full military honour.

As we returned with dazed hearts of what we just witnessed, we gave ride to some cute little Ladakhi school children who just couldn't stop talking all about themselves – looked like they found patient ears for the first time to listen to their stories. Back at Hunder, the white sand dunes were waiting for us along with herds of double-humped camels, a magnificent creature found only here in India. Our return journey via Khardung La was not as smooth as we expected, as the ride got bumpier. Across a sharp bend, a torrent of frothy water was rushing over the road (actually there was no road, only large boulders). On our left was the crotch in the mountains from where water was gushing out with increasing vigour & on the right, glacier melt plunged downwards in a waterfall. The fear of even bulky Scorpio also slipping off the edge made me stay closer to the side of mountain. Atop Khardungla top yet again we got an adrenal rush as the breeze has no leaves or vegetation to rustle through, so it uses the crevices between rocks & snow to create the universal sound of 'OM', which seems to reverberate all around.

## End of Dream Trip to Most Picturesque Place on Earth

Back in Leh for one last day, me & Deenaz - both were still under the influence of this 'dream' we were living since last two weeks which had lifted our spirits manifold, and made us think that despite the mess we've made of this world, it remains a place of infinite wonder. As we sat at a café in Leh that night, eating crepes & listening to rock music, I couldn't help think about the people of this wonderful region – for them it's just another caravan that has passed. It is a land so harsh that even nomads need to keep moving, so inhospitable that the road seems to never reach the destination, yet so beautiful that the memory of it lingers long after the road has gone. Ladakh is truly a mystical & fascinating land of majestic snow-capped peaks & enchanting valleys, of picturesque lakes & magnificent monasteries, of ancient culture & graceful heritage, a land of endless discoveries that gives you this unquenchable urge to get out there & see every last bit of it. Maybe that was the reason that brought me back to this 'Heaven on Earth' a third time....and I will keep coming here again & again, as there's always yet another road to take and yet another mystery to unravel. A sign board at Khardung La top sums up Ladakh in one single line - "You are nearest to Heaven and can have a dialogue with God" !!!

# Refer Page - 155 for Photographs of Travelogue - 5

# Canada

## A Complete Vacation Destination

### Introduction to Canadian Geography

Visiting Canada all in one trip is a massive undertaking. Over 5000 Kms separate Toronto in east from Victoria in west (about the same distance separates London and Riyadh, or Tokyo and Calcutta). To drive from one end of the country could take 7-10 days or more (and that assumes you're not stopping to sight see on the way). A flight from Toronto to Vancouver takes over 4 hours. Everything about this country is big & even bigger. When speaking of specific destinations within Canada, it is better to consider its distinct regions.

Atlantic Province is well known for unique accents, the origin of the Acadian culture, outstanding natural beauty (particularly around coastal areas), the historic beauty, and a huge fishing and shipping industry. When one thinks of Quebec, one of the first things is usually 'French'. Quebec is one of the most unique regions in Canada, and for that matter, North America. Canada's largest province by population - Ontario has endless opportunities of things to see and/or do. From Canada's largest metropolis (Toronto) to the national bi-lingual capital (Ottawa) to glitzy Niagara Falls, to the vast wilderness of Northern Ontario and the Great Lakes, Ontario is full of almost everything that represents Canada. Alberta as part of Prairies starts off with rocky terrain and flat farmland, and as one travels westward, eventually ends up at the foot of the Rocky Mountains. The region is rich in geographic variety, from rolling hills to rich canola farm fields to forests rich in diversity to outstanding lakes to rather unique rock formations. British Columbia is one of the most beautiful regions in Canada, both for those who are looking for nature excursions and those who kick it in the city. From the liberal & culturally diverse cities of Vancouver and the bustling downtown & beautiful beaches of Victoria, to Okanagan Valley which is home to wineries, graceful mountains, resorts, and retirement villages, BC is a never-ending experience. Canada's territories reside in the North Provinces. They are some of the most remote regions on Earth, which means plenty of nature to observe. The vast wilderness calls this region home with extremely extraordinary animals and vast landscapes.

### Eastern Canada – Diversity in Tourism

Somehow I have never considered going to Canada on a holiday, don't know why? Even though friends have raved about Toronto, Quebec or Montreal. Even though Vancouver has repeatedly been appointed world's most liveable city. Even though the Canadian Rockies are supposed to be spectacular. I feel we should blame America, our brains are so hardwired by US of A, that Canada doesn't come to mind when planning a holiday. So, I must confess I landed in Toronto's Pearson International Airport with not much of enthusiasm.

It was a bright summer morning, and my old classmate & friend Rinku was waiting for us at the Arrivals. So, after seeing off the senior citizens accompanying us, to their flight to Edmonton, self & Deenaz joined Rinku. It was an overwhelming feeling meeting an old classmate after 17 long years, and the towering presence of this 'gentle giant' reminded me of good old school days. The day went by catching up on our sleep & relaxing, but surprisingly, I was not feeling 'jet-lagged' at all, and by evening I was itching to move out & do some exploring. My dear friend Rinku got the hint, and he took us to Montana's – an amazing steakhouse & grill kitchen, where we dug our teeth into the most-delicious ribs.

With some guidance from our local hosts, and the rest on maps, we set off the next day to experience Canada. Our first destination was Black Creek Pioneer Village - a recreation of life in 19th-century Ontario and consisting of historic 19th century buildings, decorated in the style of the 1860s with period furnishings and actors portraying villagers. With Toronto's large transit system consisting of buses, street cars, subway lines, it was not at all difficult to move around. After stepping back in time to a period of European elegance and splendour at Casa Loma, we reached Art Gallery of Ontario. Proper internet surveys & planning got us entry into Canada's largest gallery free of cost. Along with large collection of Canadian paintings & sculptures, it has one of the world's most expensive paintings on view. Being an avid art lover, Deenaz absolutely loved this place.

> ### *Tip*
>
> *Plan your day itineraries carefully in Toronto. On specific days, all tourist attractions offer various discounts, and sometimes free entry (such as on Wed, there was free entry at Art Gallery after 6pm, which is otherwise $25).*

At Toronto, Rinku introduced us to Tim Hortons - Canada's very own answer to Starbucks or Barista. With a tag line of "Always Fresh", here in Canada people believe that they have more of Tim Hortons coffee than blood in their veins. So, filled up with a "double double" from Tim Hortons, we were ready to explore the classy & very bustling Toronto Downtown. After a quick peek at the Ontario Science Centre, we started our walking tour of downtown. It began with the world's longest street – Yonge Street, which runs 1896 km into another town. Every Torontian is proud of Yonge Street, and the Yonge-Dundas square is the hub of all activities. A must-do in this area is the Eaton Centre, a massive shopping & office complex. I was unmoved by the shops, but I was most taken up by the kind of activities in progress – a local 'Silver Elvis' dancing on a podium, street dancers doing their bit, local drummers playing their beat, The Dark Knight himself gracing the occasion & our very own Indian presence in form of IIFA pre-show celebrations – everything was engrossing.

Walking in any city doesn't feel like a structured activity (which I resist on holidays); it feels casual. Like we were walking & talking the city, experiencing it, rather than sightseeing & imbibing information. So, after wending our way past the old City Hall, where the architect had cunningly inserted visual symbols of himself into the brickwork, we headed to the nearest Food Court. With some Canadian *"poutine"* in our stomachs, we headed to the Lakefront & Harbour front where the breeze almost swept us from our feet. We gazed at the vastness of Lake Ontario, on which the city sits. It may technically be a lake, but it looks like a sea. With awe-struck views of the CN Tower & Rogers Centre at night still lingering in our minds, we returned back home.

---

**Tip**

*Tim Hortons is not only the best coffee in Canada, but also most economical. Don't get carried away by 'starry' ones like Starbucks, Second Cup etc. Best way to grab a bite is local hot dog vendors, or the food courts of Malls.*

---

Next day we wanted to explore that part of Toronto which is not found in any tourist brochure or website. After careful study of the local information, we landed at The Historic Distillery Centre - a pedestrian-only village dedicated to the arts and entertainment. Once the largest distillery in the world, it's now a working community for artists, furniture & jewellery designers, dancers and stage actors. With more patios space than any other Toronto location, The Distillery has also become a favourite neighbourhood hangout among thirsty locals. One minute you're 'in the city', the next you're on brick paved lanes amidst 13-acre charming collection of Victorian-era buildings with no cars to spoil the magic. Our pit stop was at Mill Street Brewery where we sat down on a sunny patio to taste their trademark Tankhouse Ale & Organic Lager. All the beer drinking made us hungry, and we headed to St Lawrence Farmer's Market, stretching over two buildings, with large seafood, meat and fruit & vegetables sections. It boasts of an extensive food court, with merchants often cooking food that they brought fresh that morning.

Meeting old acquaintances at unassuming locations always come as a pleasant surprise. The same thing happened when we stayed for a night at Col Suresh's place, and he was more than glad to welcome us with open arms. An old 268-er (my unit in Army) will always welcome you like a family member, and that's why 'Regimental spirit' is so very strong in Army. I ended my Toronto trip like I began, on a high. CN Tower, like Yonge Street is one of Toronto's top scorers, and with Rogers Centre being next-door neighbour, the atmosphere is eclectic.

## Road Trip to 'French Canada'

Our road trip of the eastern side began with the happy feeling of meeting my sister & brother-in-law. As we hit the cruising broad Canadian Expressways, we caught up on old times, at the same time planning for our trip ahead. The metropolis of Quebec & the second largest French-speaking city in the world – Montreal, was our first destination. We arrived in Montreal with Montreal Olympic Tower – the tallest inclined tower in the world, greeting us on the road. After getting lost in the confusing 'Ouest' & 'Est' grid, finally we found our small B & B. Without wasting much time, we moved out in spite of the big clouds hovering over the city. Montreal's downtown scene is a bustling study in contrasts. We witnessed the Victorian brownstone nuzzling skyscrapers, and the latest architectural marvels soaring beside stately neo-gothic churches. Lucky for us, but not so much for Deenaz & Reshma, International Bier (that's how they spell it) Festival was on, and as we entered the venue, it was nothing less than 'Crazy'. It was like we have arrived for the Oktoberfest of Germany.

It was the Grand Prix weekend in Montreal and the entire city was alive with street festivals, racing events & urban animation of the Formula One race. Without much delay we headed to where the whole of Montreal was going – Crescent Street, to join the largest Grand Prix party in the world and experience the incredible atmosphere. This was something I have never seen before, the whole street was one big party place, with free drinks stalls, real racing cars on display, pit-stop challenges, live Rock show – we had an unbelievable time here. Although we couldn't have enough of this place, we decided to head back, as we had a long next day.

Finally, that day arrived which was one of the main reasons of my Canada visit – Canadian Grand Prix. Under the heavy cloud-cover, Deenaz & I caught the metro train to Parc Jean-Drapeau – home of the Montreal Formula 1 Grand Prix. Sitting in the middle of the mighty St Lawrence River, these two island retreats are the hub of all outdoor activities in Montreal. A wet & exciting Montreal GP just made up my day, and after watching those racing cars zip past at an unbelievable speed of 370 kmph, I was thanking my stars for fulfilling my dream. Not to forget the mention of seeing the 'The Master' himself – Michael Schumacher, up, close & personal, was absolutely divine.

> ## *Tip*
>
> *If you are visiting Canada in June, make sure you keep the Grand Prix weekend for Montreal, but make all your bookings well in advance. The kind of party & happenings you will see here during this period, you won't see anywhere.*

So, after those unforgettable memories of Canadian GP, we joined with sister & BIL to do some more exploring. There is no place more conducive to a dreamy step back in time than the romantic district of Old Montreal. As we strolled on the cobblestone streets, art galleries, artisans' boutiques, terraces & cafes made it appear as if we were in a European town. The Gothic architecture masterpiece

– Notre Dame Basilica was as spectacular, as the Quays of Old Port of Montreal were serene. Dusk brings further enhancement, as strategic lighting brings out the loveliness of these old stone facades even more. After we explored the famous "Underground City" of Montreal, we ended our day listening & dancing to the tunes of French Music Festival.

Our next destination was Quebec City, which has an impressive location above the St Lawrence River along with its unblemished Old Town (Vieux Quebec) – filled with 18th & 19th century houses. Fortress walls still encase the upper Old city and the soaring Chateau Frontenac dominates the landscape. This Quebec iconic hotel with castle-like turrets was our first halt. After taking a quick peek inside this majestic hotel, we spent our evening at Dufferin Terrace, with breath taking views of the river & the lower town. Our stay here was at Quebec Youth Hostel which was situated in a historic building in the heart of Quebec City's old town. It had a nice homely feel about it, and we could prepare our own meals in their kitchen.

Next morning we chose to explore Quebec City at a genial pace in the charm and elegance of authentic horse-drawn carriage (*calèche*) ride. As we passed colourful boutiques, hip cafes, tempting bistros and stately heritage homes, our charming coachman-cum-guide showed us around The Citadel, the Parliament Hill, Battlefields Park & numerous other interesting sights. The old walled town with its windy streets and French colonial feel is sprinkled with churches, museums and galleries. The Montmorency Falls just a short distance from the city is a stunning experience. These falls are 300 feet and 100 feet higher than Niagara Falls, and have a suspension bridge right over the falls. We returned to Quebec's picturesque Lower Town to see the historic Place-Royale. Often referred to as the birthplace of French America, the Place-Royale is a small square with a big history. After being amped up by this awe-inspiring show, we swapped images for music and experienced some of the nightlife on the Grande-Allée – the Champs Elysées of Quebec City, crammed with great restaurants, bars and cafes.

---

**Tip**

*Minimum two days in Quebec City is a must, and you must stay within the walled Old Town, to experience the charm & elegance of this city. The best bet is Youth Hostel, which has very clean & affordable rooms, in the heart of Old town.*

---

We took the Canadian National Highway again the next morning, and drove towards the capital of Canada – Ottawa. With some pin-point accurate navigation, we reached Gatineau Park in no time, and explored this huge area full of nature with some spectacular views of Ottawa town & river. After savouring our eyes to few pristine lakes, including the very unique Pink Lake, we reached our cute little wooden Bed & Breakfast house. The French couple there treated us very warmly, and we called off the day with a quiet drink on their patio looking at the stars. A three-course gourmet breakfast was waiting for us the next morning, and we bid adieu to this wonderful French couple after that. The Canadian capital was just a short halt for us, and we spent that time at the primary attraction of Ottawa – the Parliament Hill.

Niagara Falls is to Canada what Elvis is to Maryland. This torrential cluster of three falls welcomes thousands of tourists to witness its wonder. The thrill of being on the edge, the thrill of watching one-fifth of the world's freshwater tumbling down uncontrollably, is mind boggling experience. I remember the childlike joy I felt when I first saw that enormous curtain of white. After hours of gaping at this roaring wonder, on the Maid of the Mist, at the Table Rock restaurant, in a dark room where Niagara's fury is virtually simulated, in the galleys built behind the falls – even the mighty Niagara seemed tame. We spent some time at going around the Niagara town & the Cliffton Hill, crammed with quirky museums and amusement houses, and offering some Vegas-style entertainment. The night at Niagara gave us a different spell binding experience, with the white curtain of falls painted with all sorts of colours.

---

**Tip**

*A night stay at Niagara can be very expensive. Either do a day trip from Toronto, but if you don't have own vehicle, then stay at one of the Bed & Breakfast places just on outskirts of Niagara town.*

---

### Western Canada – Picture Perfect

After a wonderful trip of the east, we finally flew to my sister & brother-in-law's home-base – Edmonton. Edmonton is the capital city of Alberta. Albertans like to claim that they have the best of everything the country has to offer. From the finest beef to the best national parks, the most beautiful towns to the oldest First Nation tribes, the largest malls to the prettiest lakes, Alberta has it all.

Edmonton is a huge city, home to 1.1 million people and is the northernmost city in North America of at least one million people. Edmonton is famous for its beautiful river valley park system, the North Saskatchewan River Valley, which offers many kilometres of recreational trails, wildlife viewing, and city views. If the great outdoors is not your target, the city also offers West Edmonton Mall, the largest shopping mall in North America. On top of that, Edmonton has a vibrant theatre community, a busy cycle of annual festivals, national sports team's active year-round, and wonderful winter recreational opportunities.

We were directly taken from the airport to my cousin's house for one activity that everybody living in Canada has to do in summers – Patio Barbeque. Kamal & Malvika welcomed us with some Glenfiddich on the rocks & delicious Grilled Salmon. They don't call this city – The Festival City of Canada for nothing. Their claims of not even a single day of the year going without some or the other festival in the city is not wrong. The next few days went acclimatizing & exploring this culturally rich city, via the means of majorly walking, and their efficient public transit. A large part of the city, built before and during the Second World War, is laid out in a grid pattern of straight streets, which make for easy navigation...a.k.a our very own City Beautiful. The walking part didn't go too well with Deenaz & Mummy, but then the sights & sojourns of the eclectic downtown & beautiful river valley aptly made up for it.

> ### Tip
> *It's better to buy a set of 10 tokens for public transit, rather than individuals – it costs less. Each travel will entitle you for a 2 hour transfer, so it's better to plan your destinations in such a manner that you can utilize the 2 hour transfer.*

The city's primary claim to fame has to be West Edmonton Mall, considered to be the world's largest retail space before a rival in the Emirates rudely dethroned it from its numero uno position. Housing more than 800 retail brands, 100 restaurants, 9 theme parks, a built-in hotel, an amusement park, an artificial beach and indoor wave pool, casino, movie theatres, indoor lake and Santa Maria ship replica, all under one roof, the sheer size & dimension of the mall are gargantuan. Among all the sight-seeing, I also got the opportunity to meet another old classmate – Tony in Edmonton. We had a great BBQ evening with Tony & Priti.

Edmonton's summer brings many festivals, as much that one can expect to find some kind of festival any weekend during the summer months and they are usually located in the central region either around Whyte Ave or downtown at the Legislature grounds or in front of City Hall – Sir Winston Churchill Square. Within a couple of days, these locations became our favourite hang-outs. Churchill Square is always packed with activities – Food streets, Works & Design Festival, Dance Festivals, Live Jazz performances, you can just pick up a home-brewed Beer & enjoy the feel of this lively city.

> ### Tip
> *Pick up the local newspapers, available free of cost all over the city, to check the current local listings of events & activities during these festivals. Most of the locals also are not aware of a number of great activities.*

Edmonton also boasts of one of the largest & most beautiful River Valley park systems - The North Saskatchewan, providing a natural corridor for all-season recreation and relaxation. The river valley is the longest expanse of urban parkland in North America – 22 times the size of New York's Central Park – with golf courses, 22 major parks and over 160 kilometres of maintained multi-use trails for walking, cross-country skiing, cycling, and more. Several attractions are located along the river valley including Fort Edmonton Park, the Valley Zoo, and the Muttart Conservatory. The 'Pets in the Park' event at one of the most popular parks in the city - Hawrelak Park, was a unique experience with numerous varieties & types of pets & their activities. Edmonton has excellent cycling routes which allow for all-year cycling. So, Deenaz & I joined the local community's favourite mode of travel – with couple of borrowed bicycles, to explore the city in a totally different manner.

> ### Tip
>
> *There are a variety of bike shops, including a non-profit bicycle co-op, edmontonbicyclecommuters.ca. You can drop in on their workshop hours and wrench your own bike for cheap. Bikes are easily available for rent with its accessories & gear. Bike maps are freely available at many places.*

## Twin 'Wild' Gems of Rocky Mountains

Our western side road trip commenced in a huge vehicle called Dodge – Grand Caravan. With my BIL on the wheel & yours truly as the apt Navigator (fully equipped with maps, GPS etc), the rest of the team was sure of having a fantastic trip. The two of the largest provinces of Canada – Alberta & British Columbia have almost everything you can ask for – from the imposing edifice of the Canadian Rockies to the vast expanse of the Columbian Icefields, the pristine infinity of Banff & Jasper National Parks, the 'tipsy' Okanagan Valley full of wineries & orchards, the world's largest gondola ride at Whistler and the sprawling skylines of Vancouver.

Elk, bison, moose, mountain goats & caribou must have established their own pathways in Jasper National Park long before humans arrived in the Canadian Rockies. Known as the gentle giant of the Rockies, Jasper - the shy cousin to bold, brassy Banff, was our first destination. "If you are really lucky, you will spot a Black Bear, and if you spot a Grizzly your life has been blessed" – a statement told to every tourist by the Canadians. With these words ringing in our ears, we entered the Maligne Valley road, and there it was...two huge Black ones, right on the road...just strolling across. So, after thanking our lucky stars, we continued our quest of exploring this beautiful valley with staggeringly deep Maligne Canyon, legendary Maligne Lake & the mysterious Medicine Lake. Finally, after soaking up in Miette Hot Springs - the hottest springs in the Canadian Rockies, we reached the small town of Jasper. It is home to the stunning Jasper Park Lodge, the superb Pyramid Lake & the historic Lake Patricia where Prime Minister Winston Churchill pulled off his secret military experiment called 'Operation Habakuk'. A perfect post-retirement settling down place, we finished the day watching some amazing fireworks as part of Canada Day celebrations.

> ### Tip
>
> *Make sure to cover the Maligne Valley on the way – all sights on this stretch are very pretty, and experience Miette Hot Springs, which are far better than their 'more-famous' & expensive counter-parts like Radium & Banff Hot Springs.*

The next morning we hit the road and caught the Icefields Parkway, often called the most scenic highway in the world. Named for the tremendous glaciers which flank its western side, the Parkway weaves up & around the mountains between Jasper & Banff National Parks, as it parallels the Great Divide. If nature was to win a prize for layout & design, it would most probably be awarded to the scenic topography of these two National Parks. The picturesque beauty of these little hamlets in Alberta put the words 'picture perfect' to shame. Everywhere we looked there was something prettier & more stunning to see.

From monolithic mountains, dabbed in shades of summery white & frosty grey, to the cloaks of green that shroud the landscape, everything about this highway is awe inspiring & scenically overwhelming. Bright turquoise lakes, fast flowing rivers, unusual gorges & canyons & an abundance of wildlife, roaming about the terrain with ease & familiarity, often stopping to stare at the weird two-legged aliens who have dared to invade their land. It's so bizarre, and at the same time, wonderful. In India, we are used to driving into national parks, going on jeep safaris to spot wildlife. Here, the animals are just there, by the major highways, and you have to stay on your toes if you don't want to miss out. Cries of "Elk Elk"..."Moose Moose"...Bear Bear"...were a common hearing, in our vehicle as well as others.

Today, Canada's first National Park draws people from every corner of the world to experience this uniquely preserved & protected World Heritage Site. Our first major halt (not considering all the minor ones – due to various 'reasons') was the roaring Athabasca Falls, where the Athabasca River funnels into a narrow gorge to surge out right beside the parking lot. The last stop in Jasper National Park, before entering Banff National Park is The Columbia Icefields. The Great Wall of China, the Statue of Liberty, Pyramids of Egypt, Taj Mahal of India...every corner of the world has its must-see attraction...in the Canadian Rockies, it's the Columbia Icefields. Composed of 8 glaciers, it includes Athabasca Glacier which is one of the most accessible glaciers in the world & is supposedly as wide as Eiffel Tower is tall. BIL & I did a touristy trek of this frigid white space which took us right to the 'toe' of Athabasca.

> **Tip**
>
> *A trip on Ice Explorer at Columbia Icefield is definitely avoidable & is not worth the money. A far better option is to trek till toe of the Glacier, to actually feel the atmosphere. There are numerable stop-overs & sights on Icefield Parkway, make sure you pre-plan the picks you want to halt at.*

We continued our journey on this unforgettable highway, providing you picnic areas, campgrounds, breath taking scenery, easy access hiking trails, and as we crossed the historic Saskatchewan Crossing, we entered what is called 'The Lake Trail'. This stretch of Icefields Parkway has some of the most beautiful glacial lakes in the world. As we moved past some Moose spotting areas near Cephren Lake, we reached the highest point of the journey at Bow Summit, overlooking a spectacular view of Peyto Lake. The bright blue & jade green glacial water of the lake & the wide view of Mistaya Valley make this one of the most scenic spots of the tour. It was aptly put by an old couple we met on our way to top who told us – "The view from top is worth a million dollars!!!" A little ahead we passed Bow Lake, with its alpine fields of wild flowers all around, as we approached what they call as "The Jewel of Rockies" – Lake Louise.

The lake itself (named after Princess Louise Caroline Alberta, daughter of Queen Victoria), is so blue, it defies words that try & pinpoint its exact hue. The world-famous Fairmont Chateau Lake Louise sits at the opposite end of the lake from Mt Victoria & Victoria Glacier. But being a long weekend, there was absolutely no space for even a good family photo. So, instead of getting jammed in the weekend rush, we continued our journey quickly towards Banff town. And the rest of Icefields Parkway didn't disappoint us as well. This highway was packed with attractions – every few kilometres you will find exciting signs. On our way to Canmore, a sleepy satellite of Banff, we came across a car stopped on the road. This generally means they have spotted an animal, so we pulled alongside & asked what they have seen. The lady at the wheel just nodded to the side of the road. And there it was – a massive Elk, a beautiful stag, giving his spreading antlers a good scratch against a tree.

The next morning was crisp & bright, and welcomed us with a grand view of the mountains outside our motel balcony, with some fantastic clear-enough-to-drink air. As we head to this extremely pretty & historic town Banff, sloping mountain-style houses & 'Animal-named' streets lined with wrought iron lamps created a beautiful picture. It's more touristy than Jasper, but a great place to walk around, among horse-drawn carriages & metal plaques of bear & caribou, and a dozen fun-looking restaurants. Of course, the most famous of them is Grizzly House which allows you to cook your own meal on hot rocks, and their menu includes almost everything from bison to elk, moose to alligators & rattlesnakes. This UNESCO Heritage town is all about pretty sights & history & fun people. An especially nice view is from Banff Gondola, with some excellent plaques on the viewing deck that spell out the town's history.

On our way out from Banff towards Golden, we decided to take the more scenic and leisurely experience of Bow Valley Parkway. This narrow highway parallels the TransCanada Highway, and is more popular with the wild animals. As we switched from these 'twin-wonder' National parks and entered Yoho National Park boasting of towering rock walls, spectacular waterfalls & numerous neck-braking peaks, it's no wonder that word "Yoho" is a Cree expression of Awe !!! And last but definitely not the least, this new National park gave us one of the rarest sights (obviously, after the Grizzly) in Rockies – the shy, very dumb-looking Moose. Its first sight next to the road got all my childhood (Ok...maybe still going) memories of Archie comics, and my first reaction was "Duh"!!!

> **Tip**
>
> *Although all these deer-family animals like Elk, Caribou or Moose don't look very dangerous, it is advisable that one should not get down from the vehicle in close vicinity. Because when a creature even bigger than a horse, with giant antlers decides to shove you, you stay shoved.*

## Exploring Few Hidden Locales Further West

Saying that Golden is one of the most perfect & beautiful locations in the world might sound like a grandiose statement, but it's not so outrageous once you look at the facts...and look out the window. Sitting at the convergence of the Columbia & Kicking Horse Rivers (famous for its White Water Rafting), Golden is the perfect getaway & four-season recreational paradise for travellers. Our first halt here was a cute little "Petting Farm". It was a home to many breeds of goats, sheep, chickens, pigs, ducks – but not just any old kind, it was a collection of rare domestic breeds – some of these animals you may not have ever seen or heard of. So, sis & Dee went ahead feeding the chickens, giving hay to goats, bottle-feeding the new born lambs, brushing the miniature donkeys & getting kissed by the alpacas (a kind of llama). One young mix of horse & donkey even fell in love with Dee. After settling down in our aptly named 'Sportsman Lodge', we nicely utilized its indoor swimming pool-cum-Jacuzzi-cum-water park. Of course, not to forget an interesting piece of architecture – the Timber Frame pedestrian bridge.

Our destination next day morning was Kicking Horse Mountain Resort – a must visit place if you are in this area. There are loads & loads of activities to do here, from mountain biking to trekking, from ATV's to chair lifts, and an actual Grizzly Bear refuge as well. The Resort's pride and joy is the 8-person gondola which whisks you from base to the Eagle's Eye summit in less than 15 minutes. There you'll find 'Canada's Highest Dining Experience' the Eagle's Eye Restaurant and Bar (great for a fancy lunch, a Ceaser or even just a quick pee) and one of the best views Canadian resorts have to offer. We had panoramic views of the Rocky Mountains, the Columbia River wetlands & the quaint town of Golden. During the journey upwards, we even got a glimpse of Kicking Horse resident Grizzly bear – Boo.

> **Tip**
>
> *Of all the Gondola rides during this west side trip, take the Kicking Horse one, it is one of the longest, has the best views from top, and is the most economical. All others are just hyped & have nothing much to offer.*

Our journey continued from Golden to Revelstoke, as we crossed Yoho National Park & entered Glacier National Park. A drive through Glacier National Park & the historical Rogers Pass was truly incredible. The giant cedar forests were like an unbelievable sight of what you tend to see only in movies. And, the Enchanted Forest took us into the Fairy Tale world. As we got out from the National Park area & got into the amazing Okanagan Valley, landscapes changed so very beautifully. The Okanagan is an ecological wonder. Its divergent terrain has created unique microclimates in various pockets of the valley. Agri-tourism is very strong in this charming region with roadside & farm-gate produce at the ready.

Our first halt in this multi-offering region was a small Cheese Farm & Factory in a tiny town called Armstrong. We savoured our taste buds with some amazing variety of home-made cheese, at the same time learning all about cheese-making from the experts. After giving them a little business of many interesting variants of cheese, we reached our beautiful farmhouse Bed & Breakfast at Kelowna. Kelowna's great climate, sparkling lake & mountain views offer visitors an array of activities, alongside discovering their numerous wineries & orchards. Our farmhouse was an old ancestral 19$^{th}$ century wooden mansion amidst vast expanse of farm land, and our gracious host Mark & his wife looked after us nicely with tours of his farm & some farm fresh eggs for breakfast.

---

### Tip

*Mission Creek Farmhouse in Kelowna is highly recommended, it will give you an amazing feel of staying right in the farm with animal stock, but at the same time, you are in Kelowna town. The décor & styling of this old farmhouse is an experience one should not miss.*

---

Once known as the mecca for 'peaches & beaches', the Okanagan Valley is now being recognized as the destination for the wine tourist. Kelowna offers you miles of sandy beaches hugging the shores of Okanagan Lake, North America's longest floating bridge & its home to dozens of wineries, ranging in size from cottage-style to large mansion-style. The entire day we spent exploring these wineries, one after the other. After we had enough of wine-tours & free-tasting, not to mention some strawberry picking in-between, we finally settled down for some chilled beer at the sparkling lakeside. When they say wines are made in the vineyard, they're not kidding. There's no way man could replicate something this dazzling in a lab. And our day finished off at the picturesque Kelowna Marina under their iconic 'Sails'. But what truly got a sense of pride in us, was a visit to Mr Sidhu's 'award-winning' Kalala Wineries. As he explained the entire process of wine-making techniques to us & simply opened his small wine-bar to us, I was ecstatic to see 'Kalala' written in Punjabi above English on each wine bottle of his.

> ## *Tip*
>
> *Don't take wine tours of the bigger wineries, they are just good to visit. Take the tours & tasting in smaller wineries – they treat you really well & offer you some of their best wines for tasting. Kalala winery is a MUST visit, they just love to have any Indians visiting them.*

As we continued our journey in this wonderful valley, it was a picture-perfect sight to have the lake running on one side of the road, and numerous orchards, wineries, fruits & vegetable gardens on the other. After the usual stop-over at Tim Hortons, we reached Penticton River Float – one of the most popular summer activities in this region. It's a man-made river-channel joining two huge lakes with a controlled gentle flow of water. People from the entire Okanagan valley & beyond come here during summers, with various kinds of floats (few as big as double beds, with seats, in-built ice cases etc) to enjoy this leisurely activity. So, we rented out a big enough float for four of us, and Splash – in we go, with beer in hand & ducks following our lead. After spending some quality time in the water & enjoying the local 'Elvis' performing by the beach, we resumed our road trip to our next destination – Osoyoos.

The southernmost town in the Okanagan, Osoyoos boasts the driest climate in Canada, with the hot, arid summers making it a popular vacation destination. The town is a hotbed for visitors year-round, who come to dip their toes in the warm Lake Osoyoos, sip fine wines and take a pleasant stroll through the downtown shops. The warm climate along with Osoyoos' complex irrigation system allows the longest growing season in the country, with crops yielding a great variety of fruit & vegetables, making this a favourite for 'Saadde Punjabis' to settle here. After doing a quick round of the lake, downtown & visiting Sandhu Orchards & Farms (picking some unbelievable sized cherries direct from the plantations), we arrived at our Countryside Bed & Breakfast amidst wineries on one side & Orchards on the other three sides. Our hosts here were George & his wife, who actually kept us just like their own guests. We had a nice Bar-be-Que party at his Gazebo in the evening, with George joining us & sharing some of his 'home-made' grape alcohol, which he lovingly called 'Antibiotic'! And they sent us off with an elaborate three-course English breakfast, very lovingly prepared by both of them.

## Double 'V' Destinations of Westernmost Part

With our last destinations in mind, we set off towards Vancouver & Victoria. As the highway goes all along US-Canada border, we crossed Princeton & Hope on our way, with a small halt at Manning Park where the ever-so-friendly 'Gophers' greeted us literally with 'open arms'. These guys look right out of a Chip & Dale cartoon, and were climbing all over us to grab a bite. Finally, our road-trip came to an end as we reached Vancouver. Arriving at Vancouver, successfully rated as the most liveable city in the world, we were pleasantly surprised by the change in scenery, temperature & demographics (not to forget the Hindi & Punjabi FM channels as well). Having spent the last eight days in hamlets & towns inhabited by mere thousands, the million-odd population of Canada's second largest city brought forth a welcome change in the form of urban adventure. Surrounded by spectacular snow-capped mountains, city-hugging beaches & dense parklands, this hip & happening metropolis is a multi-culture & multilingual paradise. We only had time that day to visit the eclectic Granville Island, with its hidden cobbled lanes & the famous Public Market along False Creek shores. With the late evening spent at the Vancouver harbour, we retired to our B & B.

Next day we switched our mode of transport – from Dodge Caravan to a Cruise liner. BC Ferries is one of the largest ferry operators in the world. Our cruise ship from Vancouver to Victoria was HUGE...a 6-deck ship with couple of basement decks for accommodating vehicles including buses, trucks etc (Imagine two football fields back-to-back). This two hour journey was one of the highlights of our trips, with everything available on the deck...from lounges to cafes, from sun-decks to shops, from activity centres to world-class amenities, it had all. And the view all along the trip was to die for. We made the most of our cruise ship, and reached Victoria, the southernmost tip of Vancouver Islands.

> ### *Tip*
>
> *A journey by BC Ferry cruise ship is a must from Vancouver to Victoria, as this is the most economical cruise ship journey you can get anywhere. For just $14 per person, it was a steal.*

Victoria is a city of energy & progress. It boasts a stunning natural landscape and is steeped in a culture that has preserved and nurtured the best of its history without being stuck in the past. It's a place where the laid-back modernization of the West Coast blends with time-honoured British, European & Asian traditions. More importantly, I was happy to be finally getting a chance to explore independently using the maps & public transport. So, here I was, back to what I do best, with a map in my hand & soaking in the atmosphere. We reached our place of stay, the first 'hotel' we checked into during the entire journey, and we were already all excited to explore this beautiful city, where the elegance of history mingles with the panache of modern life.

Our first target was obviously the Inner Harbour, an invigorating menagerie of walkers. The water here is a shimmering symphony of passenger boats, car ferries, yachts, float planes, water taxis & pedicabs coming & going. With the aristocratic ivy-covered Fairmont Empress Hotel on one side & the architectural Legislative Building on the other, the Inner Harbour comes alive with buskers, artists & musicians, mimes, sketch artists & something for everyone. This carnival atmosphere was a great way to wander away few hours. And after checking out the perennial favourite – Miniature World, featuring over 80 exciting miniature dioramas including some historic, fairy tale sections & doll houses, we caught the cute-little 'Water-Taxi' to the quirky float-home village called Fisherman's Wharf. This place offered us a glimpse at commercial fishing vessels up close & personal, with some fresh catch straight off the boats. But we headed for the main reason we came here for – to have what they claim to be the best Fish & Chips in entire Canada. We were also greeted by the friendly seal that jumps at every opportunity to grab a fish or two.

A bright & sunny morning welcomed us as we headed to the quiet & beautiful seaside location of Oak Bay, soaking up the ambience of Oak Bay Village by taking a leisurely stroll on the streets. Few more friendly Seals were waiting for us at Oak Bay Marina, as we got yet another free ride by ever-so-helpful Victoria bus drivers. We spent our afternoon exploring Victoria's vibrant downtown, with Royal BC Museum, Thunderbird Park, and the bustling Bastion & Centennial Squares, where the Mexican Dance Festival was happening. After a quick lunch at Canada's oldest Chinatown, we headed to the world-famous five-season Butchart Gardens. This piece of wonder continues to be a premier attraction impressing everyone with its unique five-season beauty. As we strolled its Rose, Italian, Mediterranean, Japanese & Sunken gardens, we discovered why exactly it has been named a National Historic Site. And, because of some good & careful planning, we became part of a fantastic performance of Rock & Roll in the evening and witnessed one of the most amazing Musical-Fireworks displays along with Night Illumination.

> ### Tip
>
> *Make sure you keep Saturday as one of the night-stays in Victoria, and visit Butchart Garden on Sat. The Live Rock shows, Night Illumination & amazing Musical-Fireworks happen only on Saturdays.*

With unforgettable memories, we left Victoria by BC Ferry & landed in Vancouver again. The day went in settling down, relaxing & a short trip to Kitsilano Beach area, where we could catch postcard-perfect shots of Vancouver's downtown & Stanley Park. A string of various kinds of museums awaits you at Kitsilano neighbourhood. Next day armed with our 'Day-Pass' giving us unlimited travel on train, bus & sea-bus, we were off to explore this lovely city. We started with the most visited attraction – Stanley Park - 1000 acres of mostly forested land at the western tip of downtown making it one of North America's largest urban parks, and quite literally, is an oasis of wilderness in the middle of the city. After wandering around in this beautiful serene park which houses Vancouver Aquarium apart from a number of other attractions, we headed to Capilano Suspension Bridge, a 450 feet span of wooden planks teetering 230 feet above Capilano River, this is a mind-blowing experience. Here, you have activities to spend almost the entire day, be it the rainforest, 100 feet high Treetop Adventure or the latest daredevil experience – Cliffwalk. This one is a chain of narrow (sometimes glass) cantilevered walkways 300 feet above undisturbed rainforest valley.

---

> ### <u>*Tip*</u>
>
> *The best way to explore Vancouver is with the Day Pass for all public transport.*
> *You can utilize services of sky trains, buses & a must-try Sea-Bus.*

After this 'deadly' experience we headed back to the Vancouver downtown, with a quick bite at the serene patios of Lonsdale Quay in North Vancouver. We made full use of our day-pass by boarding the huge Sea-Bus on our way back, which gives you excellent views of the Lions Gate Bridge on the way. The landing Waterfront station offered us magnificent views of the iconic Five Sails of Canada Place, home of the official Vancouver 2010 Winter Olympics cauldron. Downtown Vancouver has great variety to offer – we loved the stark contrast between the re-vitalized warehouses of Gastown & the ultra-chic feel of the Yaletown. It is said that Gastown is older than Vancouver itself, and when we saw the famous most unique Steam Clock, we couldn't agree more. Before boarding the Greyhound back to Edmonton, we could manage to catch a glimpse of Telus Science Centre as well as BC Place stadium. We came to the end of our western side of trip, and it wouldn't be wrong to say that Vancouver is undoubtedly the novae traveller's new-age playground.

As we arrived back in Edmonton, the countdown began, counting the number of days left to go, packing whatever we could fit in that 23 kg limit, and doing some last minute shopping. And believe me, we were actually missing India like anything, just wanted to get back to our home, although the sad feeling of leaving family was there deep in our hearts. The Canada trip was coming to an end, and lots of wrong notions about this country got cleared. When we first arrived, the notion in everybody's mind is that it's just a cold place north of USA that gives us terrors in the form of bears & Bryan Adams. It's big & rich and has maple trees, and that the Canadians get really upset when they're mistaken for Americans. But Canada is much more than that. You will like the country even better when you wake up, because Canada does breakfasts astonishingly well. Waffles, pancakes, bacon, bottomless cups of coffee, and waitresses who all but sit in your lap & ask you what India's like. Clearly, the Sikhs had good reasons to settle here. It's a shock to me, but I have to say I couldn't agree more with the statement – "When I'm in Canada, I feel this is what the world should be like."

# **Refer Page - 157 for Photographs of Travelogue - 6**

# The N-W Road Trip

## From 'Vada-Pav' To 'Sarson Da Saag'

*"Road Trips aren't measured by Kilometre Markers, but by Moments…!!!"*

## Planning Phase of a Road Journey

The concept of time, as it's commonly understood by normal people with normal jobs and normal goddamn lives, doesn't exist on the road. You never really know where you are or what time it is, and the outside world starts to fade away. Travelling across India by road is an intimate way to get acquainted with its myriad cultures, each with their unique beliefs and lifestyles. I'm a wanderer, an artist, and an adventurist. I've always loved the idea of packing a bag and leaving town for a while and it was time for me to do it. I feel as though you can't really live the experience unless you travel by car. I wanted to travel the non-interstate highways along with national expressways and stop at every small roadside Dhaba that I could find and savour the local taste of the place. One of our favourite TV shows – "Highway on my Plate" became the 'Guru' during the journey and the HOMP book became the road-trip Bible. I was hoping that this will be a successful adventure and it's something that we will be able to do every year – of course, on a different route.

The N-W road trip, or as I fondly call it as the journey from 'Vada Pav to Sarson da Saag', was on my mind since a long time. I found the right opportunity when I had to move on posting and a friend's swanky Honda Jazz had to be brought from Pune up North, and I pounced on this chance to hit the road. While I was in the 'planning phase', I avoided deciding how the road trip will go. The flow goes how the flow goes…I can't steer the river. But, I did find places worth a visit, and I did make reservations for lodging with a mix of Fauji & Non-Fauji accommodations. You could have the best checklist for a road trip ever conceived. But every road trip is unique, so there may be unique things to add to your road trip checklist.

The journey from Pune all the way up to Bathinda is a mix of state highways and national expressways, covering a distance of approximately 2000 kms. When you look at the map, it seems daunting at first – so many states to cover (six states/UT in total) and so many kilometres to cover. That's before you realize that people sometimes zip through this trip in matter of just 24-36 hours. But that could be only tried if holiday is not on your mind, because this drive is worth minimum seven, eight or even ten days. We planned the drive in a similar manner, stopping at places en route and soaking in the beauty of the journey and not just the destination.

We set off one bright, sunny morning having strapped ourselves comfortably in our sparkling blue Jazz. Me being the only driver, took the driver's seat with my wife Deenaz by my side. It was a good start : the weather was pleasant, we had peppy music and had thoughtfully stacked up on food and drinks including some chilled beer, as we hit the Pune – Mumbai Expressway. We meandered along at around 100 km per hour with a small snack halt along the expressway, before the Western Ghats begun. Another three hours of driving took us through the industrial townships of Panvel before reaching the hustle & bustle of Mumbai. Although two days was a real short duration to do justice to a city like Mumbai, but we tried to do things not done before. Being already done Excellen-Sea before, this time I selected "Gajalee" – the legendary place that serves some of the best seafood in town – as was recommended by HOMP. Gajalee specializes in Malwani food, coastal cooking that features hot coconut-based sweet & sour curries with fish and seafood. After checking out some 'live' stock of seafood, we selected a medium-sized Lobster which got cooked in a delicious garlic pepper butter coating that added flavour to the intrinsically sweet lobster meat. We couldn't leave this place without their traditional Fish Thali with fish curry, rice, bombil fry & 'sol kadi'.

> **Tip**
>
> *Highway on My Plate has already come up with 3-4 volumes and gives out authentic eating joints, mostly absolute locals, and their recommendations mostly meet the right taste bud. Do go off the beaten track a bit to try out local delicacies.*

## First Phase of Maharashtra & Gujarat

We started early next day from Mumbai, rolling up our windows to keep out city's pollution. About half an hour and many honks later, we cruised over the flyover on Sanjay Gandhi National Park and took the NH-8 for our next stopover – Daman. Driving through Maharashtra was wonderful, as the roads lay wrapped in miles of fields, occasionally separated by dry river beds. At Vapi town, we took a detour to Daman – one half of the Union Territory of Daman & Diu. As I turned westwards towards the sea, groves of tall palms lined up on both sides of the road and the sun played hide & seek behind them. I was super glad to see that Liquor shops in Daman were beating the grocery shops hands down in numbers, and I knew that I have to stock up before leaving this UT, which seems to be the perfect neighbourhood for the Gujju's and their dry state. We checked into Cidade-de-Daman at the picturesque Devka Beach, and it was that perfect getaway we were looking for after Pune and Mumbai. So, we spent the day at Daman enjoying the company of the waves with chilled beer & cocktails, and some awesome seafood.

Further on, the roads in Gujarat were lined by factories, and at some places, there were fields on one side and power plants on the other, providing a distinct contrast. As we crossed the chemical-industrial towns of Gujarat such as Surat and Vadodara on a good stretch of NH-8, my body started asking for some food – authentic Gujarati Thali to be precise. But instead of getting into the bustling towns of Surat or Vadodara, we decided to hit the small town of Anand – the birth place of AMUL (Anand Milk Union Ltd). A few quick searches on the mobile internet, and we found the best option for Gujarati thali – Divine Dining Hall, serving authentic 6-7 katori's of kadhi, sweet dal, *aam-ras*, *ringda sabzi* along with the staple *rotla, chaach & khichdi*. With our stomachs full heartily, we made our way towards Ahmedabad & Gandhinagar on the Mahatma Gandhi Expressway which was like a dream road on which we practically flew in an hour. The evening was spent exploring the well-organized Gandhinagar town and the typical Gujarati snacks fondly called as *"farsaan"*, and they say it rightly – 'any time is farsaan time in Gujarat'. With some precise information from the HOMP book, we savoured on some tasty khaman, juicy khandvi and flaky *patra* at Vrindavan Farsaan Bhandar before digging our teeth in some delicious *daabeli* from a neighbouring street cart, and finished off the evening with Gwalia's flavoured kulfi.

## Second Phase of Rajasthan

The next morning we drove on to Udaipur, as we crossed state borders from the lands of 'Dhoklas' to my home-ground – the land of 'Dal-Baati-Choorma'. The journey didn't seem tough because of the fabulous roads, as cornfields and rice plantations on either side took place of the industries, and the delicious local food at the dhabas lifted our spirits. Stone mountains lined the road as we drove into Udaipur, where we checked into the beautifully located MES Inspection Bungalow – overlooking the entire Udaipur city & the picturesque Lake Pichola. The next two days were spent exploring this "Oh So Romantic" lake-city and its many lanes & bye-lanes. The Sisodia Rajputs of Mewar migrated to Udaipur to build this fairy tale city after the fall of Chittaurgarh in 1567. Palaces and more palaces, mansions, havelis, temples & museums, and the gorgeous lakes for viewing are just like Glimpses of Paradise !!! After being done with gazing at the lake with awe, we headed to the prime spot in Udaipur – its City Palace. Most apartments are astonishing here with their craftsmanship, and the whole experience is so mesmerising. After absorbing all the history we could from City Palace, we savoured on some historic display of old wheels at the Maharaja's Vintage Car collection.

---

**_Tip_**

*Visit to City Palace in Udaipur is an absolute must keeping plenty of time for this amazing piece of history. Be careful about the narrow to very narrow lanes of Old City here and preferably park your car to take a local tuk-tuk to get the feel of the place.*

The Udaipur itinerary is impossible to be finished in just two days, but we tried to squeeze in the maximum – boat ride in Lake Pichola, Fateh Sagar Lake, and Maharana Pratap memorial with a decent dose of history-learning during the Sound & Light Show. When after all this sightseeing we felt hungry, I consulted our dear friends – Rocky & Mayur yet again, who have been constantly guiding us with HOMP throughout this journey. Based on their strong recommendation, we headed to Ambrai – the restaurant having arguably the best view in Udaipur. And, we were definitely not disappointed – a 300-year old building, shady seating on the banks of the lake and an astounding view of the City Palace, the Lake Palace Hotel & rest of Udaipur city gleaming in lights. The second night was as special as the first one, with a romantic candle-light dinner at Shikarbadi – the Royal Hunting Retreat of the Maharaja. Your trip is a real success if apart from amazing ambience, you also get delicious authentic Rajasthani cuisine. As we set off from Udaipur, barren mountains, tiny temples, black-faced langurs, and camel carts met us all along the highway. We crossed Chittaurgarh on our way, and all those childhood stories about the Rajputs who embraced death rather than bowing to a foreign power, came to the mind, as we could get a clear glimpse of Chittaur's stupendous fortifications. I drove non-stop this time with the excitement of reaching 'Home-Sweet-Home' – The Pink City of Jaipur.

Jaipur has a very 'feel-good' factor to the city – there is so much to see & absorb in Jaipur, the lives of people on the street, the exciting shopping even on pavements, the craftsmen working by the side, and above all the walled city – full of bazaars, the bustle of cows, camels & rickshaws, this city is worth exploring on foot. The visit home is never complete without savouring on the super-delicious *"Photte ka Meat"* that can only be prepared by my Mom, and she didn't disappoint me this time also, as it was waiting on the table the moment we arrived. Add some fabulous Brain Masala, and you know that you can give anything for this. Of course, we didn't miss out on some authentic Rajasthani *'Laal Maas'* & *'Gatte ki Sabzi'* along with traditional Rajasthani folk dance at Indiana – Kunwar Jai Singh's garden restaurant. Meeting & chatting with the man himself was a great honour.

## Final Phase of Punjab

After feeling fully pampered and rested at Jaipur, we finally embanked on our last part of journey towards Bathinda. The longest and the most barren stretch of journey gave us an opportunity to finally get the glimpses of some remote parts of Rajasthan with long stretches of road sandwiched between sand dunes on both sides. We had rightly stocked our Jazzy Boy with loads of chilled beer & lassi, which were like life-saviours during the entire journey. After a brief 'furniture-shopping' halt at Sardarshahar, we reached our new abode at Bathinda.

My road trip memories have always returned to me with a splendid rush of excitement, and having those road trip photos and road trip stories, makes remembering the journey a much simpler matter. Though pictures and words can never equal the magnificence of the actual road trip experience, they do offer an exciting creative outlet and a way to share your experience with those who could not come along. I find that the act of writing something down in itself helps me retain my road trip memories. And Bill Bryson aptly brings it out in his quote:-

*"To my mind, the greatest reward and luxury of travel is to be able to experience everyday things as if for the first time, to be in a position in which almost nothing is so familiar it is taken for granted."*

So, here's to this splendid road trip and looking forward for the next one.....
Cheers !!!

# **Refer Page - 160 for Photographs of Travelogue - 7**

# A Backpacking UK Trip

## Summer in British Style

### Great Britain – Country with Many Countries

Are you one of those who've always wanted to experience London madness, Welsh countryside, Irish wonders, Scottish highlands and Taste of Scotch Whisky, but who only sits around bleating about the crippling expense of a trip all around United Kingdom ??? This is for you, it's about a British holiday that stops by all major countries of Great Britain – Wales, North Ireland, Scotland & England – in 18 days, for a price tag of within Rs 1.50 lakh (That too due to the sudden untimely fall of the Rupee right during my trip – else it would have been easily possible to do it within 1.30 lakh). Mind you, this is an "All Inclusive" price tag, including return airfare along with something I normally don't do on a foreign trip – Shopping !!!

Britain is made up of the United Kingdom of Great Britain together with the Channel Islands and the Isle of Man. Britain is a diverse nation full of contrasts; whichever direction you travel you will find a wide variety of landscapes and diverse cultures to explore. There's something for everyone in Britain – from the wealth of natural and historical heritage to the vibrant and cosmopolitan towns and cities. England, Wales, Scotland and Northern Ireland are all unique countries with their own customs, cultures and traditions, and the idea was to cover all of them in these 18 days. My 'Partner-in-Crime' – Sir AJ, was the originator of the idea of a UK trip, his sister being there, and I was more than ready to grab the opportunity of exploring yet another part of the world.

For vast number of Indians who have yet to taste the deliciousness of places like Europe and UK, the boring, off-the-mill, guided package tour is a sensible introduction. For this type of trip, you don't need your own brains, as you are travelling with someone else's – and like good obedient school children, you need to just follow instructions, and it would turn out to be 'so-called' fun trip. Well, at least you will get satisfaction of 'tick-marking' places to see. For me, its 'senseless' travel option, as I belong to the "Backpacking Universe", and we function on exactly the reverse principles – it's all about 'doing you own thing'. Another guiding principle is keeping the cost down, and when you plan on your own – it's an automated aim achieved. There's nothing to it really – just trawl the web, get on for the best deals, get off and begin backpacking your way. It's possible to survive on a daily budget of 30 Pounds in UK, that's what the 'free spirits' do. As always, the plan for the trip commenced months in advance, with extensive study of travel books, online deals and precise timely bookings (yet again, mostly Youth Hostels & local train/bus journeys). So, after the usual travel research that I love doing, and a detailed, well-crafted 'UK Backpacking Itinerary', I was all set to take on the British Summers....Head On !!!

---

**Tip**

*This time I discovered something new – if you want the best deals for a country, go on their local websites & let someone local book things for you – in this case, it was all the websites ending with ".co.uk".*

---

The great high of independent travel is "Discovery". Half the fun is to arrive in a strange city, and crack its systems – orient yourself, study the metro & bus routes and schedules; find food & accommodation, and see how you can stretch your budget to do as much as possible, instead of being 'herded around like sheep'. When you're watching your wallet, you buy a good map, and the integrated transport 'Day Pass' that allows all kinds of public transport of that city and a few more pounds off for checking up with your hostel counter.

## Bit of Shakespeare & Lot of Wales

My first destination was 'Saadda Barrminggam', the pure reason for choosing to land in Birmingham rather than London was that I got an excellent flight deal for this place and because my further plan of tying up with AJ fell in place. Birmingham also offered me the chance of catching up with an old school friend – Vandna, who was sweet enough to take off from work the next day to accompany me to Stratsford-upon-Avon – Shakespeare's Birthplace which is just a short drive from Birmingham. This small tranquil town knows what its visitors want, and it delivers the Shakespeare Experience to them pre-packaged, all ready to consume. Stratsford-upon-Avon duly lives up to the connection of its famous son, presenting to the tourist a carefully crafted veneer of Shakespeareana. It's a typically English town with the gurgling Avon flowing by, old men in tweed sitting on its bank feeding the swans, boats with names like Titania, Ophelia and Juliet serving all purposes – from floating restaurants to ice cream boats, from snack boats to even tourist offices. Even the traditional English pubs in the town are named 'Othello' or 'Hamlet', and perched on a stone plinth is a seated Shakespeare, pensively thinking up a rhyme to 'thou'. After re-visiting history at Shakespeare's birthplace, a magnificent study of period architecture and design, I returned back to Birmingham to experience some of its nightlife in Brindleyplace & Broad Street areas. Tree-lined squares, international cuisine and an enviable canal-side location make Brindleyplace one of Birmingham's most exciting destinations, and in the evenings, the place comes alive with great food, music and laughter. Broad Street is Birmingham's most dynamic entertainment destination offering everything from intimate canal-side bars and international club nights, to comedy and great restaurants.

I caught the British Rail for my next destination – Wales where I was supposed to meet AJ who travelled from Manchester. We decided to explore the Welsh countryside of Conwy Valley, Snowdonia National Park & beach town of Llandudno in Northern Wales, and hence met up at the one-platform railway station of Llandudno. After checking into our cute Llandudno Hostel, we reached the medieval walled town of Conwy with its mighty 13th century castle built by Edward I to dominate and guard the banks of the Conwy Estuary. Conwy is a fortified medieval hilltop village in which time stands still and its 1000-odd inhabitants make their money from its romance. After briefly exploring Conwy by walking the narrow cobbled lanes and strolling on the quayside to see the smallest house, we caught the Conwy Valley line (answer to our Kalka-Shimla toy-train), which is one of Wales' hidden secrets, 27 miles of majestic valleys, plunging rivers, fairytale castles, picturesque villages and history by the bucket load. The 'toy-train' after going through the Snowdonia NP and stopping at tiny little stations with names like 'Pont-y-Pant' & 'Betws-y-Coed', reached the slate valley of Blaenau Ffestiniog, famous for its Heritage Steam Railway. We came back to soak in the classic Victorian seafront atmosphere of Llandudno town. To say there is more to Llandudno than meets the eye is an understatement. We did hit the pier first, which offers a fun stroll out to sea, providing fabulous views of the town with the mountains dominating the horizon. But for history and nature lovers Llandudno offers a veritable gold, or should I say, Bronze Age copper mine. – The Great Orme. Llandudno is home to some vibrant night life, and we ended our day aptly at a 'hip n happening' Karaoke place.

---

## Tip

*The best & most economical way to stay abroad is Youth Hostels – you can choose anything from a 4-bedded Dorm to a 12-bedded Dorm, from a double room to a private suite - with or without attached toilets. They have kitchenettes, information centres, internet access, a pub & restaurant, pool & foosball tables, they even update you with the latest happenings of the town.*

---

## Get Lost in Picturesque Lake District

The 3-hour train ride from Northern Wales to the Lake District is postcard heaven : black & white dappled cows grazing in green meadows, picturesque flower-studded hamlets, mist covered hills - the English countryside at its best, which can be only enjoyed by a Brit-Rail journey. Brushing up close to the Scottish border in the north and tumbling down to Morecambe Bay in the south, the Lake District sits entirely within the northwest county of Cumbria and is one of England's most celebrated and mythic landscapes. Sixteen major lakes and countless other water bodies are surrounded by brooding mountains and forested valleys; a land of plunging waterfalls and blooming meadows, where scree-covered crags team with gravity-defying sheep. The careful internet research ensured that we take the best & most economical means of experiencing Lake District – and Open top Bus. We commenced the famed Lake District with the charming little village - Ambleside, a typical Lake District settlement with wooden homes, cobbled lanes and shops & restaurants all with distinct country-style feel line its streets. Here, the unpredictable British-weather caught up with us & we had to take shelter in an old traditional English pub called "Churchills", it was a blessing in disguise as we could savour on some local brewed Beer accompanied by another local delicacy – Steak & Ale pie.

Without wasting much time, we dared the weather & took the same bus back to Bowness - the 'heart' of the Lake District, a holiday town with stunning views of Windermere Lake from its pier. Lake surrounded by mountains and thick forests tease you on a windy day like this. As the evening light starts to fade the lake's colour change and while it reminds you of a scene from *Cape Fear* there's nothing eerie about this. This is paradise, and you could actually make a holiday of just the Lake District. The weather Gods finally had some mercy on us, and we grabbed the opportunity of a scenic walk from Bowness to Windermere. Sightseeing is only one of the pleasures of travel, we could take a taxi or bus ride back, but suddenly we had a different relationship with time, and I loved the lake-breeze all along. Every corner brings a beautiful surprise – an old lamp, a hobbit door, a flower vine, and all this beauty made us crave for some wine at a cute little side-café.

> ## *Tip*
>
> *A little research on the internet about the public transport of each town/city in advance – will save loads of time asking around & at the best rates, you would be able to get top-class sightseeing experience – the way locals do there.*

## The Wonders of Scotland

We left the Lake District with heavy hearts realizing that one day was too less for this beautiful place, our swanky First Transpennine Express gave us a stopover at Carlisle for a quick morning bite of croissant & coffee. As we arrived at Glasgow – Scotland's second largest city, we found out that the stay arrangement here was at Euro Hostel – one of the best of our stays during the entire trip. This was courtesy my dear friend Shallu, who had got us a steal-deal at 16 GBP a night for a private room with attached bathroom, and such a beautiful & central location – we couldn't have asked for more. We just dumped our luggage & went ahead exploring this cultural city which few people also call Glas-vegas. What strikes a visitor to Glasgow is the plethora of Gothic-styled old structures co-existing with ultra-modern restaurants & nightclubs in the same streets. There's something for everyone in Glasgow, whatever your budget and travel agenda are. It's a walker's city; the more willing you are to explore, the richer your experience will be. We picked up the city-map from our hostel desk & commenced from the all-glass People's Palace, carried on to one of the most famous flea markets of Scotland – The Barras, and then continued our walk all the way to an attraction that shouldn't be missed - Glasgow Cathedral.

A shining example of Gothic architecture, Glasgow Cathedral has a rare timelessness. The dark, imposing interior conjures up medieval might and can send a shiver down the spine. Being a Saturday, it was the day for weddings in Scotland, and we managed to time our arrival well, as we could witness a traditional Scottish wedding – complete with the long white gown of the bride, the pretty bridesmaids, the decked up Rolls & the Father of the Bride in his traditional Scottish kilt. Behind the cathedral, the Necropolis stretches picturesquely up and over a green hill, where AJ went berserk with his SLR. The elaborate Victorian tombs of the city's wealthy industrialists make for an intriguing stroll, great views and a vague Gothic thrill. The rest of the afternoon was spent getting amazed by the architectural wonders created by Mr Mackintosh – his house, The Lighthouse, School of Art, City Chambers – each structure was better than the other. We wrapped up our sightseeing early, as it was Saturday Night at Glasgow, and we didn't want to miss out on the crazy nightlife of this place. We kick-started our eve from our very own Euro Hostel pub with Shallu & Jitesh, where a Scotland football match was on. With beer flowing like water and the Scottish-fan bartenders in good mood, I knew this was going to be a good night. As we hopped from one club to another, the streets of this industrial city converted into one big party place, and we carried on till wee-hours of the morning.

## 'Norn Iron' – UK's Hidden Irish Treasure

Following morning we had booked ourselves for a fantastic deal with National Express that allowed us to combine a Bus-cum-Ferry ride from Glasgow to Belfast, Northern Ireland's capital city. The Stenna Line Ferry service is nothing less than a proper Cruise-liner, and we cruised on this 9-storeyed majestic ship for a 3-hour journey over the Irish Sea. It's a luxurious way to travel, as the ship is all decked up with coffee house, grill, bar, cinema, duty free shopping, seating areas and fantastic views of sparkling ocean & blue skies from its decks. Northern Ireland, or "Norn Iron" as they say, is the smallest country in Britain, and its size makes it easy to travel around. For sheer variety of landscape, the country feels bigger than it is; breath-taking mountains and glens, World Heritage Sites and an inland sea - everything's packed neatly together. We had half a day of exploration in Belfast, and we commenced from St George's Farmers Market, which is home to some of the finest fresh produce & local meat. "Lazy Goose" – a local farmer couples' kiosk (equivalent to our 'tapri') served us the juiciest most delicious pork ribs I have had after Tony Ramos in Canada. With a deadly combo of 'Beer & Pork' in our bellies, we hit the Belfast streets with vigour covering the city centre, city hall, Albert clock, and Europia (the most bombed hotel in Europe), before arriving at the most-visited place in Belfast - the Titanic Quarter. Titanic Belfast there is the largest Titanic museum in the world. It contains a number of galleries, covering Belfast at the time the Titanic was built; the Harland and Wolf shipyards; the building, fitting-out and launch of the Titanic; her maiden voyage; the sinking; the aftermath and legacy; and the discovery of the wreck. We had just enough time to pick up some beer & 'ready to cook' pie or Panini from the local Tesco and head back to our hostel.

> ### Tip
>
> *Unless you are bound by time, the best way to travel to Northern Ireland is by sea-route, and if you do your 'homework' properly, you would get fantastic National Express deals which are almost one-third the flight tickets (Glasgow – Belfast return for us was as low as 70 Pounds). And it's a superb luxury cruise-liner that gives you all the comforts much better than the flight on just a 2 & a half hour journey.*

Next morning, with precise information from the internet, we hopped on the bus armed with our 'unlimited day travel' all over Northern Ireland, and began a day of touring along the glorious North Coast of Northern Ireland. Our bus-changeover was at this sleepy town of Coleraine, where we utilized our hour & a half stop to savour on delicious Ulster Fry - traditional Belfast breakfast with different types of sausage, bacon, eggs, and fried potato with bread. Our first stop along the spectacular coast was at the Carrick-a-rede rope bridge which is about 20 meters long and sits about 40 meters above the water. We explored the coastline atop these crazy edgy cliffs for some of the most breath-taking views of our entire trip, the sea was as incandescent blue as the brochures promised. This does offer some amazing photography opportunities, however you need to be careful along the edge of the cliff because there are extremely strong winds and no guard or rail to protect you from falling over the edge. All along the way on this scenic bus-ride, we got the views of Dunluce & Dunseverick Castles, Bushmills distillery & war memorial, the picturesque White Park Bay with white sand beaches, before finally arriving to The Giants Causeway - Ireland's only UNESCO World Heritage Site, North Ireland's most popular tourist destination and often called the 'Eighth Wonder of the World'. Giant's Causeway is a collection of more than 40,000 basalt columns, right on the shore of the Atlantic Ocean, as a result of an ancient volcanic eruption. The legend is that the causeway originally connected Ireland and Scotland, but a giant ripped them up fleeing back to Scotland.  As we headed back to Belfast with some unbelievable snaps of this amazing coastline, we ended up our perfect day with a perfect evening, and settled down for some traditional Irish Whisky at Crown Liquor Saloon - one of the best-known landmarks & one of the oldest Irish Pubs in the city. Its ornate Victorian exterior and delightful interior decor makes it one of the National Trust's greatest treasures. The next morning we headed back to Glasgow & geared up for one of the most excited parts of our UK journey – a 'Road Trip' in Scottish Highlands.

## 'Heavenly' Road Trip into Scottish Highlands

A trip to the UK isn't complete without a bit of exploring and a road trip is the best way to get out there to see the best parts of Scotland that you won't be able to cover by train and bus alone. Hire or borrow a car and set your own route! If you have ever had the opportunity to escape to Scotland to follow in William Wallace's footsteps, or even Harry Potter's, then hopefully you have had the chance to drive in the Scottish Highlands. Roads in Scottish Highlands are excellent and the country-side is blessed with a lot of different and beautiful terrain. Whether you want to meet 'Nessie', marvel at the natural beauty, visit battlegrounds & historic castles, or pay homage to Scottish heroes like William Wallace, "Highlands of Scotland" is the perfect place to enjoy best of Scotland's rich heritage & Gaelic culture and overwhelm your senses. The scenery is magic...I can't begin to describe how beautiful it is...I certainly wouldn't do justice to it if I tried...Sheep, highlands, lochs, and rowan trees... just beautiful!! And then there's Scotland's Malt Whisky Trail which takes you to some of the country's most famous distilleries. Our mode of transport for the highlands was a cute Toyota Yaris, the colour of which merged with the sky; we stacked up our car with all legal & some 'illegal' survival stuff. With me behind the wheels & AJ my able navigator, we set off to explore this amazing country called Scotland, considered to be one of the most gorgeous places on earth. The drive passes through some of the prettiest countryside I've seen, all jagged mist-draped mountains & turquoise lakes, first one to encounter was Loch Lomond.

The weather played a little spoil-sport in the morning, and Loch Lomond was a complete wash-out, so after a quick coffee & pancake break by the lake-side with a misty-carpet on the lake, we decided to move on further into the wild & unspoilt landscape. The more we drove, the more our jaws dropped, the kind of scenery that has to be seen to be believed. Rolling hills ablaze with heather, deep, tranquil lochs, this amazing country-side draws you into it, enveloping you in the kind of tranquil idyll that is hard to find these days. It was less of driving and more of stopping...every 100 metres we would find a 'photo-stop', which was hard to resist. And I patted myself on the back, for exploring the Scottish Highlands by a self-driven car, as it gave us the freedom to soak in the sheer beauty of this place, and also to take halts...wherever, whenever !! As we drove further into Glencoe, the roads seem to wind endlessly into the mist that descended like an impenetrable shield from the towering peaks above. Dramatic mountain ranges were split by narrow winding roads running next to shimmering lochs. While the gazillion waterfalls run from unseen natural springs into every gulley, the mottle red, yellow, brown, green, black and grey colours somehow leap off the hillsides. I was struggling to keep my eyes on the road as the sheer beauty of the place leaves you awestruck, and before you know it, it's time to pull over and take some photos...Again !!!

With the weather Gods being kind to us, we arrived at Fort William, sitting at the foot of Ben Nevis - the highest mountain in UK, and at the head of Loch Linnhe. This town has Scottish culture & history written all over it, something that all Scots are really proud of. It also offers great shopping opportunities (So, ladies – note this down !!!), however, we stuck to our agenda and after savouring on some mouth-watering 'Fish n Chips', or "Chippy" as they call it, we continued our quest of the Highlands, all along this man-made wonder called Caledonian Canal slicing through the Great Glen. Of course no holiday to the Highlands would be complete without taking some time to visit Loch Ness and the legend of the Loch Ness Monster – "Nessie". As we arrived at this small township called Drumnadrochit, Nessie was all over the town – Nessie B&B, Nessie cruises, even Nessie Bakery. After having a quick glance at the Loch Ness Centre which gives out all the myths, rumours & truth about this mysterious creature along with right dose of Loch Ness history, we managed to catch the last cruise of the day on this beautiful lake (Talk about Luck!!) which took us deep into Nessie territory & gave us splendid views of the eerie Urquhart Castle with lots of mysteries attached to it. We arrived at the gorgeous town of Inverness, which literally means 'Mouth of the River Ness', and our Bazpackers Hostel was right next to the Inverness Castle. Without wasting any time, we explored the banks of Ness River which is the hub of activities in Inverness & managed to get some beautiful snaps of this picturesque town.

---

### *Tip*

*Numerous tour operators offer various 2-day & 3-day packages of Scottish Highlands from Glasgow & Edinburgh. Initially I also planned to take one of those, however the cheapest 3-day tour was costing 130 GBP per person, and by renting the car we did the same 3-day tour...with much more flexibility & freedom of our own, seeing much much more places than what they offer on package tour – for just 100 GBP total. Hence, doing it in less than half the cost per head.*

---

It was a bright morning as we stacked up our car with the basics for our Isle of Skye trip. We followed the banks of Loch Ness yet again, down past Urquhart Castle, turned west through Glen Moriston on the way to Glen Shiel and the Five Sisters of Kintail mountains. The magnificent Loch Duich was awaiting us at the foot of the hills where we see the stunning Eilean Donan Castle in the distance. We heard the inside wasn't nearly as impressive as out, so we did all of our castle-viewing from the parking lot and from the glass windows of the cute wooden café in the visitor centre. AJ got some mind-blowing snaps of this historic castle with the lake in backdrop, but as they say it right, "British weather is like a woman's mood – totally unpredictable". The moment we went over the arch-shaped Skye Bridge, raindrops welcomed us to Isle of Skye – as if Rain-Gods were awaiting us in the Isle. Skye is one of the most popular islands to visit in Scotland, and for good reason. The cliffs on the coast, the varied landscapes, and the picturesque towns make it one of the most quintessentially Scottish places in the country. It was a pleasure to drive around, stop, drink it all in. The roads are narrow and many times you are sharing the road with animals, it's full of sheep & the 'Highland Cows' - so just be cautious! Soon we reached Portree, a small town with a harbour fronted by colourful houses that were said to ward off angry sea spirits that sought revenge when fishermen took their share from the surrounding waters. As we climbed down to the old port, where small fishing boats rocked the waves, it began to rain again, so we dived into a small traditional pub aptly named 'The Isle Inn' for a quick mug of local beer. The rest of the afternoon was spent exploring the north east peninsula of the Isle of Skye. First stop was the Trotternish ridge, for photos of the Old man of Storr in the distance, next was the mysterious geological formation of Kilt Rock, before we took a drive all the way to the Quiraing. On our way back we took a pit-stop at Talisker Whisky Distillery by the banks of Loch Harport, and did some 'meaningful' shopping from there. We took a different route back to Inverness after crossing the Skye Bridge. This was an unexplored forest route through the beautiful Loch Carron and Achnasheen, as we reached back Inverness in the early evening, in time to make use of the 'shopping' we did at Talisker !!!

We said adios to our pretty hostel of Inverness the next morning, as we took to the roads in our trusted Yaris for one last time. This time we took a different highland route going through varied landscape of mostly forests of Cairngorm & Rothiemurchus National Parks. We drove right through the heart of these national parks crossing one attraction after another – from Reindeer Centre to Sled Dog Training Area, from Cairngorm Mountain Railway to the Speyside Wildlife, and a lovely little lake covered by misty mountains. We had a quick coffee-break at the "one Horse town' of Aviemore, where the elderly gentleman at this home-run coffee shop was more than happy to meet Indians, as he had been to Mumbai years back. Our next pit-stop was Dalwahnie Distillery – Scotland's highest & one of the oldest, producing full-bodied malt with a surprisingly delicate taste. After a quick couple of complimentary drams (a Scots word for a measure of whisky) & the usual pick up of the customary bottle, we headed for the historic town of Dunkeld – Scotland's first capital. We strolled around the narrow streets of this town with brightly coloured 'little houses' & shops with unusual names (imagine a pottery shop being named 'Going Pottie'). Dunkeld Cathedral, standing idyllically amidst lawns that sweep down to the River Tay, with the old arch bridge made it a perfect postcard place. Well, we just couldn't get enough of Scotland's national drink, so we discovered yet another distillery - Dewar's World of Whisky, which combines tradition with the latest interactive technology to tell the story of the Dewar family. Here we reaped the benefits of driving on your own in Scottish highlands, the steering wheel is in your hands – turn it wherever you want !!!

We couldn't culminate our highland trip without a visit to the grand Stirling Castle & discovering the spine-chilling true story of Scottish national hero – William Wallace. When you enter The Wallace Monument, you meet the real "Braveheart" and see his awesome sword that saw action at Stirling Bridge. The true story of local hero William Wallace is even more gripping than the Hollywood legend. We didn't have much time left to explore the entire Stirling Castle, so we left it for yet another day when we may be back, and we left our 'castle-exploring' instincts for Windsor. After kissing goodbye to our faithful companion for three days – Toyota Yaris at Glasgow, we caught the night bus for Edinburgh, which was our last destination in Scotland.

> ### *Tip*
>
> *There are numerous Whisky Distilleries all over Scotland – pick & choose your options, however if you take one Whisky tour, its good enough, because all tours are the same. Yes, complimentary 'drams' you must have at all distilleries – they are happy to give. The same applies for castles in UK also – you see one from inside, you seen them all. Stirling, Edinburgh & Windsor are the worthy ones. Night buses from Glasgow to Edinburgh are as cheap as 3 Pounds one-way...do your research properly!!!*

## The Buzzing Heritage Potpourri of Edinburgh

When I arrived in Edinburgh, I had desired only to understand what all the fuss was about. I had packed plenty of scepticism that any modern metropolis could have such undiluted charms. Here I had taken a chance of booking us in an unconventional hostel, very different from existing Youth Hostels, that too in old town. But Budget Backpackers could have been the best gamble I had taken during my UK trip, with an aptly named café-cum-pub – "Kick-Ass Pub" & a donkey as their mascot straight out of Shrek series. We arrived at 10 in the night & heard a free 'Pub Crawl' is heading out at 10.30, me & AJ looked at each other - Driving since 7 in the morning for 12 hours, followed by hour & a half bus journey, then half an hour walk to the hostel with our luggage - Yes, we were damn ready for the Pub Crawl. Precisely 20-min freshening up & we were all set to hit this crazy party town all guns blazing, and we were not at all disappointed. Pub-Crawl is a smart concept of partying in UK, hopping from one pub to another meeting new people at the same time, and after couple of beers down it doesn't matter if you know that person or not, you got only 'Party on your mind' !!! I must say, Scots are freak party-animals, because by the time we decided to call it a night around 2.30 in the morning, the streets of old town had become one big crazy place with people all over the streets shouting, dancing, people falling over...but at the same time, safe...as nobody bothering anybody else, they are happy in their own world. If this was Fri Night, I can't wait for Edinburgh SNF (Sat Night Fever)...!!!

Edinburgh is entirely a different city in the day-time. I've always heard good things about Edinburgh and I have to say that it fully lives up to its reputation. It has a small town feel (which can be more welcoming and less stressful to get around), and makes you feel like you've gone back in time to the medieval era. It's a majestic and magical little city; not to mention, the capital of Scotland. There is Gothic architecture all over the place, ancient cathedrals, a great garden, small, windy streets, and historic buildings. The city is mainly composed of the Old Town of tiny alleyways and cobbled lanes and the New Town's wider, symmetrical streets – all within walking reach. We commenced our city-surfing from Sir Walter Scott monument dominating Edinburgh's main shopping street, Princes Street. As we went passed the colourful pillars of National Gallery of Scotland, we found ourselves standing at the entrance to Princess Gardens & having one of the best views of the stunning Edinburgh Castle. But we wanted more panoramic views of this unique city & the concept of fusion of old & new town, so without wasting much time we headed for Calton Hill, and here you not only get the best views of the city & castle but also Arthur's Seat, part of an extinct volcano. Climbing down from the other side, we found ourselves standing in front of Palace of Holyroodhouse – Queen's official residence in Scotland, located on one end of the famous Royal Mile. Walking up the Royal High Mile is the most historic and scenic route to take in Edinburgh, as it is literally a straight stretch of cobble-stone road that ends at the Edinburgh Castle. Being a Saturday, it felt like the whole of UK has come down to the Royal Mile – it was like a carnival of people, bagpipers, street performers, and stalls – something for everyone. We already got a slight glimpse of it a night before, Edinburgh nightlife is legendary, and you have the choice of everything from intimate bars, ideal for starting off your night, to buzzing clubs where you can really let your hair down and make the most of your weekend of freedom. And this was one of the most memorable Saturday-nights of our lives, went to some crazy places, experienced some crazy things – cannot be disclosing those details on this forum...!!!

> ## *Tip*
>
> *Edinburgh offers many economical hostel stays in old town & that is the hub of all activity. Don't ever think of taking a 'Hop On Hop Off' tour in an open tourist bus & spoil the charm of this amazing city which is "walkers paradise", and Free Walking Tours keep happening – just enquire. This is like Mecca for all you party-animals – definitely keep a weekend here & you wouldn't be sorry – look out for "Pub Crawls"....a superb concept !!!*

## The Manchester Experience

Our Scotland stint came to an end as we boarded the colourful Trans-Pennine Express with striking pink & blue exteriors. It was a mixed feeling in our hearts – on one side the sadness of leaving this beautiful part of UK & on the other end super-excited about the 'most awaited' part of our entire trip – Manchester. Well, nothing to do with the city as such, just that personally my main motive of planning this UK trip was a visit to ManU Football Club & above all, watching the God himself, Roger Waters - 'Live in Flesh', performing The Wall. We reached AJ's sisters' place at this small township called Macclesfield & after covering a lot of distance on our feet in the last few days, averaging about 10 hours walk a day, we knew that a well-deserved rest is mandatory. Not too excited about Manchester except for the two agenda's on mind, we spent some quality time with the fun-family of the Kotkar's !!!

Finally the D-Day arrived of which I was waiting for last so many days – 16th Sep. Well, it happened to be my dear sister's birthday as well, but my mind was just stuck on 'The Wall'. With some useful information about the Manchester public transport, we launched our journey with some recharged legs (I think that's how we decided to walk all the way to M'field station). Our first destination of Manchester United Football Club was interrupted by a 'factory outlet' sale just outside Manchester station, and we ended up spending two valuable hours & half the money in our wallets there. The adrenal rush I felt on the first sight of Old Trafford Stadium is unexplainable. The story of Manchester United is unlike any other club in the world. Beginning more than a century ago, it combines eras of total English and European domination with some of the greatest adversity faced by any football club. Some smart research on the net before-hand saved us two-third of entry fee to this award-winning museum & stadium tour. With jaws open in awe for the next 2 hours, we roamed around, getting closer to the world of Manchester United and sharing 130 years of football, and when we got the first glimpse of the humungous Old Trafford stadium – it was like a dream-come-true. We ended our tour with some chilled beer in the aptly named Red Café, with wall to wall buzzing football atmosphere.

And then came the time for the epicentre of the entire UK trip – Roger Waters show, and Manchester Arena is as good as it gets. I won't do injustice to this entire experience called "Roger Waters - The Wall Live" by trying to explain in words, because no matter how hard I try, I will never be able to do justice to it. So, let's just leave it by saying that be it the arena atmosphere, the crowd, the lights, sound, the visual effects, the entire concept behind The Wall, it's absolutely mind-blowing...it's a lifetime experience to watch the passion of this 70-year old man, this amazing genius called Roger Waters...!!!

---

**Tip**

*While planning your trip, do look out for some unbelievable deals & vouchers at websites such as 'groupon', 'supersaver' etc for all the major attractions in main tourist destinations. Most of the times, being unaware, we lose out on these deals which saved us half to two-thirds of the total entrance fees sometimes.*

---

### The Final 'Capital' Destination

When we left for London the next morning, somehow there was absolutely no excitement about the capital of UK, supposedly the most tourist infested city during our entire journey. For me, UK trip was already over after Old Trafford & Roger Waters, and the only thing I was looking forward to in London was to catch up with some of my old school friends. Visiting London is like getting on a giant merry-go round – tumultuous, exciting, just a little scary, but great fun... And no, I am not talking about a ride on London Eye. Don't be disheartened if you don't cover much of this sprawling megalopolis of London – giving you a list of all the things you could do in London would be a bit like giving you a list of items you'll need to build a rocket to the moon. For first-time visitors, a stroll down Thames, a tube ride, or tucking into fish & chips can be moments of high excitement. There's something for everyone, so when our first day got 'washed out' by rains after a quick glimpse of Big Ben, Westminister, Houses of Parliament & Trafalgar Square, we just grabbed the opportunity of catching a Broadway-kind of theatrical experience – "Rock of Ages". I must admit that not being too excited about the musical; I quickly changed my opinion & thoroughly enjoyed the evening with a glass of fine English Whisky. Being in the areas of Piccadilly Circus & Leicester Square, which are the hub of nightlife, we spent some more time here before picking up some delicious Chinese food from Chinatown, and headed back to our swanky London Central Youth Hostel.

God must have seen our enthusiasm & gave us a bright sunny day the next morning, and we did complete justice to it by heading for Windsor Castle (after getting a great rail-cum-entry ticket deal at the station). Built high above the River Thames, Windsor Castle has been home to the Royal Family for 900 years and is still an official residence of the Queen. After witnessing the 'Change of Guard' up-close & personal, I was convinced that catching this event here is any day a better idea than the chaotic Buckingham Palace. Next about three hours or so, we visited the magnificent State Apartments - still used for State occasions and Royal receptions, the Queen's private garden, the Doll House, explored the castle grounds and the fourteenth-century St. George's Chapel, one of the most beautiful examples of medieval church architecture in England. We didn't waste any second of this beautiful day & headed straight to the Tower Bridge & Tower of London. River Thames is at the heart of London – all major attractions on either side of it, and you just need to walk, walk & just walk, and when you get tired just use your multi-purpose 'Oyster Card' to take a river cruise, as we did & arrived at all the hustle-bustle around London Eye. With chilled beer on the serve & amazing views of London city, I knew that "Tonight's gonna be a Good Night"!!!

And damn Yes, it was a good night as I caught up with the old KVTG-ites – Sukhi, Vandy, Pali, Vasu...it was so good to meet all of them specially few of them I was meeting after almost 20 years. They all made sure we had a great time; an absolute crazy night...experiencing the best of London nightlife, details of which again cannot be disclosed on this forum...!!! With heavy hearts & some unforgettable memories, we bid goodbye to each other in the wee hours of morning. Next day was spent getting over the 'hangover of good times', strolling on the stylish Oxford Street & exploring the lively Camden Town.

Our UK backpacking trip was coming to an end, and I learnt when you're backpacking, you meet all sorts of people. At youth hostels you can ask for rooms which are gender-specific or which are mixed, private or dorms ranging from 4-bedded to 20-bedded. I learnt to sometimes ignore the sights & sounds of spontaneous dorm-romances, and instead do your own thing. But you do find lots of agreeable company in fellow backpackers, interact with them... share experiences...learn about their culture & share yours. At the end of the day, it's just not a trip...it's an experience...!!! My flight back home left early morning, and I realised I shouldn't have shelled out for another night in the hostel, but instead should have just headed for the airport and spend the night curled into airport lounge chairs, leaning on my backpack.

My dreams were only a shadow of what I've just lived. I've never had such a rich trip on such a poor budget, but then that's the best thing about budget backpacking travel. The most amazing part is that there's so much left to discover in this world – and now I know exactly how to do it.

# **Refer Page - 161 for Photographs of Travelogue - 8**

# Bhutan

## Land of "Happy" Thunder Dragon

*"Four Wheels Move the Body…But Two Wheels Move the Soul…!!!"*

**Biking in Bhutan : Happiness Unlimited**

Once a Monk told me few soul-touching lines….

*If you want to be Happy for a day…Drink*

*If you want to be Happy for a year…Marry*

*If you want to be Happy for a Lifetime…Ride a Motorcycle!!!*

Then I realised that it was one of the many Monks I have interacted with…all in my mind…and the one who told me this was my most favourite Monk - the 'Old' one…!!!

Thus began my journey of soul-searching five years back when I met my soul mate…in form of a bike - my Thunderbird. I was born in a middle class family, and I realised that it was my Bullet which made me 'Royal' !!! Hereafter, I started preparing my 'Bucket List' of Bike Rides…started with short ones including the beautiful East Coast Road between Chennai & Pondicherry and the Konkan journey, finally I expanding my horizon towards longer journeys. Having done the 'Run of the Mill' – Ladakh by Bike way back in my early years of service career, next dream route for any biker is Bhutan Bike Ride.

So, I started searching for like-minded crazy bikers, and I found my 'original mentor', someone who had nurtured and groomed me right at the beginning of my Army service, my Young Officers course instructor – Col Manoj Keshwar. I knew that with my eyes blind-folded I can put my dreams into his hands with an assurance they are going to be converted to reality in the bestest of the ways. 'Mike Sir' – as he's fondly known now, started "Viktorianz" few years back & I have been following his vision closely since then, even motivated few of my youngsters few years back to join his North Thailand venture – and they couldn't thank me enough for providing them the opportunity to experience the ride of their lifetime. So, I jumped the first instance I came to know that Viktorianz is planning a "Bhutan Happiness Ride".

Bhutan - the deeply Buddhist nation preserve the purity of their land, so much so that television entered its society in 1999 and the internet merely emerged in 2000. But you must go and experience this rare gem, especially before mainstream commercialization spreads itself which has started to set in, especially in touristy towns of Paro & Thimpu. The beauty of Bhutan can be represented by bright and vibrant colours in photos, but can only be profoundly felt in person. The happiest place in Asia puts less emphasis on GDP but so much more on GNH (Gross National Happiness). Every traveller is eventually transformed by such understated beauty that even if you're not spiritual, you will bow down to a culture that smiles in the landscapes of humility and modesty.

Her Majesty the Queen, Ashi Dorji Wangchuck, described an early journey to Thimpu over the first roads in Bhutan as "Treasures of the Thunder Dragon". She felt "sheer terror" when she saw a Willys Jeep, at its size, its noise and the nauseating smell of petrol. The trip was interrupted by landslides. That was in the 1960s, when Bhutan was still the closed kingdom, one of the last places left on earth where you might search for the mythical kingdoms of Shangri-La. In 2006, Bhutan cautiously opening up to affluent tourists, trekkers and carefully monitored tour groups, however bikers could make it to this extremely picturesque but challenging route, a little later. While independent travel to this country is not possible at the moment, the kind and humble people, along with the dramatic scenery that has enthusiastic promoters calling it "The Last Shangri-la", make it more than worthwhile, despite the barriers to entry.

> ### *Tip*
>
> *A visit to Bhutan only covering main tourist options of Thimpu & Paro, is like only 'wine tasting'. If you want to enjoy the complete bottle of wine, a road trip across the length of Bhutan is a must. The actual essence & beauty of Bhutan lies in Central & Eastern parts of this country.*

## The Start of Happiness Ride

So, here we were in Siliguri – 9 days, 1500 kms & 11 Riders, all coming from various parts of the country with different professions, different languages and different body structures, but with one common belief and motto of 'Ride to Live...and Live to Ride' !!! After an apt 'breaking ice' dinner party at Siliguri Military Station a night prior with the right mix of alcohol, delicious cuisine & rocking music, the "Happy Riders Gang" – as we called ourselves (after all we were on Happiness Ride), were all set to hit the road the next morning – all gleaming with cheerful faces & roaring bikes. But the weather Gods had other plans for us, as it rained all night and all throughout early part of morning. Mike Sir had already given us the fore-warning that it's going to be a 'wet & rough' ride (no X-rated pun intended here). As the 'Bravehearts' were preparing themselves with rain-gear, the Gods favoured the Brave by opening up the skies just at the right time, for us to kick off our Dream Ride. And to add on the zing, I had my two 'Lady Bravehearts' accompanying me – though Deenaz been on a number of them with me, this being Arianna's first mountainous road trip, all at 6 months...!!!

The 200-odd km journey within heartland of Bengal was a smooth ride, something I had already done exactly a year back on a borrowed 1996-model modified Bullet, and here I was this time with both my lovely ladies in toe.

The route meandered through beautiful tea gardens of Dooars region, and long stretches of empty well maintained roads made us zip though the distance in no time. Of course, both the mother-daughter duo had their moments on the Thunderbird during this stretch. At the fag end of the dusty haphazard Indian town of Jaigaon, suddenly an imposing gate appears at the end of road. Bright painted dragons wrap themselves up its concrete pillars, sneaking their way past lotus flowers and mandalas, and a two-tiered gilt roof rises above, ending in a pinnacle of gold. Past the gate, in the Bhutanese town of Phuentsholing, the streets are clean and lined with shops. The houses & shops, white run elaborate checkerboard cornices, fall into neat rows. Men exchange pants and shirts for the *'gho'*, a striped kilt-like full-length robe, and the women wear bright *'kira'*, which is a combination of wrap-around bottom & colourful jacket top.

The news spread rapidly through Phuentsholing that afternoon and we drew appreciative nods and gasps of awe from the little crowd that had gathered. We quickly soaked in the local attention and headed for the famous Zen Restaurant to taste some trademark traditional Bhutanese cuisine. Now, as the waiter places the Ema Datshi (Bhutan's national dish) on the table, we realise that we have ordered our deepest, darkest fear. A terror that could make us turn back because, if the waiter was to be believed, it would make its way to our table each day at lunch and dinner. For Ema Datshi, as we found, was the king of the Bhutanese kitchen; a dish that's as hot as its name is cool. A main course in which chillies (ema) are the main ingredient, along with yak cheese that hides the fiery vegetable. All along Bhutan in next few days, we discovered that most of the other names found on the menu of any small/big eating joint are a modified version of Ema Datshi, as they add various forms of meat & vegetables to make Shammu (Mushroom) Datshi, Kewa (Potato) Datshi, Shikam (Pork) Datshi and so on. We also tried some Shapta (stir fried sliced beef), Shabaley (meat stuffed pockets) with local bread Balep, and local beer Druk Lager to gulp it down with.

## Early Experiences of Dragon Country

Next day move was delayed due to time-consuming process of permits & immigration, mainly due to very-laid back attitude of the local officials. "Why in so much hurry...Relax !!!" was the usual reply we heard at most of the places. It looked like, 'Don't Worry...Be Happy' song was specially written for Bhutan population. The delay gave us the opportunity to try out Kizom Bakery of Phuentsholing – quite a landmark of this place. But the delay also ensured that we commenced our first day of ride within Bhutan in the afternoon in pouring rains. It is said that Bhutan starts where a stone rolled off the mountains slope. The road begins climbing the moments you get out of Phuentsholing. It crumples into bends and loops, and densely forested hills start rising around us, until we can't see the turn ahead. We would not be heading this way again unless officials at Thimphu refused to give us restricted area permit required to proceed beyond the capital and exit through Samdrup Jhonkar, where the kingdom shares its border with Assam. Being denied a permit is a very real possibility, because His Highness King Jigme Singye Wangchuk expressly detests hippies and backpackers.

Soon we were riding on treacherous mountain roads gaining & losing altitude like a sine curve, with roads converting to streams and the riding speed reducing to 20kmph due to torrential downpour. And soon the inevitable happened, with our first 'fall' of the ride…the rider in front rounded the tricky hair-pin curve and touched his right portion with the car coming downslope, making him skid into the ditch. The foot brake got badly damaged, but we had our 'Maestro' – Batra Ji who arrived like a Moto GP pro technician and got the bike moving in few minutes. We took a tea break halfway through Paro at Border Roads canteen, and soon everybody realised that all rain-gear ranging from 500 to 5000 is effective for initial half an hour only. By the time we resumed our ride with a well-deserved tea break, darkness had set in & the mountains were giving the haunted feel. Mist enveloped the hilly roads, and we realised that riding at night in Bhutan is not at all recommended as there is pitch dark winding roads, plus the zero visibility due to fog & mist, means that riding in the dark is not for the feint-hearted. Finally our hearts & mind needed some booster to carry on in this difficult situation, and a shot of local Bhutan Supreme whisky with black espresso did exactly that, thereafter the rest of 100 kms distance up to Paro was a cakewalk. We arrived at our heavenly abode in Paro called Kichu Resort late in the night, to some much-needed hot water shower, warm quilts & of course, the trusted 'Old Monk' !!!

> ## *Tip*
>
> *Any road trip in Bhutan should be prepared for uncertain weather conditions. Adequate back up & repair arrangements to be catered for any bike ride. Kichu Resort in Paro is a highly recommended place of stay – economical but very picturesque at the same time.*

## Twin Gems of Western Bhutan

Next day was a fresh beautiful morning when we started riding for Thimpu – the capital city. There is no other capital on earth like Thimphu. It's spiritual, deeply traditional, conservative, yet kind and generous. There's a sense of innocence in its culture, quite untainted and it's beautiful to witness. The road from Paro to Thimphu is a relatively smooth spiral staircase to enchantment. The rice fields are disgustingly emerald, and the intricate carvings that adorn everything from local bars to petrol pumps shamelessly picturesque. It's a 60 km broad, well maintained road, which in spite of being winding hilly stretch, was zipped through quickly by us in less than an hour. It was quite a welcome change from previous day's challenging experience. As soon as we approached the big traditional gateway reading "Welcome to Thimpu City", first glimpse of the capital city comes in view. Thimphu seemed state-of-the art with neatly stacked multi-storeyed houses-each painted with murals ad adorned with decorative wood-work, by order of the king – broad streets, prim policemen guiding traffic on the solitary road that loops twice around the capital.

As we entered the city, it was in a frenzy festive mood with Thimpu Tschechu in progress, by all means one of the biggest festivals in Bhutan. This annual festival is celebrated every year in the autumn season for a period of 3-4 days and is a ceremony of colours with a happy amalgamation of the changing nature and the many moods of the Bhutanese culture. The highlight of Thimphu Tsechu is the showcase of ethnic folk dance in the famous Tashichho Dzong in Thimphu. So, without wasting any time, the Royal Enfields & the KTMs zoomed through crowded streets of capital city to the imposing Dzong, literally meaning 'Fort-Monastery', beautifully located on the banks of Thimpu Chu. Like all other Dzongs, this also houses a monastic body as well as the administrative corps, catering to the spiritual as well as the temporal needs of the Bhutanese.

We braved the long but organised queue of entry and noticed that it was a carnival in the courtyard of the monastery. Every inch of space on the stairs & balconies of the monastery buildings was occupied by families who stand chatting, few sat together with picnic baskets, while the children run around. In the middle of this bedlam, hypnotically slow masked dance was unfolding. Masked manifestations of Guru Rinpoche were dancing in a circle to the beat of drums and the sound of trumpets. With every step they complete one turn, transforming the courtyard into a swirling mass of brilliant robes and flying tassels. Two clowns dressed in grubby overalls, wearing bright red masks with hideously long noses were jumping up and down, mocking people, and imitating the manifestations. A monk wearing a crinkled mask of an old lady, cradling a large plastic doll in his hands, going around asking for donations. The slow, stylised dance of the 'heavenly ladies" followed. The final dance, the dance of the heroes is, in sharp contrast, very martial. The warriors brandish their weapons, and leap into the air touching their feet to their heads.

After soaking in enough traditional festival mood, we headed straight to the main market square of Thimpu, clock tower area, which was buzzing with people, street food stalls, local products on offer...a complete Bhutanese version of our own 'Rehri Market'. It looked like the entire Bhutan was here on the occasion of Thimpu Festival. We tried our hand in some local street cuisine and brushed up our haggling skills at the stalls, and when we had enough of that, we headed straight to Bhutan Kitchen (recommended by Lonely Planet) for typical Bhutanese lunch spread. After the gastronomical fulfilment, we had to engage in some religious activity which took us to the grand 169 feet tall Golden Buddha statue with spectacular views of Thimpu valley. While at the Takin Preserve en route, where this strange creature – a sort of cross between cow and goat - takes its ease, we called off the day early at our Dantak guest room cosily located among apple orchards, sipping on premium Bhutanese whisky – aptly named after the fifth king..."K5" !!!

***Tip***

*Visit Bhutan during the annual Thimpu Tschechu Festival is highly recommended, as this time of the year, the entire Thimpu city offers you the best of Bhutanese traditional heritage & culture. Be very particular about obtaining all possible permits for visiting Central & Eastern Bhutan further well in time, as all Govt offices are closed during this festival.*

Riding in the wee hours of morning next day to catch up with rest of the group for the much anticipated trek to Taktsang monastery in Paro, maybe one of the most common landmark of Bhutan on postcards & t-shirts, and is recognized as one of the world's most important Buddhist religious shrines. Built into the side of a sheer cliff, it is believed that one of Buddhism's most revered luminaries of the past, Guru Rinpoche, arrived at this monastery on the back of a winged tiger, granting it the nickname of the Tiger's Nest monastery. After getting some strong encouragement from local staff at Kichu resort about taking new born babies to this holy shrine for blessings, me & Deenaz decided to brave it with Arianna – taking the 'most holy one' to the 'most holy place' in Bhutan. So, geared up with baby carrier in front & back-pack behind (to balance the load), I stepped up all my gas to go full throttle up on this treacherous steep trek. It's a beautiful enough walk through forests of pine loud with birdcall, Tiger's Nest slipping in and out of view, every now & then. After what seems like an eternity, we arrived at the cafeteria which marks the halfway point. After the last gut-wrenching descent down a shifty stone staircase, and a final dash up, we're there. The view is absolutely breath taking, and worth every drop of sweat & ounce of breath spent to reach there. The food never tasted as good as the simple vegetarian fare at the midway point cafeteria on way back. With great relief & immense pride of taking Arianna on her first trek all at 6 months, we returned just in time to pack up and start riding towards Central Bhutan. But not before getting the feel of this quaint & quiet town of Paro, nestling snugly in one of the most picturesque river valley in Bhutan. You realise this when you walk the winding path up to the National Museum and look down from the vantage of this erstwhile watchtower. Without doubt, this is the quaintest museum in the world.

## Out of Civilization in Central Bhutan

Our ride from Paro to Wangdue via Thimpu was one of the most eventful & 'dreadful'. For the next six hours, we drove through some of the most horrible mountain roads in Bhutan. The road to Punakha- old capital of Bhutan – first climbs to Dochu La (3,140m) from where you can see a panoramic view of the Himalaya, but only if you are very, very lucky. For most of the time, it is swathed in a mysterious fog, the way it was on that day. But in spite of the inclement weather conditions, we could manage a Biker Group photo with the 108 stupas (chortens) located atop this mysterious pass, built by Her Majesty the Queen herself, to honour the victory of Bhutanese army during a war in

Southern Bhutan in 2003. As we commenced our ride the weather opened up just a bit, maybe just to show me the glimpse of what was awaiting us ahead. I could see where the road was twisting and new gravel put down heavy on the berms. As I approached the first downhill curve I could see a lot of gravel on the turn where cars had cut the curve short and tossed gravel from the berm onto the road surface as well as from rain runoff. That made for very slow going and careful riding. It was really not any fun on this stretch...!! Every turn on this downhill side was covered in a lot of gravel due to the on going widening of the road. Most of the 150 km of this stretch was outrageously rough with massive boulders and mud/slush everywhere, at places completely non-existent roads. But Enfields just plod though everything as usual without much fuss. To add to our woes, it gets dark very soon in this part of the world, and especially with continuous rain & drizzle, the things couldn't have been better !!! So, very soon the fun ride was converted to 'follow the tail light' drill, with not knowing much where the bike was headed, and there were plenty of 'Oh My God' moments when the machine almost gone off the road...down where, can't be said also. I had heard that Bhutan is 'hobbit country' and nowhere is this more evident than on this road. At any moment you would expect to see a Dark Rider emerging from the mist, or Frodo Baggins scampering along on hairy little feet. Our ordeal became prolonged when we got stuck in landslide work on the road, just 5 kms short of our destination – Kichu Resort in Wangdi Phodrang, the last 'town' in Central Bhutan.

Next morning we decided that we cannot proceed ahead without visiting one of the two trademark Bhutan postcard landmarks, apart from Tiger's Nest – The Punakha Dzong. As we made the quick ride from our resort to Punakha, the picture-perfect view of Dzong came on one of the many blind turns. The Dzong in Punakha was undoubtedly the most spectacular we saw in Bhutan. Situated at the confluence of two frisky rivers - the Mo Chu and the Pho Chu (the 'Mother' and 'Father' rivers) - this six-storey Dzong was the seat of government for a long time. A cantilever bridge over the Mo leads to the portals of the Dzong, which had no indication that a flash flood caused by a glacial lake-burst in 1994 had destroyed Punakha and damaged the Dzong. After the customary photo-stop at this towering fort-monastery, we commenced our journey going into more interiors of Central Bhutan. The weather Gods were not so kind the night prior, so due to overnight showers, we rode through some of the most difficult stretch of our journey through mud & slush, and when we thought we have braved 25 kms of worst section, our ride came to a grinding halt with a massive landslide minutes before we arrived at the location. After analysing the situation (in true Fauji style) with Mike Sir, we decided to take shelter in a local 'Bhutanese Dhaba' nearby till the road clears.

The locals were warm and hospitable and opened their doors to us, in part because they were sure of good business from us, but mostly because they considered us a novelty. And to show how much they appreciated the adventurous streak in us, they treated us to Ema Datsi and rice. But this time I decided to not go for the traditional one, but try it with Pork or Beef. It's said that pigs are fed copious quantities of marijuana, which keeps them happy. They grow big and fat and their meat fetches a better price. Their owners are happy. And since the meat tastes better, the people who eat it, which I take to be the whole of Bhutan, are happy. And so when I tried pork, I was happy. It made sense, I thought as we waited till eternity for route to clear out, for this kingdom to measure its wealth in 'gross national happiness'. So, after eating our hearts out with all possible local dishes put in our palate, catching a nap on raw wooden benches outside & discussing everything possible with locals & few foreign tourists stuck like us, we finally took a call to head back to our resort in Wangdue. The group got the much deserved break at Kichu resort with a rocking musical evening of fun, friends & local booze...and with the Dang Chu gushing within a yard of the resort booming in our ears, it was an evening well spent.

> ### *Tip*
>
> *Keep at least a day or two as cushion while planning the Bhutan road trip, as the unforeseen delays due to road blocks & landslides are common in Central Bhutan. Do try the local cuisine with all kinds of 'Datsi' at roadside Dhabas – very economical and very very delicious.*

### Riding the Rough Terrain through Heart of Bhutan

We commenced our ride early morning next day with weather still playing devil and the route going from bad to worse, as we negotiated highly difficult stretch of hilly roads with mad hairpins to gravel to very very muddy sections caused by recent landslides. Almost 4,000 foot drops at some points at the side of the narrow roads, it was one mad but truly spectacular riding. As we came across yet another recent landslide on the road, we had an insight into everyday life in Bhutan and the unhurried, unfussy way in which the Bhutanese went about their business. The traffic was held up for over an hour on the narrow mountain road but not one horn was blown in anger. Yet again Mike sir took his 'Trusted Lieut' ahead to analyse the road block status, and we took a call that this time we won't be wasting more precious time, and decided to take our Mean Machines over the landslide boulders & rubble. Now this required great amount of team work & motivational talk, as also some skilful riding, but the group pulled it off like experts. But the ordeal was far from over, as the road & weather ahead made us think twice, maybe it was a good idea to have not crossed the landslide. The amount of mud & slush on the road kept increasing as we rolled & slipped & skidded our way through the road which was extremely narrow and full of loose gravels & heavy slush, it was difficult to grip and the bikes faced skidding in couple of places and once we escaped by an inch from a straight fall into the valley. After some time, we again found a dozer removing stones and we kept waiting for almost 45 mins before it gave us an extremely narrow space to pass.

Beyond Wangdue, the road ascended to the bracing Pele La (3,420m), where the temperature dropped considerably. Through a thicket of prayer flags, we entered Central Bhutan. The descent was rapid, the hillsides lined with dwarf bamboo, lush evergreen forests taking over and, in the lower reaches, broadleaf species. The deeper we went, the more overwhelmed we were. Finally, the Dzong of Trongsa slipped into view, seemingly suspended in mid-air on the other side of the valley. The road then switchbacks into the valley, crosses the raging river at the very end, before turning back to approach Trongsa. Trongsa enjoys a strategic location, with the sole road between eastern and western Bhutan running through it, and tradition dictates that the crown prince must serve as *penelop* (governor) of Trongsa before ascending the throne. The air in this sleepy town was scented with cypress, betel nut and Bhutan Highland whiskey, the latter two consumed in huge quantities by the locals. We halted for a quick lunch break here at a typically local eating joint that gave us the insight into their lifestyle away from mainstream towns. The place had an extensive Bhutanese menu, neatly written on a white board...with all sorts of "Datshi" on offer, apart from the staple rice, beef & pork delicacies.

Without further delay, the bikers geared up for the second half of the journey which was less eventful, as the road & weather conditions both improved. The two-and-a-half-hour drive from Trongsa to Bumthang tackled the Yotong La (3,425m). From there, the road began to descend and the vegetation undergoes a sudden change. On the way you also encounter Bhutanese peasantry and realize how different they are from the pool-playing, disco-going populace of Thimphu and Paro. They stand like sentinels along the road, their faces etched and creased like prehistoric rock. As we approached one of the most picturesque parts of Bhutan, valley widened and opened up, landscape dotted with small farms. The mountains were magnificent, the countryside green, the air pure & unpolluted and the architecture striking. Then we were in Jakar, a windy little town at the bottom of the valley, its main artery clogged with charming wooden shacks selling everything from strips of dried yak cheese to enormous wooden phalluses. In Bumthang and elsewhere, homes & shops are decorated with paintings of flying phalluses. The Bhutanese are puzzled when foreigners giggle and gawk – as for them, phalluses are a sacred, lucky symbol. The phallus belonged to a monk, Lama Drupka Kinley, *"The Divine Madman"*, as he is also called, he is Bhutan's most beloved saint, who in the 15th century subdued errant demons by striking them on their heads with his penis. So scared were the demons, that even a mural of the phallus scare them nowadays.

We reached our heavenly abode – the Jakar Lodge, which was a stunner, and more importantly, it was unpretentious, the flavour all local, the structure all traditional, and with Jakar Dzong towering its presence over it, this is definitely one of the best stay options in Bumthang. I was welcomed by the traditionally dressed, but fluently English speaking caretaker-cum-owner, the lodge was owned by his grandfather (retired Royal Bhutan Army officer). The conceit is that this is a residence and the staff your family. So no over-fussy service here, even though your every whim is catered to. As we were surrounded by so much of local feel & air, we decided to savour the in-house product Raven Vodka & Misty Peak Whisky in the evening, along with some free history & nature talk by the owner himself. The dinner consisted of a simple chicken broth, braised yak cheese datshi and buckwheat noodles (a Bumthang special, buckwheat being the area's chief crop).

## The Bhutanese 'Swiss' Experience

Next morning we decided to explore this beautiful valley, and on top of our wish-list was the visit to local cheese factory (Swiss style) and the Red Panda 'Weiss Bier' brewery (German style). Bumthang is noted variously as the valley of the beautiful girls (bum) or the spiritual hear of the kingdom (after bumpa, a vessel of holy water), depending on your priorities. We got the glimpse of the 'bums' of this valley in the one-street Jakar market inside most of the shops. They also call it the "Switzerland of Bhutan", the scenic beauty of this region is mesmerising.  It also has the 659AD built Jampey Lhakhang, one of Bhutan's most worshipped temples. Despite a few additions over the centuries, the primary shrine retains a modest grandeur of its own, which few of us had the chance of locating & visiting. At Bumthang, I learnt the secret to happiness at a curio shop. Garuda, the legendary eagle who stares down from above the main entrance of houses and dzongs, shreds all forms of evil that tries to enter their lives. I bought the story, and the souvenir. Call it superstition, but our journey from then on was a dream. The days were sunny, the roads were like any Biker's dream, and we managed to traverse through the most picturesque part of Bhutan in the best possible weather.

The ride to our next destination, Mongar, took us through some splendid and varied terrain, definitely was the best part of our ride. The scenery for first three hours was comparable to the Alps highlighted by Bhutanese villages. Fantastic twisty sections on empty roads, children all waving and shouting as we passed – everyone really smiley as ever. Water cascading off the rocks onto us riding on the road below – like riding under a waterfall. There was only one pass today, the *Thrumshingla Pass* at 3750m – the highest motorable pass in Bhutan. But before that, we rode past vast meadows of dwarf bamboo where some yaks were grazing, and we descended into one of Bhutan's quietest but most breath-taking valleys – Ura Valley. We took a short unplanned halt, just to lie on the grass of this vast plateau overlooking Ura village, and to soak in the splendid views in front of our eyes. The air here was so clean and clear that when the clouds disperse the views of the mountains take your breath away. We zoomed on the wide & empty roads all the way up to Thrumshing La Pass, feeling on top of the world at 12000 feet. After crossing the pass we were officially in 'Eastern Bhutan" and to celebrate, the road descended 2800m within two hours. Along with the disappearance of any possible 'altitude headaches', the temperature and vegetation also changed. The roads were dramatic with cliff-hanging scenes in many places, but the extensive growth of rhodendron flower all along the way kept us spell-bound. The rainforest also brought along with it, huge waterfalls falling off the steep mountainsides, in fact at one place, we were almost blown off the bikes by the huge blast of wind and spray created by the sheer volume of water. Mongar lies before a range of mountains which runs from north to south, all the way from Tibet to the Indian border. It's a small sleepy town, an overnight stop for people travelling from one side of Bhutan to the other. A couple of hours' drive north is the small town of Lhuntse, known for its spectacular Dzong. But we didn't have the time for it, instead we checked into the beautifully located Wangchuk Hotel in time for guzzling down our Red Panda stock picked up from the brewery.

> **Tip**
>
> *Central Bhutan has some of the toughest but most picturesque roads in the entire country. Stay options in traditional Bhutanese lodges & resorts are economical and extremely comfortable, along with getting the real feel of the country's rich culture. Don't miss out on the local 'beer' of this place.*

## Wild Wild East of Bhutan

Heading out of Mongar the next day, the road climbs considerably into some challenging hilly portion of the ride, but the decent status of the road condition makes it a challenging but pleasurable ride. On this stretch from Mongar to Trashigang, you can experience and sharpen all your biking skills through twists & turns on the offer. While you are still marvelling at this bit of the ride, please take extra care as soon the not-very-wide road clings to the side of a cliff for some way. It also passes through small villages like Yadi Mongar, where the road is lined with trees laden with oranges, which look like Christmas baubles that someone's forgotten to take off. As we rode through forests of oak, with a thick undergrowth of ferns, orchids and bamboo, a band of endangered golden langur were seen playing on a tree. The quick-fire ride brought us to the best stay option of the entire ride in my opinion – The Lingkhar Lodge – a traditional Bhutanese cottage lodge overlooking picturesque valley & meadows. I couldn't leave Bhutan without trying out the local liquor – 'Ara', and as luck would have it, I found it at the last halt in Bhutan, here in Trashigang.

With the customary group photograph wearing "Bhutan Happiness Ride 2015" t-shirts, we commenced our last day journey in Bhutan and to commemorate the occasion we were to be riding some very winding roads, majority of which was under road-widening work by the Indian Army Border Roads Organisation. All the way the vegetation is lush and green with many pine, fir and chirpine forests along the way. The Sherubtse College, Bhutan's only centre for degree studies also falls in this route. Fold after fold of mist-covered mountains lie stacked on the horizon during the initial portion of this stretch from Trashigang. Tall white vertical flags (*manidhar*) erected by families in memory of the departed flutter high up on the hillsides and on bends in the road. They're a comforting and reassuring sight in the middle of this lonely landscape. This was the longest portion of journey we took in a single day, of more than 300 kms to be done, one-third of which is within India. The mountains finished in Bhutan, as we descended rapidly on winding gravel roads full of rubble, approaching the last civilisation in Bhutan - Samdrup Jhonkar. And as you enter the Indian border town of Darranga, not only the weather changed to hot & humid, but the chaotic traffic conditions also changed dramatically. But beyond this point, the road is a straight stretch all the way till Guwahati via the military cantonment town of Rangayia. We reached Guwahati just in perfect time for chilled beer and paranthas in the Army unit, which was also official termination of our fantastic Bhutan Happiness Ride.

It's rightly said... *"Sometimes, you find yourself in the middle of nowhere...and sometimes, in the middle of nowhere, you find yourself..."*. Having returned from a nine-day bike ride in Bhutan, I am pleased to say it was one of my favourite places that I have ridden in. The scenery, roads, culture and people are all wonderful. The country is amazingly diverse, from lush green farmland to spectacular mountains and quaint happy towns & villages enroute. The Himalayan Shangri La of Bhutan is one of the best kept secrets of Asia and offers pristine nature to its few numbers of visitors. The few who do visit this magical place find an ancient Buddhist culture thriving in a landscape of incredible natural beauty. The mountainous roads in Bhutan, reaches heights of 4000m and offers the most romantic sights of the Himalayan ranges, the rides are through various types of vegetation ranging from sub-tropical to alpine vegetation, in the valleys passing through many villages of terraced rice fields and fairy tale rivers. There will also be sufficient time to stop and explore the ancient white walled fortresses and monasteries, known as Dzongs.

Myths and legends are woven into the landscape of this country. Temples pin turbulent demons down, guardian spirits reside in rocks and rivers, the ghosts of monks keep benign watch over villages and must be offered buckwheat noodles and home-brewed wine, though in a pinch, *Koka* (Bhutanese Maggi) and Red Panda beer will do. There are many things wild and wonderful about riding through Bhutan : streams thunder down steep hills, cicadas screech all day, autumn explodes in a riot of colour, painted phalluses on walls of houses keep demons at bay, Gods are appeased with ema datshi. We saw them all on our way from Phuentsholing to Samdrup Jhonkar, packed into the 1000 plus kms that took us through eight of the 20 districts in Bhutan. The unpredictable weather conditions made it a perfect mix of adventure and pleasure for any biker. It certainly was an experience I won't forget in a hurry, as it was everything that a long distance motorcycle trip should be.

*Happiness keeps you Sweet,*

*Long Rides keep you Strong,*

*Sorrow keeps you Human,*

*Life keeps you Humble,*

*Riding keeps you Growing...*

*But Motorcycles keep you Going !!!*

# **Refer Page - 164 for Photographs of Travelogue - 9**

# Backpacking with a Baby

## Europe & Scandinavia

### The Travel Bug Further Transfers in 'Little' Hands

Travelling is an art which comes from within and passionate travellers also have fears and apprehensions about not being able to continue this passion of theirs forever due to major incidents / changes in life such as getting old, getting married, having a child etc. These are very genuine concerns and actually have effects on any kind of passions & dreams in one's life. But I have never let anything come between me and my passions of life, and have always taken such challenges head-on. And I have always been very fortunate to get such people in my life who have supported my dreams & accepted my passions, my small baby being the recent one of them all.

This brings me to the newest and the most exciting phase of my travel-journey – 'Travelling with a Baby'. The more I got to hear that "Now you have a baby, your life is going to change, you won't be able to do all those things you did before", the more my will power increased. The same statements I had heard on getting married as well, but nothing changed; in fact things became much better and more beautiful. As both me and Deenaz had decided mutually that in her first year, our daughter Arianna would have her first major road trip (Bhutan road trip happened at 6 months only – refer my travelogue) and then her first backpacking trip to a foreign locale before she turns two, we put our heads together to decide on the destination, and what better could be than Europe…!!!

But the first thing which comes to mind is, 'Backpacking' and 'Babies' - two words you would not automatically put together. But just because you've had a child, either recently or some time ago, doesn't mean you've given up the right to live your life your way. Nowadays, more and more families are taking holidays, to see a bit of the world and have the 'trip of a lifetime', or to just break from the monotony. So, if you've ever dreamt of doing something really special with your family, such as travelling, I suggest not waiting for the so-called right time – it is now or never. We are all mature travellers but with children in tow to share the experience, it often brings a more enriching dimension to travel, meaning you will get more from it and see things through a child's eyes.

In today's high-tech, fast-paced world, where our lives are increasingly 'timetabled' and constricted, taking time out to travel as a family allows you to spend proper, quality time together, enjoying a special experience that each member of the family will cherish for the rest of their lives. Of course, you need to be realistic about the pressures of living out of each other's pockets for an extended period of time specially on a budget backpacking trip, and there will be trying moments, but the chance to see a bit of the world, experience different cultures and meet a whole host of friends along the way will usually more than make up for the more challenging elements of adventurous travel. And there's the added advantage of travelling with babies or toddlers, as it's often cheap or free, and offers parents a chance to do something special before their child starts school.

## The Challenge of Planning with a Baby

Obviously no trip should be undertaken without some thorough research into your preferred destination, as well as careful consideration of practical issues such as money and accommodation and transport etc. This brought us to the most difficult choice – Where in Europe? A proper itinerary is essential if you want to go backpacking cheaply in Europe. It can be very difficult to narrow down exactly where you want to visit, and a lot of travellers can really struggle with the decision. It takes a lot of creativity, and you'll probably spend many days trying to nail down your itinerary. Keep in mind that the length of your trip has a huge impact on how much of an itinerary you'll need. Basically, the shorter your trip, the more you need to plan.

Few things we mulled upon is length of the trip, budget involved and most importantly how much our little one be able to take it, keeping in mind it's going to be a budget backpacking trip. It was an experiment for us, and quite a brave experiment which we had taken upon us. Finally, we homed on to a 3-4 weeks of trip in total but we didn't opt for the 'mainstream' Europe, instead we went for the region that's called "Crown of Europe" and considered to be one of the most beautiful and picturesque regions of not only entire Europe, but of the World – Scandinavia. But with it came the challenge of planning a Budget Backpacking trip to one of the world's most expensive destinations. It's a question I get a lot from friends and family, "So how much does it cost to actually backpack through Europe?" – The answer is obviously as subjective as you want it to be. Everyone travels differently, and people like to do various things – with some of those things being more expensive than others.

Planning for any kind of trip is a daunting and overwhelming task, especially if it's a backpacking trip and that too with a baby. So naturally, you want to know at least how much money you will need so you will have peace of mind knowing that you don't have to die in the cold because you run out of money and can't afford a sandwich and a dorm-room in a hostel. But mainly because I have already done two backpacking trips – one of mainstream Europe and the other of entire UK, it assisted me a lot to plan this one. There are multiple strategies for traveling, and it's up to you to find the one that works the best for your journey. There are so many amazing places to visit in Europe — you could travel for over 12 months and still feel like you've missed a lot.

So, armed with internet as the strongest tool along with 'Europe on Shoestring' bible from Lonely Planet, we started the daunting task of planning the trip. Of course, our Life Membership cards of Youth Hostels were going to assist us in the accommodation portion, but we still had to choose apt stay keeping in mind that we are travelling with a 15 month old baby. I got benefitted from past experience of not going for to & from tickets, and in the bargain got some pretty good deals of air tickets, and was also able to add on Turkey in my otherwise purely Scandinavia & Northern Europe. We went in for a mix of local airlines, Eurail tickets, Scandinavia Eurail Pass and also a Cruise to cover the internal travel within Europe. The accommodations were mainly Youth Hostels with couple of B & B's thrown in between (as we got some very good deals online).

> ### *Tip*
>
> *There lies different kind of challenges while planning a Backpacking trip abroad with a Toddler. But here lies mental flexibility as it's not very difficult. Take care of few basic things like packing essentials, flexible itinerary and safe stay options – and you are good to go !!!*

## Fusion Istanbul : A Turkish Delight

Our first destination was the mesmerizing Turkish capital – Istanbul. As the cliché goes, Istanbul is where east meets west, or vice versa. This unique location combined with its history and occupants of different cultural background make this city a true melting pot. Here century old buildings stand near modern skyscrapers. In the same area mosques, churches and synagogues call for devote inhabitants. Liberal and conservative Muslims peacefully live side by side, together with people from a dozen other religions or beliefs. However, they all have one thing in common: the world famous Turkish hospitality. We had booked a cute little hotel through AirBnB, right in the heart of city – The Blue Tuana. There was slight apprehension about Istanbul as there was a major terrorist attack on its international airport just days before we arrived, but we decided to brave it out, and were right away out exploring the city. To our delight, the main Sultanahmet Sqaure was just 5 mins walking from the hotel, which has all the sightseeing heavyweights packed together with must-see Blue Mosque, Hagia Sofia, Topkapi Palace, Basilica Cistern and the Grand Bazaar.

We had half a day with us that we made complete use of, starting out with some local street food – *Bazlama & Soslini*, Hamburger Islak and Cinnamon Roll for Arianna, which she was happy to feed more to the Turkish pigeons than herself. This was a landmark moment for us, as she found her best friends on first day itself which were going to give her company throughout the trip. And I could just recollect the epic scene from DDLJ – "Aaao...Aaao...!!!". After getting awestruck with the architecture of Blue Mosque which gets its name due to blue iznik tiles inside, we headed for the (in)famous Grand Bazaar - a labyrinth of passageways and corridors with 64 streets, 3,000 shops, 22 entrances and 25,000 employees, and its huge range of goods. But instead of getting involved in the maddening barter system, we opted for a traditional cup of Turkish tea at a local sit-out before heading back to Sultanahmet Square to catch the mesmerizing Dervish (Whirling) dance performance at Dervish Café. We wrapped up the day with some of the most memorable sights of our trip – beautifully lit up Blue Mosque and Aya Sofia and some chicken shwarma for dinner from a local outlet – the owner of which developed special liking towards Arianna.

Next morning as we started exploring this historic city a little more, we realised why other cities claim to be at the crossroads of Europe and Asia – but only Istanbul can legitimately claim to straddle both continents, being split by the Bosphorus. That's where we headed after going through the gigantic Topkapi Palace, as we took the local tram to Eminonu, the main harbour of Istanbul. Without wasting any time, both of us being Foodies, we headed straight to the line of seafood specialising restaurants under the main Bosphorus Bridge for a typical Turkish spread of fish dishes with a glass of their national anise-flavoured drink – Raki. After savouring our heart's full we crossed over to the other side for some more exploring of Tunnel Square, Taksim Square and the buzzing Istiklal Caddesi. After covering Istanbul above ground, we went underground literally, in the fascinating Basilica Cistern for an experience of a lifetime. With its dimmed light and classical music to the background sound of dripping water, some find it romantic while others experience it as slightly spooky. We treaded the slippery walkways in between the 336 columns, all the way to the end to see the Medusa heads, placed upside down as the base of one of the columns.

## Stylish Sweden's Stunning Capital

We bid adieu to Turkey and headed to our main destination – the Scandinavian region with Stockholm being our first base. The countries of Denmark, Norway, Finland and Sweden form the Scandinavia, and are filled with amazing architecture and beautiful sights. Scandinavia will surely satisfy any globetrotter who wants to collect unmatched experiences to bring back home. The best part of it is Scandinavians are exceptionally friendly and hospitable. Forget about Disneyland, Norway and Denmark have been ranked as the #1 and #2 happiest places in the world. As we landed at Stockholm airport we were about to know why this region is one of the best to visit in Europe. We caught the most economical and convenient transports out of Stockholm airport - Flygbussarna Airport Coach which dropped us just a short walk from our Youth Hostel – HI Zinkensdamm. But this walk seemed the longest of our entire trip as we experimented all combinations of carriage of luggage and baby together – but we soon mastered it using the baby stroller in a smart manner.

---

*Tip*

*There are some simple ways to stay within your budget in Scandinavia. Stay where the locals do—at youth hostels, private homes, and B&Bs. Compare the best deals for train and air travel before you go. The famous cruise on Baltic Sea is very affordable. With a little bit of planning, the only bite you'll feel is from the icy breeze coming off a glacier.*

We checked into this old yellow & black stone building of HI Zinkensdamm and straight away fell in love with this place. But without getting carried away with our newly found love, we snapped out of our dreams as there was more important task at hand – to explore Stockholm. Wedged between Lake Malaren and the Baltic Sea, whose calm and yacht-speckled waters brought in Viking ships a thousand years ago, Stockholm city sprawls across 14 islands, each with its own personality. Kungsholmen is the thriving city centre; Sodermalm is the youthful island where we were staying; and Gamla Stan is the nautically strategic 'old town' of palaces, churches and cobblestones, offering a smorgasbord of sights. As we skinned the onion of this old town peel by peel, exploring the cobbled alleys (much to annoyance of Arianna as she tried to sleep in this bumpy ride in her stroller), we realised why this place is mecca for lovers of architecture, museums & palaces. The narrow alleys, one of which narrowest - Alley of Marten Trotzig, brought us to Stortorget, or 'big square', which is at the centre of this touristy but romantic neighbourhood, and houses the Nobel Museum and a pretty fountain around which street musicians play soulful tunes. As we walked around it to the grand Royal Palace (Kangliga Slottet), we were just in time for the Change of Guard and could witness the Swedish military drill much to the amusement of Arianna. Right next to it was Storkyrkan – the Royal Cathedral which was having an Organ Orchestra Show in the church. We wrapped up our day with a visit to the tiny adjacent island of Riddarholmen - the old town centre which offered us breath taking views of the elegant waterfront City Hall where the Nobel Prize Banquet is held each year. Arianna had sea gulls to give her company, while we settled for locally bought beer and bacon-wrapped hot dogs from 7-Eleven giving us company.

Scattered across a series of islands, Stockholm is one of the world's most beautiful capitals, and it is best seen from the water. We did exactly that and instead of taking one of many organised boats tours, we took the public ferry which showed us the same scenes from the water at less than half the cost. Our next very obvious stopover was Djugarden, the activity hub of Stockholm. As you approach ferry bay of this picturesque island you could see the many rides of Tivoli amusement park from the ferry itself. We decided to explore this gem by foot and went through long queues of Nordika and Vasa Museums, as the place is full of most of the touristy museums of Sweden. We decided to go with Arianna's choice this time – Junibacken, a magical fairy-tale world that can provide inspiration for a lifetime, with Europe's best children's theatre, exhibitions, and the fabulous Storybook Train through some of Astrid Lindgren's tales. This was truly an experience worth the hefty entrance fee kept by them, but our li'l one thoroughly enjoyed this children's museum. Their café opened its doors to us, and my first impulse is to fetch myself a cup of tea from the cafe. But that would be sacrilege in Sweden, a country of coffee fanatics. So instead we enjoyed a *'fika'*, or a coffee break with chocolate cake on the side, which is a social institution every visitor to Sweden should know and partake in.

---

> ### *Tip*
>
> *The cheapest breakfast in Europe is arguably also the best : the stop at the local bakery or pastry shop. Throughout Europe, you can find delicious tastes from baguettes and croissants to pretzels and apple tarts. These delectable & filling delights cost just a few euros and leave you not only satisfied but also is pocket-friendly.*

---

We continued our quest for some more exploration this time taking the old blue tram to Ostermalm. Swedes love their meat, but they're equally fond of the creatures of the sea. At Ostermalms Saluhall, a gourmet market inside an antique brick building, there are rows of giant fish for sale alongside fresh cheeses, veggie and locally-produced condiments. And we tried them all, warm-smoked salmon with cherry tomatoes and lemon wedges, served with melted butter, while the cold herring and shrimps were served on crispy slices of bread making their national delicacy – Smorgasbord & Raksmorgas. All this was nicely accompanied by their local freshly brewed beer, of course what we couldn't eat there we packed it, like the raw pickled herring, something of an acquired taste - a Scandinavian sushi of sorts. It is preserved with sherry, mustard or cream sauce or with dill and pink onions. Finally we ended up the evening at the buzzing bar of HI Zinkensdamm with couple of friends.

### Picturesque Baltic Sea Cruise & Mysterious Finland

Next day after a hearty breakfast at Youth Hostel, we proceeded for the most awaited part of any travel itinerary in Scandinavian region – Cruise on Baltic Sea. When I had booked this all-inclusive two nights cruise between Sweden & Finland for just about 10K for an independent cabin, I was not hoping this kind of luxury. But our Viking Line cruise ship was magnificent...a 6-deck ship with couple of basement decks for accommodated vehicles. This two night journey was one of the highlights of our trips, with everything available on the deck... from lounges to cafes, from sun-decks to shops, from activity centres to world-class amenities, it had all. And the view all along the trip was to die for. We checked into our cosy little private cabin with four bunk beds, and Arianna immediately fell in love with it, for it had the most amazing play area for her apart from magic shows, dance shows, live bands, and loads of other fun activities on the menu card. We didn't miss any of those, but only after enjoying the mesmerising views of Swedish Archipelago & its 14000 islands from the top deck with cool breeze and chilled beer. Once we got enough of Baltic Sea we hit their main Lounge-cum-Party place which had a Live Band playing some awesome Retro numbers. Arianna was the star attraction of the place, doing the jig initially with Daddy dearest, followed by sandwiched in-between both of us while we managed to enthral the crowd with our Salsa & Cha Cha moves, with the baby tucked in her carrier in-between.

**Tip**

*All cruise liners in Scandinavian region have duty free shops on board, ideal for shopping alcohol and other goodies which will be double the cost in any Scandinavian city. We stocked up from Viking Line for the rest of our trip within Scandinavia till flying off from Denmark.*

A night well-spent was followed by a heavenly morning with first views of Finland from the sun-deck café and the combo of coffee & croissant to go with. We were welcomed by a chilly weather at Katajanokka Harbour of Helsinki – our day stopover in Finland. Deenaz & Arianna braved the cold nip in the air and commenced their walking tour with their trusted tour guide – yours truly. Sophisticated Helsinki is an intimate city filled with cafes, parks, markets, beer terraces, funky bars and some beautiful architecture. After a quick "Awe" at the redbrick Uspensky Cathedral with a golden dome, we landed up at their main Market Square by the waterfront to find a local flea market to our delight – with locals from all over Finland including up north snowy regions, selling their local products. After savouring some yummy waffles and *'pirong'* (meat pie) and gifting Arianna her first Mink Fur Mittens, we took shelter in a building to save ourselves from the sudden drizzle. The building turned out to be Helsinki City Museum which opened doors to us free of cost. The rain gods actually brought us to this lovely place with the unique Museum of Broken Relationships and Children's Museum, where Arianna quickly transformed herself into a village belle from higher European regions back in 1950s.

Helsinki reveals itself best through aimless wandering and inward reflection. Walking about is rewarding here. There's quirkiness to the heritage architecture, Russian touches here, Greek Orthodox there; or figures from Finnish myths. We continued our walking tour to the Russian inspired Senate Square & the stately chalk-white Lutheran Cathedral, which had an art exhibition in its basement. We walked all the way to their Central Station which in itself is a landmark architectural wonder, before hitting Esplanadi – their main boulevard. It runs east-west, like a little equator, and is a good way to mentally map this very compact city. It's two one-way lanes with 200 feet of shaded garden in between, as we walked among the picnicking families and the gulls, and past the statue of Runenberg, Finland's national poet, the boutiques, cafes and stores line up on either side of the streets. Soon we were back at the waterfront on opposite side just in time to enjoy a soulful performance of a street musician – in Raj Kapoor style. All the walking really built our appetite and in just about perfect timing, as we entered the red, white and yellow-brick Old Market Hall (Vanha Kaupahalli) which houses 30 delicatessen stalls, as well as restaurants and cafés. It has been named the best market hall in the world. Being by the sea, how could we have missed on fresh catch, as we dug our teeth into Flamed Salmon Rolls, Fried Herring and Mini Mackerals with freshly brewed Finnish Beer, saving our food from the notorious sea gulls as we sat down by the waterfront watching boats, ships, cruise liners of all shapes & sizes go past us.

We made our way back to the cruise liner and bid adieu to Finnish capital with some amazing memories in a day well spent. But the whole day of walking around didn't deter our enthusiasm & zeal of enjoying our second evening on board Viking Line, as we enjoyed yet another night of fun, music & some late night shopping from the ship duty free for our trip ahead. On our way back we could finally get the glimpse of the concept of 'Midnight Sun' as we strolled on the deck at ten in the night with bright sunshine. On arrival at Stockholm next morning, we had to rush to the train station for our next part of journey. So after air, bus & sea we had to complete our transportation quadrant with the best & most scenic means – Scandinavian Rail, and what better way than taking a Scandinavian Eurail Pass (which we had bought from India only). The picturesque rail journey kept us hooked onto the windows gazing outside as the Scandinavian country side enthralled us including Arianna who enjoyed her first Eurail trip mostly running around the Train Café while we enjoyed our wine with some shrimp salad.

> ### *Tip*
>
> *If your trip extends south of Scandinavia, consider the flexible Eurail Select Pass, which allows you to choose three, four, or five adjoining countries connected by land or ferry (for instance, Germany-Sweden-Finland-Norway-Denmark). Rail passes also give you extra money-saving bonuses, such as free or discounted use of many boats (including Stockholm to Finland). Also, consider the efficiency of night travel—a bed in a compartment on a night train is a good value in Scandinavia.*

## Cultural City of Oslo in Viking Norwegian Land

Ok, so we expected to visit the land of Vikings and the fjords with our shoestring budget in place, and here we were standing outside the central station wondering where to head. Norway is expensive and Norwegians proud of the fact, but we were prepared for it with all the budget info we could gather before-hand. We quickly figured out our way to Citibox Oslo, just a short walk from station, this was one of the most cost-effective and funky stay option of our entire trip. As we arrived in this luxurious hostel, we realised that this place was absolutely free of any managing staff – the whole place was running on technology & gadgets...How Cool !!! After checking into our spacious & very comfortable room, we headed out to do some exploring in whatever time at hand. Oslo is also an incredibly walkable city. The streets are clean, the architecture is gorgeous, and there's a lot of nature even within the city. I read somewhere that Norwegians are a stiff lot, but smile, be friendly and seem interested, and you will be surprised by the warmth and generosity you will receive in return. We wandered around from the vibrant Youngstorget Square to trendy St Olav Circle, from enjoying the sun at Parliament Square to the main boulevard Karl Johans Gate, all the way to the majestic Royal Palace. Wrapping up the evening in the courtyard of National Theatre with a quick bite from local supermarket and picking up our late night snack & breakfast items for the hostel, we carried a very tired baby back to the room.

Our day started early next morning with a bright & sunny day at Oslo Opera by the waterfront. There are plenty of Operas around, but this one is quite new, and is definitely trying to be up there with the Opera in Sydney. And it pretty much succeeds with a fantastic structure and the "tourist" thing to do here is to walk on the roof. However, seeing the madness of crowd doing the same, we simply skipped that – didn't quite understand what thrill they all were getting from it. Instead we headed straight to Oslo City Hall or the 'Radhus' as they called it all over Scandinavia. Splendidly decorated with motifs from Norwegian history, culture and working life, the city's political and administrative leadership is based here, and it is here that the Nobel Peace Prize is presented. The roof of the eastern tower has a 49-bell carillon which plays different tune every hour – a treat for the ears. On Deenaz's special request, we headed to The National Gallery, which houses Norway's largest public collection of paintings, graphic art, drawings and sculptures. The gallery features more than 300 masterpieces, including works by renowned artists such as Munch, Monet and Picasso. The painting "Scream" from Edvard Munch is the most iconic painting in the world besides Mona Lisa. It looked like being inspired from Macauley Culkins "Home Alone" pose, as well as the horror mask in the Scream series of movies. This experience was truly once in a lifetime, and just imagine Arianna gawking at works of art without blinking an eyelid at the age of 15 months...!!! We also had a quick glance at Museum of Contemporary Art for a different kind of experience. But all this artwork made us hungry...very hungry, and we decided to treat ourselves to a nice Norwegian Lunch as it started to drizzle a bit. Out came my handy pocket guides & brochures, and we found ourselves at one of the oldest cafes in Oslo – Kaffistova, serving traditional Norwegian food since more than 100 years. This lovely restaurant serves what Norwegians often eat at home, and we had our fill with authentic dishes such as steamed Salmon with cheese sauce, grilled Reindeer meat, Lamb meat cakes and Beef Curry with Potatoes. Armed with our Day Pass, we caught the next tram to Vigeland Park, one of Norway's most popular tourist attractions with more than one million visitors a year. This unique sculpture park represents the life work of sculptor Gustav Vigeland with more than 200 sculptures in bronze, granite and forged iron. We culminated our day at Arek Brygge, the hip waterfront area with line of cafes and live music all along the pretty backdrop of Arkenhaus Fortress.

## Danish Treat : Buzzing & Bustling Copenhagen

We took our next train ride from Oslo to Copenhagen with a change over at Goeteberg, literally 'encroaching' a private cabin illegally in the X2000 Express train – one of the best in Scandinavian Rail circuit. With precise details from our host, we arrived at "Kenneth & Shindi's B&B" using city bus from the station. Kenneth welcomed us into his cosy apartment which we had booked through *AirBnB*, and immediately loaded us with all kinds of info, maps, travel guides & public transport pass. We also didn't waste any time to head out in this compact world-class city of Copenhagen, with rich history & a burgeoning bar, café & restaurant scene. It was clear Copenhagen had surrendered to its cyclists who have convinced the city authorities that a two-wheel ecological contraption is the solution to 21st century urban challenges. The Danish capital has over 1,000 km of cycle track, and is still obsessed with new traffic design ideas to get more people to choose bikes over cars. Copenhagen is proof that cars do not make a city. With just the evening available to us, we caught the bus straight to Kongens Nytorv Square landing up straight into the most commonly seen postcard picture of Denmark – Nyhavn Canal waterfront lined with bright gabled houses now containing cafes and restaurants. From here, tourists take sightseeing trips on ferries along the canal and nearby harbour. Here I understood how & why they call the Danish capital as the liveliest & most entertaining Scandinavian city and why the outwardly sensible Danes as the craziest party animals, as the whole canal side was buzzing with side café's, musicians, party groups – it was like one big carnival. We settled down at one of the bustling café on the cobbled street with full moon beautifully playing in the waters, and enjoyed a traditional Danish Platter consisting of *Smorrebrod*, buttered rye bread with various brilliant toppings-smoked salmon, cod, cheese, beef carpaccio, pickled herrings, boiled eggs and spreads, with Akvavit or Schnaps shots to go...which I must say, were quite strong.

Copenhagen is a gem among walkable cities. Having undergone many efforts towards pedestrian-friendliness, now it is a delight to explore on foot. From a walker's perspective, Copenhagen is a labyrinth. Walk; do not take a bus tour here – and that's exactly what we did the next day, after a hearty breakfast with our hosts – Kenneth & Shindi. As we disembarked from the bus at Radhuspladsen (by now we knew this is City Hall Square in Scandinavia), the historic Danish City Hall opened its doors for us to the engrossing 'paper-mache' painting exhibition and the amazing Jens Olsen's World Clock. From this huge square, a narrow opening introduces you to this unassuming lively, crowded series of streets & squares called Stroget which runs through the city linking Radhuspladsen to Kongens Nytorv. The walking tour through Stroget is an experience not to be missed in Copenhagen, for its crowded street shops, lively squares, beautiful fountains, Our Sacred Lady Church, Round Tower among many other gems hidden in its maze-like alleys. After savouring on traditional choco-softee and chocolate balls filled with fluffy egg white at an 1800-vintage store and some chilled Carlsberg (How can you not have this in Denmark !!!) under shadows of Christiansborg Palace at Gamla Strand, we caught the bus to the famed Little Mermaid – a massive tourist attraction, which tends to disappoint all with its 'overwhelming' size, except the most steadfast Hans Christian Andersen fans like Deenaz. Seeing Arianna's wide-eyed expressions looking at the turquoise blue waters with shining streaks of sun on it, we decided to walk all along the harbour front, stopping over at Amallenborg Palace – the winter home of Danish Royal Family. Now this is the advantage of exploring any city on foot – you discover hidden gems not mentioned in any travel guide or itinerary, as we noticed Papiroen – Copenhagen's Street Food-cum-Party Hub, open 24x7 and home of some of the best street food of around the world. We dug our teeth in some of the yummiest world cuisine, it was like the whole city pouring in from all directions into this huge waterfront party place. While returning late night, we realised we are actually in the 'Freetown' of Christiana – a self-declared independent state.

Next day was one of the most eventful days of our trip, as we caught the local Scandinavian Airlines flight from Copenhagen to Paris just in the nick of time, after getting our names announced all over airport, as we got so engrossed in digging our teeth in the goodies at Burger King. We landed in France's bijou extraordinaire – Paris, the City of Love & Lights in the evening and headed for our HI Hostel in a beautiful neighbourhood. When they upgraded us to the VIP room on top floor for no extra cost, we were delighted to find our room to be at par with any 3-4 star hotel at almost one-fourth the cost. After the fury at Copenhagen airport we decided to take the evening at leisure at the underground Pub of Youth Hostel itself, cooked our own meal and enjoyed with the 'duty-free' Coffee Liqueur picked from the cruise. Hostel cooking can be loads of fun apart from being highly economical on pocket, especially if you can rally up some fellow backpackers and share the meal along with making new friends & learning about new cultures.

> ## *Tip*
>
> *The entire Scandinavia region is famous for its rich heritage and museums, look for specific days & timings for discounted museum tickets (sometimes you may get lucky to get free entry also). All major Scandinavian cities have excellent local Farmer's Markets/Street Food Hubs – to experience the right kind of localised feel of the place.*

## Romantic Rendezvous in Paris

With both my girls super excited about exploring Paris which remains the benchmark for beauty, culture & class the world over, we headed out early morning to make the most of just one day available there. And yes, we didn't have Eiffel Tower as No.1 on our list, but rather it was Pere Lachaise Cemetery – world's most visited graveyard, with over 70,000 celebrities buried here. We got mesmerised by the stunning architect of the graves and the eerie atmosphere of the place, as if walking amongst the celebrity spirits including its most famous tenant - Jim Morrison, whose grave was like a pilgrimage for both of us. Without any further delay, we caught the Paris metro (which is spread all over the city like a spider's web) to the City Centre which is hub for all Parisian landmarks. One of the best things about Paris is the sheer number of things there are to see and do - and, of course, eat! The intimate pleasures of Paris include a cheese platter and bottle of wine by the seine river, strolling through Champs Elyseese on a breezy afternoon, feeding pigeons at Tuileries garden, and cruising on Seine River while the sun sets in the late evening. And yes, we could easily do all of this in one single day.

A little pre-research had informed us about the *"Paris Plages"* during the weekend we were in Paris, wherein all along the banks of Seine, pop-up beaches are created, each section with a distinct theme and it's like a carnival atmosphere. So after going through the spectacular interiors of Notre Dame (braving the long queue) we hit the crowded 'artificial' beaches of Seine enjoying our Rose & Blanc, while Aria was having the time of her life with music & fun activities there. With a hangover of good music & wine, we made our way to the "must-do-in-any-itinerary" walking trail in Paris between Louvre and Eiffel, through Tuileries Garden, Place de la Concorde, Grand Palace and Arc de Triomphe, burning out the memory of our camera & mobiles with photos in the bargain. The irony was that we had already spent most part of the day in Paris without even getting a glimpse of its most iconic monument – The Eiffel Tower. Somehow, there was not much of excitement for that, and it was proved right when we reached this 325m tall iron lattice tower, it was like Chandni Chowk of Delhi or crowded Colaba market of Mumbai. So, instead of joining the madness, we decided to spend some quality romantic time under the shadows of Eiffel in Parc du Champs de Mars. We took the metro back from there to arrive just in time for our sunset boat cruise on Seine River picking up the customary wine bottle enroute. The cruise of course gives you the most stunning views of all its landmarks, especially in the pre-dawn twilight of late evenings and the glitter of illumination being introduced all along Seine. While I & Deenaz nicely cozied up with our wine glasses, Arianna got busy trying to strike a deal for the mike with the pretty commentator. The day came to a perfect culmination at the Love Lock Bridge where three of us also declared our eternal love for each other.

## Tubingen : Hidden Gem in Southern Germany

Our rush to catch the flight on dying moments continued as we boarded the Air France flight to Stuttgart, from where we caught the bus for our first destination in Germany – charming little university town of Tubingen. We arrived in the town in midst of their annual Triathlon event, and knowing the size of town we knew that the whole town was closed for the same. Somehow we made our way through the crazy rush crossing Necker River with our baggage & baby to reach this lovely apartment (booked through local German Bed & Breakfast site) located in the heart of town, right next to the market square & city hall. We met our sweet & warm landlady - Claudia who showed us our beautiful 'Yellow Room' overlooking the narrow cobbled alleys down below, this place was like straight out of an old German Folklore, with exquisite woodwork and painted interiors. My old classmate Kamal gave us a surprise visit with his family, as we caught up on old times and he also introduced us to something which was going to be my nectar for next couple of days – local Neckermuller Beer. We went out for an evening stroll navigating through cobbled alleys to find a cosy little traditional German Pub serving freshly brewed beer and *Swabian* delicacies. In search of some more late night grub, we discovered the 'Food Mecca' for students – fast food joint called "X". We picked up Schnitzel Wiekel & 'X' Burger along with couple of local bier pints, and sat down to enjoy our late night binge at Marktplatz, the medieval town centre lined with spectacular buildings like the Rathus – Town Hall, beautifully lit up at night.

I was up pretty early the next morning, and was straight away out while my two girls were still nicely tucked in the bed. To my delight, the market square was hosting the weekly farmer's market. Europe's fresh produce markets are a downright bacchanalia of tastes, colours, and lively social interaction. This is a miniature world in which farmers, tourists, locals, and chefs collide and interact. Not only could I find delicious and fresh fruits and vegetables, but also fresh-baked artisan breads, marinating olives, and farm-fresh cheeses. I explored a bit more down the old university hall, past the Burse and the famous Holdiner Tower, walking all along Necker river with the *'punting boats'* lined up in a picture perfect frame, all the way to Necker Bridge. I picked up some fresh pretzel with coffee, to have all the ingredients to make a wonderful option for a budget breakfast. Back in the apartment we cooked up a hearty breakfast together before heading out to Tubingen University. We explored this pretty university town bit more, visiting their Student's Administrative Centre, New University Hall & Old Bibliothek (Library) buildings, wading through the lovely lanes dotted with shops, cafes and inns. And to my absolute delight, the wine shops were in plenty selling exotic German & other European wines at unbelievably low prices. Stocking up for our rest of the trip, we climbed up to the town's Schloss (Castle) lording over the town which was still part of University having couple of departments. All the walking made us very thirsty & very hungry, so taking a cue from Arianna, we headed to the place of her choice - Necker Muller Brewery by the banks of Necker River. The day culminated perfectly with fresh local dark & pale Ale along with *Flachermuchen* (kind of German Pizza) and Steak with traditional *Scheike* noodles, watching the sun go down behind the punting boats on the sparkling waters of the river.

> ### *Tip*
>
> *Renting an apartment or finding an accommodation with a small kitchen allow you to indulge in family fun of cooking own meals together at a fraction of a price of restaurant meals, prepared with fresh ingredients from local markets. And the whole experience of buying from these jolly local vendors itself is a feast for the senses, with people of all ages buying & selling.*

## The Extravagant German Capital City

We took the journey next day in one of the best train among Eurail – ICE Express from Tubingen to Berlin, in which we could get hold of a private coupe and Arianna made the most of it – playing, shouting, jumping, eating & even getting her diapers changed in private. Berlin is a city like no other, it thrives on variety and takes great pride in catering for every taste & budget. Boasting of some unique features and startling contrasts, exploring the many shades of this shape-shifting metropolis could take a day or the rest of your life. As we stepped out of the main station, we were overwhelmed by the variety of public transport Berlin had to offer – S Bahn, U Bahn, Strassenbahn (Trams), Buses, Ferries – it has all. A short tram ride took us to our Studio Apartment here which again was a 'human-free' fully automated kind of stay. As it was bit late in the evening, I decided to just step out for checking out the neighbourhood, unaware of the 'Gold Mine' I was about to discover called *The Kaisers* – a departmental shopping mall (a mix of Walmart, More & Reliance Fresh). With stuff cheaper than even street vendors and alcohol lower than duty free shops, this place became our haven for next few days here in Germany.

It was a cloudy day as we armed ourselves next morning with rain gear, umbrella and *Tageskarte* (Day Pass for unlimited travel) – Alexenderplatz was our first destination, named after Tsar Alexander I. In spite of the gloomy weather, the scene here was that of carnival as some local festival was on, with beer stalls, street food kiosks serving all kinds of *'wurst'*, dance & magic shows all over the buzzing square. We caught the S Bahn from there to witness the longest surviving stretch of Berlin Wall which has been converted into a permanent open air art gallery – East Side Gallery. After getting mesmerised by the works of famous graffiti writers & artists, we returned back to Alexenderplatz to start our walking tour towards Berlin city centre. The famous Berlin TV Tower was souring above the city, as we walked through the Berlin Dom on one side & Palace of the Republic on the other, on to Unter den Linden boulevard which has some of the greatest surviving monuments of the former Prussian capital. As we were getting late for a dinner date with some old friends, we caught the metro straight for Tiergarten – the huge city park. Walking past the famous Victory Column we strolled through the interiors of the park (much against the safety norms of late evening with a baby) to reach our destination – Café Am Neuen See, an absolute hidden gem by a small lake. Meeting up with Ana & Sophie who had told us about this place was super fun, as we drank, ate & roamed about till late at night.

We were excited & eager to get on with a beautiful bright sunny day the next morning, as we caught the S Bahn to Oranienburg for a visit to the famous Nazi Concentration Camp – Sachsenhausen. This was the place where more than 2 lakh people from 22 different countries were imprisoned between 1936 & 1945, and wherein more than a lakh of them died of starvation, disease, mistreatment & the 'death marches'. Not for the faint hearts, this tour features a visit to the punishment cells, gallows, gas chambers and burial pits located inside the prison. Hearing stories of prisoner bravery as well as the chilling atrocities that took place at the camp through our Audio Guide, we were stunned. A visit to this 'model' camp which now serves as a national memorial to the prisoners who lived and died here is an absolute must in Berlin itinerary. We headed back to Berlin city centre as all the main attractions were still balance, and rightly so we started from Brandenburg Gate – the symbol of Berlin and once the boundary between east & west. We walked past the majestic Reichstag building (German parliament) to arrive at the mesmerising maze-like Holocaust Memorial commemorating killing of more than 6 million Jews. As we went by the ultra-modern Potsdamer Platz, it was a pleasant sight to see 'Amrit Restaurant' as one of the busiest & poshest restaurants in the area. The unique open-air architectural complex - Topography of Terror along with 200m of original Berlin Wall gave us the goose bumps, as Arianna was enjoying her ride on Daddy's shoulders. We ended our walking tour at the Hollywood favourite featuring in many WW II flicks – *Checkpoint Charlie* which was a major crossing between east & west during Cold War.

## Here's to Many More Backpacking Trips with the Baby

It was time for me to bid adieu to this fantabulous backpacking trip the next morning, as for Deenaz, another week of real challenge was awaiting. We frantically sorted & re-sorted our luggage, trying to pack judiciously & intelligently, so as to keep all basic essentials with my two brave girls who were attempting the unthinkable, at the same time ensuring not to burden them with heavy loads. When I said goodbye to both of them at Berlin Central Train station, my heart came into my throat just seeing them being left all alone in an unknown country among unknown people, to rough it out continuing their backpacking trip for another week in Germany. But soon the feeling of pride overwhelmed the scary feeling in me, as I really wanted Deenaz to go through this lifetime experience of backpacking in Europe with an infant. I travelled in the metro and then throughout in the flight back to India with thoughts & memories, writing this post in my head. I wanted to put together something really useful, to help people take this dream of travelling around Europe with their family, and make it a reality. My belief got stronger of the fact that traveling domestically or abroad with your family is a wonderful experience; it brings you closer together while expanding your cultural appreciation as well. And it becomes all the more memorable if the region visited is as picturesque and lovely as Scandinavia - home of sleepy isles, big-city beauty, fantastic fjords... and humbling costs. While you may not have a Viking's plunder to pay for your vacation — particularly with the unfavourable exchange rate for Indians — a Scandinavian trip can still be reasonable, even for a budget traveller.

# Refer Page - 166 for Photographs of Travelogue - 10

# North Thailand Ride

## A Superbiker's Dream

*"No Matter how Bad your Day is…*
*Your Bike will Always make you Feel Better"*

## Introduction

Whenever anybody mentions a trip to Thailand, it brings couple of usual images in mind – those of crazy nightlife, sin cities of Bangkok & Pattaya, beach parties of Phuket and all-in-all a Bachelor's Paradise. But there's an entirely different side of Thailand when we talk of Northern part and its famous mountainous road trips. From buzzing & energetic small cities to preserved nature and from rich heritage to heavenly hill towns, North Thailand has something for everyone. This part of country will stimulate you by its cultural richness, and let you relax at the same time. By spending time on the roads here you will soon realise how important 2-wheels are to the Thai people. Long distance motorcycle trips in Northern part of Thailand are usual and the cafes you will encounter are a testimony of this bike culture. This was one trip I have been trying to take with Viktorianz since last more than three years now and finally I found the window of opportunity in January 2017 to make that dream come true.

Somebody asked me – "What's so special about North Thailand Bike Ride? And if you want to enjoy Thailand, experience the 'touristy' Bangkok & Pattaya – Why trouble motorcycling in the wilderness?" Well, my response came out in form of my favourite Bike Quote…

*If you want to be Happy for a day…Drink*

*If you want to be Happy for a year…Marry*

*If you want to be Happy for a Lifetime…*

*Ride a Motorcycle !!!*

Just picture lush jungles & rolling hills, breath taking scenery & authentic local culture – not to mention the thrills that come from navigating sharp descents, high-throttle climbs and the tricky loops on some of the best super-biking circuits in the world – this indeed is any Super-Bikers dream route. Starting from Chiang Mai - the city which is heart & soul of this region, this bike ride will show you the real & authentic Thailand, with exciting stop-offs along the way and also challenge you into a whole new biking experience, especially for those who dream of zooming on magnificent open roads with curves & loops to die for (not in the literal sense). On top of all that you can enjoy some local street food and let yourself be surprised by spontaneous meeting with the locals in quaint little Thai-towns. And if this complete dream package is offered to you by a perfectly planned itinerary with excellent stay options, most reliable & choicest of super bikes and a highly professional team of 'Viktorianz' leading the way, you can be rest assured that it's going to be "Trip-of-a-Lifetime" !!!

## The Route

North Thailand Bike route takes off from Chiang Mai and consists of two main circuits – The Mae Hong Son Loop (famously known as 1864 Curves Ride) via Pai district and The Golden Triangle Loop (infamously known as Opium Ride), returning back via Chiang Rai. The Viktorianz planned it to the perfection and combined both these circuits to make one superb ride. The 6-day ride was beautifully thought & worked out to give just about right amount of mileage covered in a single day, with few tourist attractions & sightseeing sprinkled in-between and hand-picked meal/snack breaks as toppings, and you have the recipe of a perfect dish.

- **Day-1** : The ride commenced from Chiang Mai on the big wide Highway 108 all the way to Chom Thong where you turn on to very tricky & twisty Highway 1009 taking you to the highest point in all of Thailand – Doi Inthanon. You carry on through dense & pretty Dio Inthanon National Park down to valley towns of Mae Chaem & Khun Yuam to get back on 108, and then it's a zooming ride till the pretty township of Mae Hong Son.

- **Day-2** : The second day of ride is full of great stop-overs & the first one is a quick rendezvous with pretty ladies from Karen Long Neck Village, and then you are back on Route 108 which later turns to 1095 and goes via Pang Mapha to oldest & most famous of more than 200 caves in this region – The Lot Caves. Post a hearty lunch at Cave Lodge you catch Route 1095 again all the way to Pai.

- **Day-3** : Ride's third day brings you down from the hills into the plains for a while through sharp descent wherein from Route 1095, you turn onto Highway 107 and reach this pretty little town of Tha Ton on the banks of Mae Kok River. It also covers the customary visit to Chiang Dao Elephant Camp located by the picturesque stream. This part of ride gets somewhat bumpy and challenging due to type of roads encountered on this stretch. However, the lovely Maekok River Village Resort at the end of the ride makes up for it.

- **Day-4** : The fourth day sees the most twists & turns in the ride and also is the most eventful of the complete trip, with the visit to (in)famous erstwhile opium hub of the region – The Golden Triangle. The first phase takes you up & above to the Royal Villa at Doi Tung and then you get on the heavenly Route 1290 and come on to the banks of Mae Khong River bordering Thailand, Burma & Laos – The Golden Triangle. The ride from here is very much straight on Route 1016 to the second largest city of this province – Chiang Rai.

- **Day-5** : The fifth day is reserved for the most awaited sightseeing of the entire trip – Wat Rong Khun or more famously, The White Temple. From here its zooming on the super bikes in full throttle reaching some of the highest speeds in this ride on Highway 118, as the long stretches of this amazing road terminates in the maddening traffic of Chiang Mai.

> ### *Tip*
>
> *Viktorianz is a Gurgaon based adventure travel company run by Ex-Army guys and is an excellent choice for bike rides all across the globe. They have highly professional people to arrange for various types of rides and North Thailand Bike Ride is one of their trademark trips.*

## Preparation

Any bike ride needs careful & deliberate planning & preparation – be it choosing the right kind of bikes for the route, places to stay overnight, fuel top-ups, eating breaks and of course the correct biking gear. We were fortunate that we had to only worry about the last part out of all these as the rest was meticulously planned & worked out by Mike sir & Gary sir of Viktorianz. A good helmet with an unscratched visor is the foremost & most important part of gear and that's why most of us decided to carry our own from India. A well-padded riding jacket, preferably riding pants, protective gloves, knee & elbow guards and riding boots provide additional safety. Protective gear is a matter of personal choice as it becomes difficult to put on & take off, so it needs to be comfortable. As motorcyclists it is always better to carry lots of bungee cords, a multi-utility kit, a torch, riding glasses/goggles & a sling bag to carry important documents. A rain suit and basic inners will be add-on assists in the time of need. And of course, a little internet research on things to see & do in each of the towns where we were going to halt for nights did ease out making the most of evenings available to us everywhere.

## North Thailand : The Region

Northern part of Thailand has been central to the history of imperial Sim. Over the course of the 13th century, the capital of the Lanna Kingdom moved south from Chiang Saem to Chiang Rai, and eventually to Chiang Mai. The hills of Northern & North-Eastern part stands at one of the most important historical crossroads of South East Asia, where people from China, Laos, Myanmar and Thailand have long bartered both goods and cultures. It's also the home of Thailand's hill tribes – the Hmong Mien, Thai Lu and Phun. Along with Sukho Thai further south, it was the first Southeast Asian region to make the transition from domination by Mon and Khmer cultures to being ruled by Thais.

## Pre D Day Activities

The best part about these bike rides are that you get to meet like-minded people from different parts of country or world, with different backgrounds, leading separate set of lives but having one common passion – that of 'Riding'. So, here were 13 Riders from absolutely diverse streams of life and parts of country (including two highly-spirited female riders) that got together on 22nd of Jan 2017 in Raming Lodge, our first of the hand-picked stay options located absolutely in the heart of Chiang Mai. I landed up with my set of adventure already begun as Malindo Air left my main bag in Malaysia where I switched flights, so I had to head out straight away to fetch up some basic essentials. Gary sir brought in the 'Beasts' which were going to be our inseparable companions for next one week in the evening, and the mandatory checks, inspections & trial rides were carried out. I had opted for a Honda 500X which as per the experts was best bet for a Bullet-rider like me who was going to have first-hand experience on any superbike. We also got introduced to Bobby – who was going to be our ride leader, interpreter, guide, philosopher, mechanic – our all-in-one *Man Friday* for this trip. Irish by origin, Thai since last decade, a farmer by profession & a rider by passion – what an amazing fellow !!!

The others got our taste of Army functioning as evening saw everyone gather around in hotel lobby for Ride 'Briefing' and basic introduction of each other. Quick earmarking of duties was done in precise manner by Gary Sir and we all knew that we are in good & expert hands. I couldn't let the evening go by in a city like Chiang Mai, as I wasted no time to head out & found myself on Loi Kroh Road – the buzzing hub of nightlife here. To my delight I found a cart right outside our Lodge having 10-12 different varieties of creepy-crawlies, just the thing I was hoping to lay my hands on when I landed in Thailand. So I got a packet worth of 50 Baht & when I was asked – "Which ones?", I could not resist grinning when I replied – "Whatever are your specialities !!!". So, armed with choicest of crickets, grasshoppers, beetles & worms in one hand and local 'Chang' pint in the other, I headed out on this crazy & wild street where beer bars & massage parlours were fighting with each other for space, and every now & then a strip-club used to pop up – it's an experience in itself just to walk on Loi Kroh Road. Not getting too distracted with the 'attractions', I spent the eve at Boy Blues Bar at Kalare Night Bazaar, simply the finest place to enjoy live music in Chiang Mai.

---

### *Tip*

*North Thailand is a region famous for bike rides especially on Super Bikes, as this part of Thailand is unlike the other more (in)famous parts of this country. This region is mountainous, picturesque and extremely laid back with lovely villages enroute offering highly economical stay options and off-the-beaten-track sightseeing options.*

---

## Day – 1 : Mae Hong Son Loop

Finally the day arrived as we all geared up after a hearty breakfast at Raming Lodge, the excitement was pretty much evident in the complete group of riders. After the customary group photo for the start of ride, as we all were told to start our bikes, I remembered reading an apt thing somewhere about motorcycles – *'You Start a Car...But you bring a Motorcycle to Life'*. So, we did bring our bikes to life and soon found ourselves on Highway 108, that typical adrenaline rush came within the moment wind started to cut across from both sides. On the smooth & wide highway, the motorcycles were soon in their element, however a sudden disturbing sight moved everybody as we passed a very recent motorcyclist crash right in front of our eyes. So, with complete concentration on road & quickly trying to get used to this new 'Beast' between our legs, we followed Bobby like disciplined followers. To my delight, Honda 500X was an absolute dream-of-a-ride and I was riding like a pro within first 20-30 kms. Overtaking vehicles was a pleasure knowing that you are fastest thing on the road which was quite reassuring not only boosting your road confidence but self-esteem as well. The mini windshield added to the comfort, cutting out drag you feel at high speeds.

After the initial somewhat drab stretch, things changed quickly as we turned onto Route 1009. We approached the huge artistic gate reading 'Doi Inthanon National Park', and realised every few kms they had a waterfall signage. We ignored these distractions and soon were riding into the clouds, literally, and realised why Doi Inthanon ride is counted as one of the trip's major highlights. You will also pass plenty of hill tribe market stands along the roadside selling local produce. Just before the summit we came across two impressive Royal 'Chedis' standing majestically on the side of the mountain. This spot sometimes offers a good view of the valley below, however most of the time visibility is masked by the clouds due to the high altitude, as was the case that day as well. But the 'Roof of Thailand' – as commonly known, Doi Inthanon top had crystal clear weather, and standing atop 2500 m at the highest point in Thailand feels quite ethereal. Moving downslope was the trickier part as we negotiated twists & turns carefully down to the base of Doi Inthanon and were soon into a little civilization of Mae Chaem, a traditional town home to a mix of hill tribes such as Lisu, Hmong & Lawa. That's where we halted for lunch, as I challenged some more of my taste buds with stir fried sweet & sour seafood and some locally prepared minced pork with their staple sticky rice.

We re-joined Route 108 at valley town of Khun Yuam and as I was caressing the curves, I observed quite a few small shacks selling strawberries & some other local berries. I stopped to taste some as they looked real good, and soon GS Sir joined me. Nipping at strawberries, we tried to make conversation with the friendly fruit-seller who was selling fresh produce from her farms. Though she was unable to communicate due to language, but was far from being shy and seemed eager to offer us the fruits. At the bottom of valley was 'The City of Three Mists' - Mae Hong Son, in the shadow of the mountain ranges that form the border of Burma and Thailand. Its remote location gives it a secluded and tranquil feel, while its proximity to Burma gives rise to the mix of people who reside there : Burmese, Shan, Thai, and hill tribe groups. This volatile blend of people and cultures gives Mae Hong Son a very distinct feel. We checked into this lovely highway resort just short of the town called Imperial Resort. A little pre-research told us that in town, by the Jong Kham Lake, is a lively open-air street market with stall holders selling a wide range of arts & crafts along with some traditional barbequed Thai dishes. Few of the enthusiasts among us could make it for this and enjoyed lakeside dinner.

## Day – 2 : Route 1095 to Pai

The next morning I was up early as I wanted to check out the twin temples of Mae Hong Son that I had read about. The twin Shan-Burmese-style *'wats'* of Wat Jong Klang and Jong Kham and their reflections on Jong Kham Lake make for the classic Mae Hong Son photo. The brilliant white and golden chedis mesh with the green roofs and their yellow edgings to form a glistening mirage across the surface of the lake, broken only by the lake's fountains. It was worth every effort of riding early morning into this sleepy town. Our first destination on the second day of ride was a short stop-over at famous Karen Long Neck Village. It was an eventful ride as this was the only stretch we made through very narrow forest lanes interspersed with plenty of streams flowing over the route which we had to negotiate. Once I entered the village l saw the bamboo stalls lined on both sides with the women selling crafts. Of course, everyone comes here to take pictures but I felt it would be weird pulling out my camera and taking snaps of them as they were just going about daily life and they didn't look keen to have their pictures taken. I tried my hand at their traditional bow & arrow and also bought some souvenirs as I strolled down to the end of the alley.

As we got back to the road, we realised that the segment on Route 1095 from Mae Hong Son to Pai is arguably one of the most scenic drives in the north, but is not for the queasy. This mountain road is reputed to have curves more than what a certain 'Pam & J Lo' can offer together, and that's how at the end of it you find big signboards reading – "Congrats on completing Mae Hong Son Loop - Winner of 1864 Curves". The jolts and bends on this road make it an absolute delight for any super-biker, and the continuously spectacular views just makes it doubly delightful. By this time I had got fully set on my bike, as it was going around corners quite beautifully. With increased confidence & with Bobby leading the way just up ahead of me, I had started going faster around the bends & began leaning into the curves. There is nothing extraordinary about leaning into a corner, but going fast on twisting roads require an upright, alert riding position. And then there was the scenery, the vista changing dramatically every few corners – it was a perfect ride, the sort you remember and share with other motorcyclists.

This portion of journey can be broken up in few very interesting stop-overs such as Pha Sua waterfall, Tham Pla fish cave and Tham Lod, the last being a favourite among tourists was aptly chosen by Viktorianz as our next stop-over. Tham Lod, which means *"coffin cave"*, is famous for its stalactite and stalagmite formations and ancient wood coffins. A river flows through the caves and you can hire a guide to float through them on a bamboo raft to explore the cave. At certain points you can climb up stairs and ladders to explore the stalactites and stalagmites up close as well as the numerous ancient ceramics and wall paintings that are scattered throughout the complex. After getting mesmerised, and tired by all this 'Indiana Jones' kind of exploring, it was time for a sumptuous lunch at The Cave Lodge. This was an interesting place as some very interesting information I could find pasted all over the restaurant of this lodge in form of colourful charts, giving out the entire history & geography of the region and how about more than 200 caves have been discovered by a mix of foreign explorers, mainly from Australia. Of course, how could I let it go unnoticed, one of the yellow charts reading – 'Thai Stir Fried Crocodile'. As I shared this yet another 'exotic' dish with my fellow riders, they pretty much enjoyed something different apart from the usual chicken & fish.

We rode on Route 1095 for rest of 50 odd kms without major hic-ups and reached the last destination on this particular loop – the 'hip & happening' town of Pai, an unexpected find in a remote mountain valley. Few years ago the town of Pai was a few dirt roads and shops. As tourists discovered the natural beauty of Pai River and its surrounding valley, businesses and development followed not long after, and it turned into the little backpacker settlement that it is today. Our resort here – 'The Quarter' was one of the better stays in our entire journey, lovely & cosy glass-walled cottages, traditionally done up central area and a lovely pool in the middle, and that's where we all headed straight away with our chilled Chang & Singha beer. Once again some prior readings on internet about Pai told me about Pai Walking Street. As we headed out, we were pleasantly surprised to discover that this little town was buzzing with Bohemian vibe along with hip music & art scene with lots of watering holes apart from its amazing walking street, which was filled with food vendors & market stalls selling everything from quintessential hippie clothing & jewellery to post cards & local handicrafts. The selection of culinary delights was absolutely delightful : Sushi, Indian food, BBQ meats, fresh fruit smoothies, noodles, snacks, pancakes and deep fried everything. You certainly won't go hungry! Then there was this unique herbal tea stall giving out aromatic tea in bamboo, which was quite refreshing. It seemed that everyone ends up at this street market most nights so the people watching is great here, and it's lined by all regular cafes, bars & pubs too which makes the scene more lively & bustling. We homed on to the place here most famous for its live band performances called Yellow Sun, run by a welcoming bunch of long-haired south Thai guys. As we entered we could see a pool table, comfy chairs, some good music and a local Thai band preparing to go live. The moment it started off with "Wish You Were Here", I thanked my stars in selecting this place, and from that time onwards it was an unspoken friendship that got established between me and the band members with common taste of old time rock music as our means of conversation. As we reluctantly called it a day, I realised that Pai was a sort of place where you come for a day and want to stay for a week – a hidden tropical island in the mountains.

> ### *Tip*
>
> *The globally-famous Mae Hong Son Loop, or more popularly known as 1864 Curves circuit is any super-biker's dream route and is a must on this trip. Pai is a quaint little Thai town offering lovely stay as well as nightlife options. The Pai Walking Street is a fantastic night bazaar for local food & shopping.*

## Day – 3 : Pai to Mae Kok River Valley

We were back on the road after a hearty breakfast at The Quarter and this last stretch of 1095 started climbing steeply immediately on exit from Pai town, and we soon found ourselves on the most tricky & winding portions of the whole ride. The loops & hairpin bends were far from over & their frequency as well as degree of difficulty kept increasing as I used all of Honda's 500 CC/50 HP power to negotiate the twists & turns. We zipped through pristine virgin forests where a ludicrous amount of green shades surrounded the mountains. The sturdy wheels of Honda 500 and the bike's ability to swerve quickly but stably along the bends on the narrow road made it a safe & confident ride; the fact that there was much lesser traffic on the road also helped. However, the conditions deteriorated further as we turned onto Route 107 where the steep descent was interspersed with broken & pebbled road, which made this as one of the most challenging part of ride. Bobby's skid right in front of me taught me one very important thing about biking – it's a game of concentration, even an eye-blink of loss of concentration can make the most experienced also fall. An interesting sign board reading "The Witch's Café" made me take a much-needed coffee break, as I noticed an entire witch-house with all the spooky works amidst the forest out in nowhere. A hot, strong cup of coffee for rejuvenation, and some candid photography and we were again good to go.

Our next halt was that for lunch, and Bobby had chosen an absolute delight of a place, kind of oasis in the deserts. The complete food joint was like a mini traditional village, with murals, artefacts & other Thai knick-knacks thrown over all over the surroundings which had bamboo as the main ingredient used for doing up the whole of the place. Lovely little bamboo thatched roof huts, small ponds & lakes, innovative fountains & water falls, cute wooden bridges, even a rain forest – all thrown together to create a beautiful locale, just perfect to unwind & try out their traditional Thai dishes. And as the 'Experimental Foodie' of the group, I once again tried to enchant my taste-buds with some sushi-kind of crab sticks, traditional fish cakes & their local speciality of whole fried fish with varied herbs & garlic. And adding onto all this, Bobby introduced us to one of the most favoured local dish of North Thailand – *Tom Yum Gung* – a superbly flavoured soupy dish with strong Thai spices & delicious whole shrimps along with other veggies.

With heavy stomachs from one of the most amazing lunch meals and a small cat-nap, we were back on the road zipping away on a beautiful stretch of road. With lush greenery, smooth but curvy turns and not a car in sight; we had the road all to ourselves. We made it to this pretty little town called Tha Ton on the banks of Mae Kok River in quick time. The Mae Kok's shores are truly picturesque: paddies in places, teak plantations in others; on occasion, a hill rises directly from the water's edge, or a hot spring bubbles not 20 feet ashore. The small town of Tha Ton lies very close to the Burmese border, and is most often visited as a stopover on the Chiang Dao-Fang Mae Salong loop or as the departure point for the popular Kok River boat trip. As I rode past the huge blue & golden ornamental gate of this town, I couldn't help but notice the hill-top temple - Wat Tha Ton, which overlooks the town spectacularly. I also noticed plenty of *Akha* women in their regalia in the town selling their knick-knacks. Our resort for tonight was Mae Kok River Village Resort, picturesquely located on banks of Mae Kok and managed by a British guy called Brian who showed us around the unique concept of Outdoor Training Camp which he runs as part of his resort for children from all over the world. It was amazing to see the kind of infrastructure he has built in a short time and here he organises everything from team building to personality development and from obstacle courses to hobby sessions. We called off the evening sitting at the pool-side bar with drinks on GS Sir for the 'good news' he had just received in earlier part of day.

## Day – 4 : The Golden Triangle Ride

Today was another relatively early start, as the rugged mist-shrouded mountains awaited us all along the way. We waded our way through fog & mist as the visibility was reduced to minimum, however one could still catch the glimpses of huge statues of Buddha in various forms & moods which were popping up on every corner, conjuring up an evocative & exotic image of this mesmerising countryside. The mountains of this region include Doi Mae Salong, Doi Chang and Doi Tung (*Doi* means "mountain" in the northern dialect - if you hadn't guessed), and they are truly spectacular but descend abruptly into a wide valley, broken with occasional low hills interspersed with remote hill tribe villages. These comely hills used to be prime opium country, central to the infamous Thai-Burma-Laos "Golden Triangle" that supplied much of the world's narcotics until recently. And we did get our history lesson also from few of the locals who told us that on each hill, opium would be sown on the sunrise side and marijuana on the sunset.

Our first halt for the day was The Royal Villa Doi Tung, the steep climb towards this beautifully located royal residence of Princess Srinagarindra atop the hill giving stupendous views of the valley. The place turned out to be a typically touristy affair, with souvenir shops both sides of road, restaurants & cafes, guided maps, an audio guide tour of the villa and a botanical garden. The customary audio guide tour of the villa gave us an insight into princess mother's life history, but the old-fashioned interiors of this lovely royal villa was what took my interest rather than her story. Mae Fah Luang Garden a little way down below was just like umpteen botanical gardens back in India, so I quickly made way to the most interesting part here – a local flea market by the road. It had some unique knick-knacks, local produce & fruits and quite a few Thai street specialities to satisfy your stomach. We quickly made our way down the winding roads hitting the main Route-1 heading towards the famous Golden Triangle, which is where Thailand, Laos and Myanmar meet geographically. But not before taking a required lunch halt at an interesting buffet place having a vast spread of dishes, and because we were so close to borders of three countries, the dishes had influence of all three countries local cuisine. The short stretch of Route-1 was left as the same goes all the way up to Thailand-Myanmar border check post and we had no intentions of crossing over illegally, so we took the turn onto Route-1290 and it was a pleasurable ride all the way to Golden Triangle. The landscape was hilly, with Ruak River up ahead which flows into Mekong River. These rivers form a natural boundary between the three countries – Laos (to the east of Mekong), Myanmar (to the north of Ruak) and Thailand (to the west of Mekong).

Historically the Golden Triangle has been an area well-known for the growing of opium, and the name comes from a US State Department memo on the practice. These days, though, the place lives on the cultivation of tourists, and this is undoubtedly the largest tourist trap in northern Thailand. As we approached Sob Ruak town which has come on World map only because of Golden Triangle, I was aghast to see a series of increasingly bizarre attractions that have been erected by the riverside; there's a giant golden Buddha on a ship, elephant statues where you can clamber to pose atop a palanquin, elaborate shrines to the royal family, half a dozen signs stating that yes, this really is the Golden Triangle and, inevitably, river cruise touts, souvenir shops and Western-style cafes. We got onto this rustic looking country boat and it chugged north towards the confluence of the Mae Khong with the Ruak river, Burma was up ahead across the Ruak, Thailand was to our left, Laos to the right, and China just 275 km upstream. But all I could see was the river, and a building claimed to be a casino on Burmese land. We were brought across to a small island named Don Sao, belonging to Laos. No visa for Laos is required to make this trip. This is popular among tourists, as the island is in Laos, and should you be so inclined you could claim to have visited the country, but more for the reason of grabbing some illicit Chinese goods and the (in)famous "Snake & Scorpion Whisky". After some frenzy bargaining with the locals here on calculators and couple of local liquor out of containers with snake/scorpion/other creepy crawlies freely floating inside, we were back on the road.

We continued on 1290 with the mighty Mae Khong giving us company all along till Ton Pheung making this an absolute cracker of a ride with bikes matching wind speeds of riverside. Leaving our companion for this short duration, we turned onto Route 1016 which further re-joined us on Route-1, the main route till the city of Chiang Rai. There is an alternate route if you continue on 1290, however being a longer route and Gary Sir heading back to Tha Ton, we decided not to venture into unknown territory. I took the role of bringing up the rear in absence of Gary Sir, and for a change had the pleasure of riding in a relaxed manner enjoying the surroundings rather than zipping through. We arrived in Chiang Rai just after last light. Despite being older, the town is nowadays more of Chiang Mai's snotty little brother than any miniature version and, somewhat lacking in charm. Chiang Rai forgoes the narrow lanes and spectacular ancient temples that characterise its larger southern neighbour and presents itself as a rather featureless town; many streets look similar and many are one-way, so it can be a confusing city to negotiate.

Without wasting any time, we decided to check out the famous Chaing Rai Night Bazaar, on the lines of the one in Chaing Mai, but this one is more pleasant and fun place with excellent option for local street snacks, chilled beer and catching live band and stage shows. As we entered the lanes of mayhem, we soon realised that there are two adjacent sections, one having more touristy flavour to it, and another more aimed at locals with aluminium chairs and staff in jeans and T-shirts. The former had all the usual Thai dishes being served in a central tasteful, traditional place with the (in)famous 'Lady Boys' show on stage and a local guitarist singing Hotel California between dances, while the latter had live Thai pop and country singers, cheap draught beer, lots of fried insects and street seafood, and the local buzz I was looking for, and that's what we chose to experience. The insect stall was my first target as I asked for a 'Mix Bag', I noticed how the lady picked up a bunch from more than dozen varieties of insects & worms, tossed them in wok for half a minute, and sprinkled some salt. The rush of flavours in each one was quite unique and gets on your taste buds very quickly, and then I just couldn't stop myself from popping one after another. After a fun-filled night of savouring on loads of local snacks & food, chilled beer and listening to Thai bands, we retired back to our hotel.

> ## *Tip*
>
> *Golden Triangle on this route is a unique experience wherein three countries are so closely connected with each other through a river. Shopping and bargaining skills at Laos street market can fetch you some excellent deals. Their (in)famous snake/scorpion liquor is pretty strong & local, but gives you a kick due to its unique experience.*

## Day – 5 : The Last Ride

The last day ride had mixed emotions of the sadness for we were to part ways with our faithful 'Beasts' at the end of this day, and joy for being able to complete this amazing & challenging ride incident-free. Our first halt just on the outskirts of Chiang Rai was this lovely Elephant Camp called Chang Puak Elephant Training Centre. Here, we met our three little new friends who not only entertained us, but also gave a nice 'Thai Elephant' massage to me in their own unique style. After getting enthralled by their tricks & talents, we headed to the must-visit destination on any North Thailand tourist's list. A visit to the famous 'White Temple' or Wat Rong Khun, has become absolutely *de rigeur* for any visitor to Chiang Rai. Just 15 kms south of the city, this highly ornate, all white, icing sugar temple is either described as spectacular, spectacularly kitsch or just simply kitsch, and it certainly draws attention and varied opinions as well. According to the artist/architect, the white plaster coating symbolises Buddha's purity, while the pieces of glass stuck all over the walls represent Buddha's wisdom. Wat Rong Khun displays perfectly a mix of traditional and modern imagery, with interior murals combining scenes from the life of Buddha with sci-fi, superhero and pop star images such as Keanu Reeves from The Matrix, Elvis, Michael Jackson, Superman and so-on. As we entered the temple by a bridge over a sea of demons, skulls and grasping hands, which is supposed to represent the transition via hell, from earthly existence — the start of the bridge — to nirvana on the far side of the bridge, and then entry into heaven being the temple entry itself. Gaudy, sacrilegious or a work of art — regardless of what you think, the temple certainly brightens up the ride between Chiang Rai and Chiang Mai and is well worth a visit if you're staying in Chiang Rai.

We left the White Temple after an early lunch of traditional Phad Thai with shrimps along with staple mango & sticky rice and soon parted ways with Route-1 at Ban Rong Sala to get onto the wide expressway kind of stretch of Route-118, which was an entirely different type of ride – long stretches of smooth spotless roads, with spiffy signs, past police checkpoints with a smartly dressed men. The windings in the route changed from going in left-right direction to now being in up-down direction, it was an entirely different thrill of zipping on a roller-coaster ride of vertical rises & drops on the road. I must say that North Thailand's civic infrastructure was first world, there was not a speck of trash anywhere, urban or rural. As we rode through picturesque hills of Doi Luang National Park, pure fresh air creeped in from the sides of helmet to tell us how clean things were in this part of this beautiful country. The customary coffee stop-over at one of many hot springs was refreshing, as I read the signboard proudly flashed in the coffee shop reading – "Nine One Coffee – Winner of Best Espresso in Thailand Indy Barista Championship". This being the last stop over before we culminate the ride, all of us didn't leave the opportunity of getting our photo-shoots clicked by our main camera guy – Shoaib.

As the mountains gave way to plains...the hilly winding roads gave way to six-lane expressways...and the clean fresh air to city winds of Chiang Mai, the sinking feeling came in for this mesmerising ride coming to an end. The big hoardings welcoming us to city of Chiang Mai announced our arrival back from what was a lifetime experience of a bike ride. Finally it was time to bid adieu to our faithful companions from last one week as we arrived at 'Pop Rider Bike Rental' to return our bikes and had the pleasure of meeting 'Pop' himself – the man behind starting the biking culture in North Thailand and the oldest in business here. While Chiang Mai does have the remains of both the city walls and the moats, it is every bit a modern city with the advantages of great geographical good fortune and a history independent from the South. Like most other Southeast Asian destinations, Chiang Mai has a vibrant street food scene. Stalls open late and stay open well into the night and its endless eating for tourists and locals alike. In spite of being drained out from last five days of non-stop riding, we couldn't miss the opportunity to explore the very buzzing nightlife and street food culture of this city, especially when we knew that this was our last night together. Luckily for me Chaing Mai is small enough to allow one to get a handle on its basic geography fairly easily. And it helps that, unlike its more chaotic cousin, Bangkok, this is a friendlier town where no one really seems in a mad hurry. And staying in the heart of city (Thanks to Viktorianz' immaculate planning) helped in that even better.

To our delight, the main night bazaar was in the backyard of our new residence – Hotel Porn Ping (Yes, I got the name right !!!). This bazaar is full of local handicrafts, latest fashion clothes & shoes, delicate silver jewellery and almost every possible fake branded item. For the more adventurous and less inhibited there is the option of getting a massage. Rows of reclining chairs are planted across the length of the market and you can have a surly looking man pop your neck for you or a pretty girl give you a pedicure. Once again a live band playing in a local pub caught our attention and soon we were swaying to the band's tunes. This was followed up with some exploration of the (in)famous Loi Kroh Road. Being in a bigger group, we didn't hesitate to venture out into couple of 'Beer Bars', where one couldn't help notice all the pretty young Thai arm-candy on grizzled white men. After gulping down anything & everything that came across – both in liquid & solid form, it was time to call it a night in the wee hours and we retraced our steps back to Porn Ping.

## The Last Word

The last day saw us packing our stuff not only with personal items, but with loads & loads of amazing lifetime memories of the trip (except that of last night – which is highly confidential). When you go through hardship together, you forge a special bond, especially when you are vulnerable on two-wheeler and facing some really tricky mountainous roads. Reminiscing about the highlights of the trip, we agreed that this was one route that was bound to bolster your soul. Imagine driving over mountains with jungle, rice fields and lovely countryside as far as the eye can see - the sun setting and it's just you and the open road. The best word to describe this feeling is "Freedom"!!! You stop in a small village where you are greeted warmly with a smile & you fill up your gas tank sometimes from Coca-Cola bottles filled with petrol. This is the Thailand that few get to see; the part that has been largely untouched by the tourism industry.

North Thailand Superbike Ride is definitely a lifetime experience, especially with Viktorianz. As you get to go to where few travellers have ventured, you follow some of the most challenging but picturesque mountain roads, where you will see hilltop towns, indigenous people, 1864 hairpin bends, the Golden Triangle and vibrant Night Bazaars. You get to eat some of the wackiest &

craziest local street food and get to stay in choicest of hand-picked resorts and hotels as you venture through the most scenic areas in Thailand. And of course, meet lots of like-minded people and make some new lifetime friends. It is an exhilarating and freeing experience to ride the bike on these roads, making it one of the most memorable trips of my life. Travel is not about the destination, but about the journey and this is an 'Epic' journey!

*I Ride to Fly...to Feel...to Touch...*

*To Breathe...to Laugh...to Soar...*

*To Overcome...to Belong...to Heal...*

*To Feel Strong...to Love & be Loved Back...*

*To Communicate without Words...*

*I Ride to LIVE...!!!*

# **Refer Page - 169 for Photographs of Travelogue - 11**

# Trekking & Camping

## Sojourn In Parvati Valley

### Hidden Valleys of Himachal Pradesh

There's a certain allure to a holiday that requires absolutely no effort on your part once you get there, where you're not compelled to 'go see this' or 'go do that' because doing nothing is the order of the day. You can do all the 'Nothing' you like and then some more of it. That's exactly what we were looking for as a perfect break from the mundane routine which was going on since quite some time now. But we did have few things to do in our minds, as I wanted to expose Arianna to the natural beauty of the mountains in its purest form, along with some trekking & camping in the hills. Himachal was the obvious choice due to its close proximity and good approach routes. But at the same time, I didn't want it to be the run-of-the-mill touristy trip of Shimla or Kasauli or Manali or Dalhousie. So we opted for a hidden treasure of Himachal (not so hidden now) on the Manali route – Parvati Valley.

If you're driving to Kullu-Manali and have not heard of Parvati Valley before, there are chances you might completely miss it. But take a little detour from the main road towards this valley with quite a few petite hamlets in terms of hill-villages, and it will give you enough reasons to stay here rather than going to the tourist frenzy of Manali. I've as such always thought of Kullu and Manali as concrete-ridden-hill-stations packed with honeymooners, beer-guzzling white water rafters and psychedelic cafes that serve desi lasagne. There are few places where driving within a destination is as dazzling as driving to it, and Parvati valley is one of them. This place is meant for relaxing & rejuvenating with long walks along the river, trekking in the woods and staying with the locals. There's little otherwise in terms of activities, but it's a place that lends itself to indulging in complacency. This part of Himachal offers well-known nature's gift to the earth like Kasol, Manikaran, Tosh and Malana. Feast to your eyes, these destinations can give you the full and the real enjoyment. Surrounded by the spellbinding, splendid and magnificent contours of the forest and hill alike with glorious horizon in the backdrop, this region is as close to nature as you can get.

Luckily I got in contact with this young duo of Anshul & Prakul, thanks mainly to some lovely reviews about them on the net, who have started few properties in Parvati valley...and guess what, with the name of 'Parvati' into them. All the properties of theirs - Parvati Woods Cottage, River Cottage and Woods Camp are within few kms of Kasol town and Manikaran, which is much talked about among the tourists due to its hot water spring and one of the most pious religious Gurudwaras located on the banks of ice cold Parvati River. At the same time, Kasol village has catapulted into becoming a hub for backpackers who get attracted to the scenic valley, untouched hills and great climate throughout the year. It is the perfect place for the nature lovers, for which overwhelming & positive reactions from tourists never cease.

## The Unusual Introduction to Parvati Valley

So, we stacked up our Ford Ecosport with all the essentials required (mainly for Arianna's needs), but at the same time being very careful not to overdo the packing as we knew our first stay itself is a place where you got to trek down steep mountain trail with your luggage. We hit the highway from Ambala and the initial portion we zipped through Kharar and skirting Ropar, leaving the main highway at Fatehgarh we started the climb towards Swarghat and Bilaspur. There was little respite from the sultry & humid weather until we passed through Mandi later that afternoon, when we were treated with sudden downpour. The drive from Mandi onwards was beautiful, particularly when we crossed Pandoh Dam, with the Beas gurgling to my right and the sheer rock face on the left kept me on the look-out for any falling stones at the same time.

At Bhunter we were supposed to phone our host for the next few days, 'Ruchit'. To get to Parvati River Cottage, Ruchit explained that we needed to turn off the main highway at Bhunter onto the picturesque Parvati Valley road towards Manikaran and reach this small village in the hills called "Jari". When I asked about any landmarks in the village, to my delight he mentioned to just stop in front of the only 'Theka' or the liquor shop of Jari. Now that's one landmark I was sure everyone in a mountain village would be aware of. "And when you reach the parking area with few more vehicles, just give a call and we will come and get you down to the cottage", he mentioned. It was late evening by the time we pulled up next to the Jari Liquor Shop and were guided into this small parking space next to it with an old but very attentive lady who was taking care of her cows, she was up & above to guide us to the parking spot for our car. As we were struggling with our rucksacks & backpacks & the baby, a hefty looking guy with specs & look of a mix of hippie & intellect, earphones & harem pants approached us. "Hello, I'm Mahin – your guide till the cottage", he spoke in impeccable English. Then he guided me to the luggage trolley which would take our 'heavier' stuff down to the cottage. A one inch thick wire hung across the valley and the river, with a metal basket hung from it on two pulleys. The metallic contraption wasn't much bigger than a baby's bassinet. On my surprise question whether this squeaky thing is going to hold the weight of our luggage, the smart young guy handling it declared very confidently that this thing can even take me across. I simply & quickly believed him and left the luggage in his experienced hands and walked off before he could get any more ideas of putting me into the *"Span"* – that's what they called the trolley system in these parts. I obviously preferred the foot journey rather than being suspended on a metallic wire with pulleys over the roaring river.

Following our guide along a stony path that went through the village houses initially and descended into a heavily forested & tricky trek, all the way down to gushing sound of Parvati River. As I struggled with Arianna on my back in the carrier and backpack in front for balance of load and Deenaz carefully following on our guide's footsteps, we finally gazed upon the creaky wooden suspension bridge over the raging river. It was tough, adventurous and thrilling – all at the same time, both because of the difficult steep trek and due to the fact that darkness & drizzling had a combined stamp on our craziness, which we just did with a two-year old kid.

As the treacherous trek of around a kilometre of steep descent into the valley, with loads dangling on our fronts & backs, came to an end and we arrived at the cottage which is going to be our haven for next few days, I inhaled the surrounding wilderness and smiled euphorically. Because all the 'crazy' aspects mentioned before took a back seat when we arrived at this amazingly picturesque cottage by the Parvati River side. And by the river is an understatement, it's literally 'On the River'. The cottage is in two parts - one which is a little away from the river has rooms with common/shared toilets (but extremely clean & hygienic) and the one which is absolutely overlooking the river has rooms with attached toilets. The five immaculate and warm guestrooms specially the two on the first floor facing the river are filled with basic but very neatly organised items. This particular cottage is almost as if overhanging onto the river, with views from the balconies to die for, raging Parvati river underneath, beautiful mountains shadowing over the property & serene jungle treks all around, this is closest to *'bliss'* you can get (of course, only after you have dared to cross over the creaking n shaking wooden bridge over the river). I knew that this was going to be no ordinary week in the hills. Next came dinner, which was served nicely in our balcony overlooking the river and it was like literally sitting on the edge and eating our meal. Pepper, the cute little Alsatian-cum-Mountain pup nuzzled up to my foot, and begged for scraps. Arianna couldn't keep her hands off her for next four days and fed her more than her fill every day. Our first night, we ate Indian, the chef's deft hands reinventing simple dishes into local flavoured delicacies. All veggies here are organic and freshly grown on the premises itself or nearby. The valley's symphony – river and crickets – coaxed me into the deepest slumber I'd had in weeks after the long drive.

> ## *Tip*
>
> *Parvati Valley in Himachal Pradesh has much more to offer than just the famous Manikaran and the in-famous Kasol. Look for few excellent traditional Himachali home-stay options here, a bit away from usual hustle & bustle of Kasol town. Getting 'off-the-beaten-track' is the Mantra over here.*

## An Insight into Himachali Rural Region

We started off our first morning sipping tea on the balcony outside our room almost touching the gushing waters of Parvati River and observing the racket it was creating. I was wondering how the 700-800 metres climb down from the main road spelt the difference between tourist mayhem and a slice of paradise. That's when I was introduced to the entire staff working here; a bunch of guys who themselves have chosen to leave the luxuries of city life & the mundane lifestyle to work here. So, they are kind of 'Volunteers' doing what they love to do, each one of them from a different part of country and extremely courteous & hardworking. While Shamsher & Vishal are soft-spoken, ready & eager for any kind of assistance, there's Mahin who is like a Work-Horse, a Bangalorean who suffers from diabetes due to his 'sweetness'. Then you have Saddam Hussain (Yes, you got the name right) who is an excellent cook, always ready to go that extra mile to please you with his cooking and even going away from the set menu, exercise his culinary skills. Last but not the least, there's the Manager-Caretaker-Gardener-Guide-Handyman-Companion, an 'All-in-One' guy - Ruchit. Most importantly, he will be like a close friend within a day of your stay. A beautiful human being, he's a gem of a person who is always ready to give you any assistance, any time of the day, that too with a big smile. A corporate professional, Ruchit gave up city life to manage Parvati River Cottage on his own and now he is half a mountain man himself.

It's impossible to travel to Parvati River Cottage and not be touched by the lives of the local villagers. In fact, a guided tour of surrounding villages is a must-do for any of the guests visiting this beautiful homestay. Tucked behind the cottage is a magical forest, complete with a little stream, a broken bridge and all. One such evening we headed out with Ruchit, our companion-cum-guide during the stay up to nearby Baladhi village and beyond. The trail was just like taken out of a fairy tale, firstly going along the white waters of Parvati River and then climbing up through narrow foot trails flanked by natural spices such as pudina, tulsi etc growing in abundance in the region. The view from top was breath-taking. The residents of the quiet village told us that Parvati valley is beautiful in every season – while the summers brings out every possible colour in the valley, the winter landscape is desolate & warm, twiggy & cedar-green. There were moments on our hike and even during our stay at the cottage, when we were out of signal range and that had become kind of benchmark for wilderness – places beyond the reach of Airtel or Reliance or Vodafone. Next few days we kept on taking off in different directions every now & then from the cottage to do some exploration of the places around. During all of these treks, if it hadn't been for our guide Ruchit explaining the finer points of 'Ganja-making' as we passed these plants several times (they are in absolute abundance here...growing almost everywhere), it would have been a mundane activity. Indeed it had plenty of beauty to offer, but not much of excitement. The tales of villagers, their lives, the *'Cream'* & *'Lugdi'* existing in their lives, were the ones which kept us going all the way in spite of the difficulty of trail or the load of Arianna on my shoulders.

One of the evenings there, I asked Ruchit if we can get hold of some local liquor, as that's what I have done during all my trips – from 'Chhang' in Ladakh to 'Toddy' in Kerala, from 'Feni' of Goa to 'Tongba' of Sikkim. He looked at his watch and then at me, it was 9.30 at night, and the village folks have their lights out by 8, but my 'Yes Man' agreed. So, armed with just 50 Rs in my pocket and a dirty bent 1.5-ltr empty Pepsi bottle in our hands, we commenced our trail towards the village – in pitch dark through the jungle. When I tried to switch on the torch, Ruchit stopped me saying it would attract animals. I didn't know whether he was talking about local village dogs or otherwise, in any case I didn't dare ask him. We arrived at this small mud hut, size of a locker where an old couple was fortunately awake. After the basic pleasantries in local language, the old lady took the bottle quietly inside and told us to wait, and suddenly Ruchit had a big smile on his face, I knew we were in luck. It took the lady about 15-20 mins to appear again and to my delight the bottle was filled with white fermented freshly brewed local beer called 'Lugdi'. And this big a bottle worth just 50 bucks was a steal, also for giving a warm smile to her we got a glass full extra as bonus, for the trek back.

Back at the cottage, we sat around the fireplace, and drank "Lugdi" and the Fauji Old Monk. All around us were symbols of serene domesticity. The two resident dogs, Pepper and Timmy were curled up close to the fire. There could be few better ways to signal our commitment learning about the indigenous culture than sipping a little country made liquor. The 'staff' at Parvati Cottage was more than happy to share the local fermented rice beer and the hard-hitting fauji drink, along with that sharing their stories and experiences of the region, as all of them come from such varied backgrounds and from totally different parts of the country. When asked about reason behind their choosing this property out in the wilderness instead of a more rewarding main-stream one in Manali or Kasol, one of them brought it out very aptly, "Actually it's more of a homestay, I do it because I enjoy it. It allows me to get acquainted with different people."

> ### *Tip*
>
> *Parvati River Cottage is totally cut-off from the world and you are absolutely on your own, with few very friendly 'hosts'. They do have more accessible property also called Parvati Woods Cottage for non-trekkers. But try this 'non-accessible' property to just unwind yourself from mundane daily struggles of life.*

## Exploring Parvati Valley till End of Road

In our quest to explore more and more of this mesmerising valley, one day we set our eyes towards Tosh – the culmination point of this valley by road – the last village where the road ends. Tosh valley attracts mountaineering enthusiasts from all over the world for moderate to professional trekking with Barshaini being the take-off point for most of the moderate treks going towards the tri-villages of Kalga-Tulga-Pulga and ahead towards Kheerganga and Mantalai lake, and further on all the way across Pin Parvati Pass. The more seasoned trekkers take on the difficult treks towards Papsura & Dharmsura, Kullu's highest peaks. Also nestled here is the beautiful Sara Umga Pass which dips into the Lahaul valley beyond. This offbeat trek rises up from the green dales of the Tosh valley and crosses over into the wilful wakes of Lahaul, offering some of the best views in the region.

Keeping all this information about the region at back of our minds, we trekked up from the cottage to village Jari. The ascent proved to be quite an effort for Deenaz and me also. Though done couple of times before already, but this time with Arianna's 15 kgs on my back and another 5-odd kgs of backpack in front, it proved to be reasonably tough. As we managed to reach our car in the parking, another challenge was awaiting us with one of the tyres flat. I quickly got it repaired at a workshop within Jari, and we set off further ahead towards Tosh, crossing Kasol, Manikaran and Barshaini in the bargain. The roads were dusty and never-ending, but it didn't matter much to us. The picturesque mountains were there for the company. The road was broken in between, strewn with pebbles and rocks at quite a lot of places, but hardly any traffic on the road, and a serene bluish-green Parvati river ran alongside all along. It was a stunning sight, the sun was in & out of the clouds, and we played soothing Floyd instrumentals enroute.

The fun ride ended as soon as we turned onto road to Tosh just ahead of Barshaini town. They called it a 'road', but it was quite difficult to locate also, because when we arrived at that junction, it seemed as if the road has terminated here. But then somebody pointed out that Tosh road is in that direction, to which my reaction was, "Which road...Where's the road...!!!" And then I looked towards the directions he was pointing and I could see some rubble & boulders paving way to so-called 'road'. The drive up to Tosh village and back, though precarious due to the width of the dirt and rock track, is an amalgamation of vertigo and wonder. The track is so narrow that it seems that the mountains have reluctantly relented just enough width to make motoring possible. The road itself is barely the width of a truck and there are outcrops to facilitate two vehicles to pass each other but more often than not, one of them has to reverse to the nearest outcrop or wait if the driver spots an oncoming car. It's truly a nerve-wrecking drive where you require all the road discipline you can gather. We were fortunate that we didn't face too much of oncoming traffic.

We arrived in Tosh with lots of expectations but it was kind of let down, with dirty & slushy village pathways welcoming us and quite a few 'youngster' groups thriving the place. However, as we went ahead in the village we could see why this place is sought for by the wanderers, it had breath-taking views of the valley as well as the snow peak ranges up ahead and a perfect place to unwind. We gave the skip to the usual known Cafes like Pink Floyd Café (which apparently doesn't have any connection) or Shiva Mountain Café or Jackie's Place and made our way through the narrow alleys towards 'Pinki Didi's Café' or as they have aptly named it – 360 Degrees Café because it has some of the best views Tosh can offer. Another board at this pretty little cottage-cum-café read 'The Last Resort' – don't know if it had anything to do with the famous track by Eagles. The setting of this place is simply amazing with both inside seating as well as outside one offering excellent options. The variety of tea and food options are plenty and we even tried the famous handpicked 'luxury' mushrooms of this area – Gucchi. Of course, you don't have to get scandalised by the innocent remark endorsed in their menu saying – "Please don't grind *Charas* on the menu...Thank You" !!! Well, we didn't want to brave the route back in darkness, so we called off Tosh visit quickly and headed back to our cottage stopping enroute in this beautifully located camping site bang next to Parvati River called Kasol Camps, for a cup of tea & some hot *pakoras* & sandwiches.

As I sat outside the next morning on the porch with the green mint tea in hand and feeling like a local headman, I could hear the merry river almost touching the base of wooden balcony and looking back at the sheer mountain-face that stared at me. Once you've made yourself comfortable on the balcony of your room, getting up to do things becomes altogether unnecessary. The rain-gods had opened up their fury today so we generally stuck to the cottage itself, as Ruchit tells us that this is kind of off-season that has started due to rains in Parvati valley. The night brings a sudden calm after the violent rains and a star-decked sky beams above. Give me off-season any day, crisp clear skies are best left to the tourist.

---

**Tip**

*There are plenty of options for stay in smaller villages such as Tosh, Chalal etc, but these are very basic accommodation and can be given a skip. Barshaini and Tosh are the base villages from where quite a few treks commence, such as the famous Kheerganga trek. Most of the stay places can organise these treks for additional cost with guides etc.*

---

## Over to the Manali Trance

After extending a day out of our original itinerary at Parvati River Cottage due to the sheer beauty of this stay, we finally decided to bid adieu to this heavenly homestay, to dare the mayhem of Manali. But for all its rustic simplicity, a sojourn at Parvati River Cottage is no leisurely picnic, it can be best savoured only if you're bodily fit enough to do a fair bit of up-and-down treks on tricky mountainous trails and your mind is expansive enough to delight in the splendid isolation of the place. It offers simple but comfortable accommodation, with no TVs or phones in the rooms, and the staff though pretty friendly is quite laid back to hustle up anything for you. But if it's a place where you can hold infinity in the palm of your hand, you just don't mind it. This is as close as possible to the life of locals you can get – it is a sort of 'un-resort'.

We hit the road again after four days of experiencing heavenly bliss in the Parvati valley. When we arrived at Bhunter junction I decided not to cross over the bridge on Beas to come on the main Kullu-Manali highway, but to take the left-bank road towards Manali which is a lesser used route towards the hill station. The road may not be as smooth and wide as its main counterpart, but it's having at least one-tenth of the amount of traffic you will find on the main artery, and it passes through numerous small hill-hamlets that have retained their sanity and solitude, one such place is Naggar. As we climbed a steep ascent after the fish-haven of Patlikuhl, a series of hairpin bends through apple orchards and fragrant cedar forests brought us to Naggar, the capital of the Kullu Rajas for over 1500 years.

Naggar is an enchanting picture postcard village with terraced fields, thick forests and superb views, with a majestic little castle as an added attraction which is now a heritage hotel run by the Himachal Pradesh Tourism. Located on a wooded slope, it commands a magnificent panorama of the valley, with the Rohtang to the north and Kullu valley to the south. Naggar also houses Roerich Art Gallery in what used to be the home of the Russian artist Nicholas Roerich and his wife Devika Rani. The diversity of this town from that of Kullu-Manali was evident when we saw the locals still going about their daily chores in traditional clothes, unlike their more urbane valley cousins. It was already lunch-time and our rumbling stomachs made us drive straight to Naggar Castle which houses a picturesque restaurant dishing out local Himachali cuisine. As we walked in the castle, we noticed that this was hardly like a conventional castle, with no ramparts or minarets. The only ghost from the past here is that of a medieval queen who is said to have jumped to her death from the *verandah* overlooking the Beas valley. Soon we plonked ourselves on the wooden outside deck of the restaurant with a view so breath-taking that not even a ghost could spook us out of having a meal here. We stuck to ordering local Himachali dishes which are simply delicious here. Our first usual choice was the speciality of the region - a whole Manali grilled trout served with sauté vegetables and fries. British anglers introduced brown and rainbow trout into the Beas in early 1900s. A cousin of Salmon, trout thrives in icy cold mountain streams. An abundance of wild trout still draws anglers to Kullu-Manali, but the Government is keen to take up commercial cultivation of these. This HPTDC run restaurant of Naggar Castle didn't disappoint us at all with Siddu (country cousin of Momo), the Anardana Chicken oozing with local spices, Himachali Pulao cooked to taste and the trout grilled to garlicky perfection.

As we commenced our journey towards Manali town with extremely satisfied stomachs & hearts, we decided not to go all the way to the main town but instead searched for local homestay cottage on Naggar road itself, as there are plenty of options here. We got lucky that in spite of the crazy rush due to being the weekend, we found the perfect location with the name of Manali Village Cottage, nicely tucked at a little distance away from the main road and about 10-odd kms short of Manali. We entered this sweet wooded cottage through an ornamental wooden door, into a fully wooden decked lobby complete with a fire place & all, walked up creaking wooden staircase, into our extremely spacious wooden room with wooden flooring & wooden roof & wood-panelled walls – this was like an overdose of 'wood'. As I stepped out in our balcony (Yes, you guessed it right – wooden balcony), I thanked my lucky stars that I didn't pre-book one of the umpteen resorts in mainstream Manali, because I had a view which can run in the 'Best View' competition in this region, giving a panoramic shot of the complete Beas valley, Manali town and the snow-capped mountains. We were especially glad as we were getting to stay in this room for a cost which was almost one-third of what we would've to shell out otherwise anywhere else. As we were in no mood to try the local cook's trial dishes here, I went in search of something better, and found this roadside café called Pizza Olive with its Tibetan owners/cooks. An atmospheric little place set in a garden, it serves high quality pizzas and pastas and it definitely didn't disappoint.

Next morning we were off to explore Manali town, with Deenaz & Arianna all excited to see & experience one of the most famous hill-stations of North India. As we fought & struggled our way out of bumper-to-bumper traffic to just get inside the town, Manali town began to sprawl around us, with an explosion of signage reading 'Gujrati Thali, Marwari Thali', 'Sher-e-Punjab', 'Kalinga Restaurant', 'Madras Hotel', 'Delhi Chaat Bhandar' and 'Annapurna Bengali Restaurant'. As the road curves up to Old Manali, the national diversity display of the honeymoon hill-station gives way to an exhibition of bohemian tourist fashion, interspersed with budget homestays in all shapes and sizes. But just to cover this two km stretch to reach Old Manali bridge, it took us more than an hour and all the old 'Delhi Driving Skills' I could garner to manoeuvre my Ecosport through what looked like line of vehicles till eternity. We parked our car at the very first space we could lay our hands on and set out to explore the lanes & bye-lanes of Old Manali.

## Manali with a Different Perspective

Old Manali is more popular with North Americans, Europeans and upper-middle class Indians, it has less of the doped-out hippie haven nowadays. Israelis, while still the largest single nationality among Manali tourists, have reduced in absolute numbers and as a proportion of the tourist population. Our first stop over was the Lonely Planet recommended Lazy Dog Lounge, which actually lives up to its name perfect to spend a lazy afternoon. It was set up in 2008 by the spiky-haired Gopal, a friendly Delhi-ite who abandoned a 15-year career as a television producer to do this. If it's a cold evening, the cosy wood-panelled interior is the place to try their signature dishes. But as it was a bright sunny afternoon, a table in the rocky outcrop of a garden outside is perfect to enjoy some chilled beer watching the river roar spectacularly below. The transformation of Manali's culinary experience from generic 'tourist food' to a variety of specialised cuisines owes a great deal to the non-locals who have settled in Manali and decided to make a living selling their kind of food. The Korean partner at Lazy Dog is one such example.

We explored some more of this much saner part of Manali with ascending alleys and shops & cafes on both sides, offering some very interesting things & food options. After engaging in some local shopping and endearing conversations with the shopkeepers there, we settled down in another one of Lonely Planet & HOMP recommended cafes – Dylan's Toasted & Roasted, serving some of the best freshly-brewed coffee in all of Manali. Our next stop-over was at this rustic looking place called Café 1947. Nothing patriotic about this place but quite a relaxing ambience with beautiful views of the river outside and an apt quote of the café saying – "Eating is no choice but Taste is". They serve amazing variety of tea and are also famous for their evening chill-out music sessions. After savouring our taste buds to heart's full in Old Manali, we decided to give a skip to rest of Manali and returned to our cottage. Yes, that's all of Manali we saw – no Mall road, no Hadimba Temple, no Rohtang Pass. Instead we spent the evening at this lovely garden restaurant close to our cottage called 'Fat Plate'. It's a family run place by an old couple with Nepali gentleman & Punjabi lady. The food is otherwise unremarkable, but the ambience is cheerful and welcoming. The lady even sat with us for a while telling us the story how she had come to Manali for the first time almost 60 years back and was in complete agreement with us about how this beautiful hill-station has become a crazy touristy mayhem now. When we asked her what kind of cuisine Manali offers you, especially with hoards and hoards of restaurants and eateries spread out all over this hill town, she told us that there's no such thing as local Manali food. "They all eat tourist food nowadays", she mentioned. Tourist Food – a term that one might think conveys nothing at all, but in fact it's surprisingly descriptive. In India, at least, it conjures up a vision of pasta in white sauce, chocolate banana pancakes and mango lassi in an uninterrupted chain all the way from Goa to Pushkar and from Varanasi to Manali. Well, nothing against these dishes as such and I am as much fond of chocolate pancakes as anybody else, but do we need to follow this firang-backpacker-trail so blindly, can't we have our own backpacking style as Indians. Well, a Food-for-Thought !!!

Next morning when we checked out of our beautiful cottage, we decided to explore one more part of this region – the village of Vashishth, which is famous for its hot water springs and another haven for hippies. Accordingly, apart from some regular visitors who either have genuine love towards peaceful environment and tranquillity, and who want to be away from the hustle & bustle of Manali – and trekkers and nature lovers – Vashishth have now started getting loaded with car-loads of tourists specially at the height of the 'seejun'. Inevitably, they are disappointed by the narrowest of the roads, few commercial shops now opened up and a small temple up the road dedicated to Sage Vashishth. We skipped all this and headed for the sunny terrace balcony of the World Peace Café that serves as the outdoor café looking out over the complete valley and the Himalayan ranges. You can also look up, up and away for a glorious view of sky and snow-capped peaks. Once the food arrives, though, there's no looking anywhere else. The breakfast here is simply delicious and the place lives up to its name by serving best of world cuisine under one roof, specialising in Israeli dishes. The prawn omelette and the Israeli breakfast platter with the trademark hummus, pita, chips & salad were the highlights of the meal. On our way back to Parvati valley, we took a small stop over at Kais for a visit to Dhakpo Shedrupling Monastery. Arianna was quite thrilled being among the little monk kids playing around within the complex. After savouring on some fresh apricots, peaches & cherries picked up from the road side, we arrived at Parvati Woods Camp, which was to be our base for next three days.

> ## *Tip*
>
> *Manali as a destination has lost all its charm and beauty due to too much of tourist influx and unplanned chaotic development. It's advisable to stay on outskirts of Manali and old Manali-Kullu road (also called right bank road) has plenty of charming cottages to stay at very competitive rates, and is a far better option to stay than in the madness of Manali town. Old Manali and Vashishth are the only two worthwhile places to visit in & around Manali.*

## Camping & Trekking in Parvati with a Baby

At a height of 1500 metres, Parvati Woods Camp is surrounded by towering mountains on all sides and is set on the banks of Parvati River that surges through the valley. Now Parvati Valley & especially around Kasol, you have lots of camping options. In fact almost every other property is trying to cash in on the camping craze currently in that area. What sets Parvati Woods Camp aside from others, is their location, their excellent service & the fantastic staff. They have this personal touch which wins your heart. This place is beautifully nestled amidst the higher mountains of Himachal ranges next to Parvati River, in an area which is within the valley but still have enough opening to give you amazingly picturesque views, that too right outside your tent. They are conveniently accessible from the main Kasol road, just 2-3 kms short of main Kasol town, but at the same time, tucked in nicely to give you the feel of being away from hustle & bustle of the crowd. They have basic type of tents of two sizes, with common toilets, but very nicely maintained. They got their own running Cafe called "The Bunker" for reasons best known to them, a trout farm next door and some great treks to offer from their locale - Soma Rupa. We arrived here by the evening and quickly settled down in our tent, with Arianna already making friends with the camp furry animals. After the meal, as I sat there sipping at my Vodka under a beautifully clear star-lit night, listening to the river (sounding ominous in the dark of the night), I could clearly see my future home in the hills. That's the charm of this camp, it perfectly blends the simplicity and indulgence to create something of a fairy tale feel.

I poked my head cautiously out of the tent early next morning, I could see a pale pre-dawn light had lit up the sky, but the sun hadn't hit the mountains. There was silence all around. As I was debating going back to sleep a mug of hot tea was deposited in my hands, and I retreated back into the tent. When I poked my head out again, the sky was ablaze and the first rays of the sun had struck the massive mountains all around. There are options aplenty here if you want to simply laze or angle for trout by the river, but I highly recommend that you go on at least a few treks here. It is ideal for that first real introduction to nature for your kid even if she is just two years old, because this would propel her on for that further longer hikes later on and that's why I was glad we braved Arianna on this trip. We didn't want to let go of this beautiful sunny day and quickly packed our backpacks as well as Arianna, and set out for this gorgeous trek from Soma Rupa to Kasol via Katagla & Chhalal.

We shouldered our packs, crossed a slim, broken suspension bridge which could take load of only one person at a time, and commenced our trek. The trail initially skirts the Parvati and is largely free of Bisleri bottles and wrappers. Beginning our ascent towards Katagla, we came across villagers taking their livestock to graze, as also the loaded ponies huffing & puffing on the trail, greeted us warmly. A bridle path ascended through the village and the fields. We set a leisurely pace, giving ourselves time to get into the rhythm of the climb and I was busy arriving at the best setting for the baby carrier so that Arianna is properly & comfortably tucked in and my shoulders & back also don't take too much of strain. As we got higher the hubbub of conversation from the cafes and small homestays along the trail faded away leaving only the rustle of leaves and the gentle wheeze of the breeze as it forced its way through narrow gaps in the rock faces. The path made its way through the initial narrow alleys of Old Katagla towards a cleft in the hills rising steadily into a very tricky stony trail with steep drops on one side. The sun did get strong but the dense cover of oak and deodar kept it cool. The sunlight played hide & seek, as it filtered through the trees in small patches, we walked on a path filled with fallen leaves as we could hear the probing tap-tap-tap of the Himalayan woodpecker from the hidden corners all around.

The climb got steadily more difficult as the rock-strewn pathway climbed relentlessly up. Our camp location appeared more than a kilometre below us, and views of valley stretched out from where we stood to eternity. As we huffed and puffed, village folk carrying huge bundles of leaves came skipping down the path, disappearing quickly around the bends. "Bas thodi si chadhhai aur hai...!!!". Each time a 'pahadi' man uttered those reassuring words, the barometer of suspicion in my head would go shooting up. Because a phrase like 'thodi si' has different meaning for different people, and especially for people staying in mountains it just multiplies manifold from our definition. As I put one dogged foot in front of the other and braced my lungs for my further assault towards this picturesque but daunting mountainous trail with Arianna happily sitting in the rugged carrier of hers on my back, I realised my baby has gained quite a bit of weight in last few months....or was it a bad idea to give her those Aloo Paranthas in the morning, the calories of which were now showing on my back.

We reached Chalal which is a village with just over 50 homes, mostly converted into homestays and cafés and settled for a place called Shiva Garden Café opened in a small green & pink cottage, but what attracted us was King of Pop playing there. Couple of youngster groups were sitting out, a guys & a girls groups separately, happily rolling their 'joints' oblivious of the world, but we could see that surprise look on their faces when we arrived at this backpacker's haven in the woods, with a two-year old kid on the back. Taking that welcome break after reaching the highest & half point of our trek, we ordered the Israeli speciality *Shakshuka* and some Maggi for Arianna, who was happy dancing on MJ, much to the delight of people around. Chalal is the destination to hit if you are looking for some peace & tranquillity, it is what maybe Kasol was couple of years back. It's almost criminal if you're a wanderer and haven't set foot in Chalal yet. So, recharging my energy levels by adding fuel to my body from my 'Hip Flask', mixed nicely in the fresh watermelon juice, I once again picked up Arianna on the back and commenced the trek. We started our descent into the forest with gigantic trees of deodar & oak, horse-chestnut & spruce. Moss, fungi and ferns covered huge fallen logs, the air was cool and moist, and the sound of birdcalls all around. As we rested on a rock, a sunbeam broke through the trees and shone on a scarlet green of the species swaying on top of a deodar. Parvati River again appeared as the ever faithful companion all along our trek as we could now see the habitation of Kasol town across the river. This last stretch of this amazing trek was truly serene, walking all along the raging milky river, till we came across the cable supported bridge over the river which took us away from the wilderness into the rush-hour of Kasol town. After the hard work of last couple of hours, we headed straight for Evergreen Café – arguably having the best food in the entire region, to answer the call of our stomachs. And the place didn't disappoint, with beautiful setting both inside & outside, great music in the background and delicious international cuisine on offer. We tried their pasta & Jerusalem Mix which was an Israeli mix dish of all kinds of meat. The evening at the (in)famous Moon Dance Café terrace was just the kind of culmination we were looking for. Back in the camp location, we could still feel the untouched beauty of the trek we had been to in the day.

## A Bit More of Himachali Heaven

A lot more of exploring was on the cards on our last day of the trip, as we set out to finally scan the Kasol town. I must say that every orthodox tourist normally scans a destination before heading out and scrolls through various information about the places to see and things to do. And you always expect the chaos of a 'travel guide tour' which will help you touch every checkpoint in the region. But that's not the case with Kasol. The town hasn't got monuments or other such sightseeing points, but the natural beauty that the heart craves for is in abundance. You need to walk to commute here. Kasol was also known as the mini Israel of Himachal Pradesh because of the many Israeli inhabitants one can see there. But I'll be honest here and say that Kasol is no more than a smoker's paradise now. Family trips are seldom seen here, as there's a whole lot of foreigners and young kids getting high everywhere. Notwithstanding that, the town has this nice feel about it and is also a shopping paradise. Junkie sweatshirts, harem pants, animal face mufflers, reggae T-shirts and a host of trekking gear are a few of the things worth shopping for in Kasol. Hand painted psychedelic T-shirts and jewellery made out of wood are unique specialties there. But keep your bargaining skills ready for striking good deals. We freaked out on some authentic 'Hemp' handmade products, and even bought them for Arianna. I'm just waiting for her to walk into her first day in school with the Hemp school bag, and can't wait to see that look on her teacher's face. We also tried some authentic Tibetan momos from this small eatery called Yantling Tibetan Café.

We still had one last evening in this heavenly destination which we made full use of, by heading out for another small trek in a different direction along the river. We also stopped over at the neighbouring Trout Farm to pick up some fresh silver trout for dinner. I couldn't resist going down to the water line of the river for Arianna to at least have the feel & touch of the water she has been seeing from a distance since so many days. As we went further deep into the forest on our trail, we entered a patch of forest that had run amok. Huge trees towered hundreds of feet above us. The path was strewn with fallen tree trunks, moss covered every rock surface and the thick smell of decaying vegetation hung in the air. I decided to put Arianna down from my shoulders for a while, and suddenly she was like a free bird, running around taking those baby steps around those huge trees. Without any map or compass or any guide, we didn't realise that our long evening trail had brought us back to our camping site from the other end.

We spent the evening around a bonfire while head chef Praveen doled out pan fried trout which was hand-picked by us absolutely fresh from the Govt Fish Farm. Believe me, everything they say about local seeds and organic farming is absolutely true, the food here tastes fantastic. I kindled a few more small logs separately in our fireplace right outside the tent and soon after all three of us were snuggled together in the chill of the night, watching the surrounding mountains lit up beautifully by the starry night and literally going 'Comfortably Numb', which coincidently was playing in the background on my phone. As I took a late night walk from my tent to 'The Bunker', I found the camp manager Jeetender a.k.a. Jeetu Bhai star-gazing in the courtyard where I joined him, as he narrated his story of migration from Jammu to Himachal, that too courtesy a 'Colonel Saab' only. He also told me about how the camp came into existence and how this place is the conviviality of families and friends looking to enjoy a slice of wilderness in the picturesque setting. I listened to his narrations for a while, but then got lost in the sounds of crickets and the clear black sky on top which didn't have space to hold its stars.

> ### *Tip*
>
> *Parvati Woods Camp is a very basic tented stay option with choice of putting your own tent as well. But it's extremely clean & hygienic and managed by a very passionate & friendly staff. Numerous trekking routes are available from here and you can dare to do these treks with a two-year old as well. Kasol can be kept as day & evening trip from here.*

## The Final Goodbye

With heavy hearts and amazing memories, our Ford Ecosport vroomed out of Parvati Woods Camp, bidding adieu to our newly formed friends that included the owners of the place – Prakul & Rakhee, as well as the friendly staff of Jeetu & Praveen. The drive back till you hit the main route of Kullu-Manali is in itself quite a challenge. It is the combination of the geographical dynamics and dangers this region offers which makes driving across the Parvati valley such a thrilling and adventurous experience. We took a deserving lunch halt just short of Mandi at this restaurant called 'Roti' to try some of the local Rajma-Chawal. That evening as we sat at the roadside Sethi Dhaba on the Chandigarh-Ambala highway eating hot Tandoori Paranthas with the trademark 'Cutting Chai', I played the last week plus back in my mind. We had seen a not often traversed region of Himachal, arguably one of its prettiest and done unthinkable things with a two year old kid, and also collected some of the best lifetime memories in bargain.

In this part of the region, we learnt that rural Himachal has the best of both worlds. Schools and health services work in the remotest of villages. The roads are good, and everyone, including the shepherd, has a mobile phone. The villagers in these parts are fairly well-to-do. Their livestock, fields, forest and fruit trees give them enough in cash and kind to live comfortably through the year. Of course, not forgetting to mention about the *'herbal medicine'* few of them depend on to make that fast buck. Many of the men we met had worked outside Himachal Pradesh, but were now content making a living at home. A word about this picturesque Parvati valley of Himachal, here you cannot be in a hurry because nobody is. But this slowness is full of possibilities and improbable conversations and it gently mocks the self-important stress of city people. Most of the people in this region are peasants; they usually have some land or the other and tend a cow or few sheep. Every home, however impoverished, will have at least some organic vegetables growing in the backyard, if not already growing in the wild. This is a region where seasons dictate activities, and you can't hurry the seasons.

Now about all the places I stayed in, while almost all other hotels & homestays are constantly vying for visitors' attention – with advertising boards making claims that range from the fantastic to the bizarre, all the properties of Parvati cottage are based on word-to-mouth publicity. So, unless you're in the know, you'd have no idea that you could stay in these beautiful properties right on the banks of Parvati River, just a few kilometres short of Kasol, but a whole world away from its madness. That the resident dogs are friendly, happy and healthy might give you an idea of how special the places are. And they are a far cry from the touristy Kullu & Manali beat. In Parvati valley, you can actually believe that the villagers converse with the Gods, invite them to meals, and that the local *'goors'* can speak of medicine, the future and the divine.

# Refer Page - 171 for Photographs of Travelogue - 12

# New Zealand

## The Southern Heaven

### The Kiwi Intro

Do you fancy the corner slice of a delicious cake? The one with extra cream on top as well on side and the one with additional cherries on top? New Zealand happens to be exactly that little piece of heaven – it is found in the corner of the world map, and has the added goodness of being a complete tourist destination and also a country you can relate to in many ways. New Zealand or Aotearoa, as the native Maori's call it – is extraordinary. It has miles of open country, and farms with deer, emu, antelope, sheep and cattle, which you can drive across – with silent hopes of great meals as well. Sealed roads, negligible traffic and ever-changing scenery, along with the fact that it's all a right-hand drive with Indian driving license valid there, making it an ideal destination for Indian tourist to drive around with ease.

Having your own sibling in a foreign locale makes it a preferred destination to plan for, and that's exactly what we did during the start of brand new year 2018 (The Indian winters – but Kiwi summers). So, we decided to visit my sister & brother-in-law who have now moved to the Kiwi-Land from Canada (I like it when they keep moving from one country to another – it gives me more opportunities to incite my Travel-Bug). Our first introduction to the Kiwis was a bit confusing – Kiwi being the New Zealander, the flightless bird and the fruit – but all has nothing in common !!! Apart from a deliciously indifferent accent, it's their hostility with their 'Bigger Cousins' – the Aussies, that makes the Kiwis much more interesting. In fact, I read a cell phone advertisement somewhere in Auckland which referred to call rates getting cheaper to 'call across the ditch' – referring to Oz. Then there was another interesting statement elaborating the differences with their big neighbour, stating "We are smaller, friendlier and we didn't descend from a bunch of convicts."

Well, leaving these differences for them to sort out either politically or on the cricket field, we caught the Malaysian Airlines from Delhi for Auckland via KL (which happened to be the shortest one-stop flight between India & NZ – and one of the cheapest). Arianna was obviously super excited to take yet another overseas destination with her 'Nomad' parents (Her tenth country before she had even turned Three), and she couldn't stop grinning bagging the window seat. I wanted to check out the reason of her happiness when we were getting closer to our destination, and as I glanced out of the window at the endless blue Pacific merging with the horizon, broken at places by white swirls in the water,

I could clearly see the reason. As the aircraft came down more & more and the land came closer & closer, the mesmerizing sight of this paradise island became clearer & clearer. By the time we landed, I also had a silly grin plastered on my face that refused to quit.

But soon that grin had to give way to bit of stress on the face, as we went through series of tough but friendly security checks at Auckland airport. Anyone going to New Zealand knows just how strict they are, about not letting in any organic material, including all food. There was already so much planted in our heads about this aspect as we landed in Auckland airport, and there were warning boards all over – the bags were scanned in detail. Heaven help you if you have an unnoticed orange or packet of half-eaten chips in your backpack. If you like living dangerously, try carrying fur coats to NZ, or flowers for your relatives – and you will feel the full effect of Kiwi customs. But with extensive research on the internet and much more brain-washing by my dearest sister, we sailed smoothly out of the Auckland airport.

## Auckland – Harbours & Volcanoes

As we drove out of Auckland airport, soon I realized why my sister & BIL chose to migrate here. Not because it is the largest city in New Zealand which is set between three beautiful harbours and dotted with 48 extinct volcanic cones, but it is the diversity of experiences in such close proximity that makes this city unique. One of the most fun cities in NZ, it's got a happening night life, a bunch of whacky sightseeing options and tonnes of activities to try. There's never a dull moment in this city with its bustling waterfront at any given point of time. Its two active harbours, Waitemata and Manukau, give you plenty of water related activities, and the city's volcanoes dot them like punctuation to a sentence.

Next couple of days went by in acclimatization & taking things easy (Sudden change of weather took a bit of toll on us), but that gave us time to plan things ahead, and also to catch up on some 'bro-sis' times. True to my colours, I got busy with maps & guides to do my research on New Zealand (Well, Travel-Research could be my PhD thesis subject – seriously !!!). But I wouldn't just do the usual tourist-as-herded sheep tour thing. I soon learnt that best way to go about in this city is doing a bit of research and booking something – anything available on numerous 'coupon sites'. This is what Aucklanders do, always happy to indulge in the pleasures of one of the most activity-based cities in the world. Though they are known as JAFAs (Just Another Effing Aucklander) to outsiders, but they welcome visitors with open arms. Follow their lead and you'll be greatly rewarded. And if there is really nothing you want to see or do, one can at least just sit and stare at the beautiful harbour (and the iconic Harbour Bridge, of course) at one of many bars & cafes at Viaduct Harbour while enjoying fresh fish & chips along with locally brewed craft beer with a kiwi twist. That's exactly what we indulged in whenever we got a chance, soon figuring out the limited, but efficient local transit system.

On one such bright & sunny day, we found ourselves exploring the buzzing heart of Auckland – twin 'royal' streets of Queens & Princess. Being in the heart of a city and not doing what the locals do, does not fit into my itinerary of things, so we checked out the local music festival going on there and tasted some street food from the local 'food-trucks'. From the hustle & bustle of Queen's Street, we set off on a self-guided tour of Auckland's 'Hidden Secrets', wandering through the back lanes of the city centre, to discover layers of the city's history in the historic Auckland University buildings and the iconic Auckland Museum located in this vast green pasture right in the middle of city, called The Domain. We also explored many other varied styled neighbourhoods of Auckland such as Remuera, Parnell, Ponsonby and Mt Eden – each having its unique flavour. One such drive along the picturesque Tamaki Drive, took us to Auckland's most popular inner city beaches, Mission Bay. Here one can take a dip in the sea, hire a kayak, try stand up paddle boarding, throw a frisbee around or just enjoy an ice cream on the beach. For the more adventurous, you can jump off two of Auckland's iconic landmarks, the Harbour Bridge and the Sky Tower, or even walk its edge - 192 m above ground level.

Auckland is New Zealand's most multi-cultural city, and later arrivals too have made their presence visible through the plethora of little Chinese, South East Asian, Italian and Indian eateries in the city centre. In this emphatically foodie city, everyone pronounces as authority on food and wine. In fact, as we discovered more and more about food here, we realized that it's almost impossible to eat badly here, or to have a glass of wine or a coffee that's substandard. After all, there's so much to choose from – it just feels that every third shop here is an eatery, that too of varied cuisine from a different country. While we tried a lot of new and unfamiliar foods, after a while our desi hearts were craving for some butter chicken and shahi paneer. In New Zealand, especially in Auckland, you should never fear – Indian food (which of course predominantly means North Indian tandoori meals) is quite easily available. *"Paradise"* came to our rescue as my sister & BIL introduced us to this hugely popular chain of eateries located in an area which can easily claim to be a mini-India, called Sandringham. Really, this sums up Auckland completely – a bubbling, cosmopolitan experience that's not to be missed, but still holding on to an unusually old-school charm.

> ## *Tip*
>
> *Auckland as a city has a plethora of activities and eating places to offer. Most of the activities within the city are costly, but the eating options are in plenty with almost every type of food available here. Exploring the city on foot is the best way to get the feel of the place.*

## Hidden Gems Around Auckland

Auckland has long been known as Tamaki Makau Rau – *"The Spouse Desired by a Hundred Lovers"*. Well, I had no inclination in knowing the reasons behind this particular term, but this was maybe due to the fertile volcanic slopes which sheltered fishing sites and access to some of the great waterways, that so many desired it. The city has grown up quite a bit in last decade or so, and has been re-invented by its people into a wonderfully varied, international and multi-racial culture capital of this wonderful island country. The next we discovered that there lies many more surprises all around Auckland, within short drives away. The first one of our mini-getaways was towards the West, where the first stop was this lovely animal farm out in the countryside. The farm stretched over 4000 acres and was home to countless native animals, from sheep, goats & cows nibbling at the grass to all sorts of farmland bird species scampering through the undergrowth. They had their very own 'Furry House', with rabbits, bunnies, hares & hamsters in all shapes, sizes & colours, that we lost count of how many types we saw and played with. Then there were puppies, emu, horses – all having their own names, and then of course there were Alpacas – New Zealand's answer to the Himalayan Llamas, extremely cute & friendly animals who loves to eat out of your hand. It was like a dream-world for Arianna, being such an avid animal-lover – she just went bonkers with so many types of farm animals and those too, in such close proximity, that at one time she was being overwhelmed by the little goats, lambs & calves eating out of her hands – all at one time.

As we drove ahead, within just 45 minutes out of the city, we found ourselves in the middle of a rainforest. Yes, I thought it was ridiculous too, as this is supposed to be a city – right !!! This dense rainforest forms the Waitakere Ranges, a regional park and city's water reservoir. As the dense tree-infested mountains started, we came across Arataki Visitor Centre which gives out a descriptive introduction to New Zealand's flora, especially that of giant kauri trees. We drove further towards western coast to come down to the dramatic Piha Beach, the sand of which is almost black and also magnetic because of the large quantities of iron ore in it. This beach was like one big party destination, with people flocking from nearby in their cars, bikes, RVs – camping by the beach, on the beach – just about everywhere, and few trying their luck at climbing the nature's wonder – Lion's Rock. You can also check out the more rugged Karekare beach close by with the stunning Karekare falls just a short trek away.

Not feeling fulfilled yet, I did some more exploring in the coming days around nearby areas and on one such day with overcast, I reached the Waitemata Ferry Terminal from where you can get a ferry to almost everywhere. This efficient mode of transport gives you an economical and quick way to explore many islands of the Hauraki Gulf such as Waiheke Island with its numerous wineries, or volcanic Rangitoto Island that dominates the seascape. While Waiheke Island is the ultimate island retreat where a wine tasting tour is a must, Rangitoto is a dormant volcanic cone famous for its trekking & walking trails. I decided to keep these two for yet another day and took the short ferry across the Waitemata Harbour to the small North Shore hamlet – Davenport.

It has two panoramic look-out points, namely Mt Victoria and North Head, having commanding panoramic views of the entire Auckland harbour & its skyline on one end and the beautiful Hauraki Gulf on the other. The ferry ride itself had splendid views of the iconic Harbour Bridge thrown free of cost in its ticket. I decided to explore Davenport village by foot and first headed to Mt Victoria braving the slight drizzle, but the spectacular views from summit more than made up for the weather. The highest volcanic cone on Auckland's North Shore was established as a fort in 1889 to protect against the imagined Russian invasion. After walking back to the ferry terminal, I decided to walk all along the waterfront, with splendid view of 'City of Sails' on the other side. The trail culminates at the Naval Museum at the base of North Head, one of Auckland's most treasured historic reserves. It's also known as 'Volcano with a View' and I found the reason for it as soon as I reached the summit. It has incredible 360 degree views of Auckland City skyline, the Hauraki Gulf, crescent-shaped Cheltenham Beach & the Victorian architecture in Devonport's historical village. After getting the quota of the overwhelming views, I took a tour of the bunkers and gun emplacements and tried to find my way through the maze-like tunnels which might have been extremely useful during the war time of 1880s. Davenport also introduced me to Esplanade Hotel by the ferry terminal, where later we had a fantastic dinner to celebrate our 10th Anniversary (their Seafood Platter is a must-try which gives you almost everything moving underwater on the plate).

Now if you are in a country which has two of its largest industries in agriculture & dairy, where the last census count had more number of cattle & sheep than humans, how can you not have the concept of Farmer's Markets. And this country has almost every small town & village boasting of one of its own, with fresh produce, gourmet food, condiments and more. My sister did give me a small glimpse of it within Auckland city also in terms of the famous Parnell's French Style Farmers' Markets, set up every Saturday and Sunday morning. But to get more authentic rural feel, we crossed over the Harbour Bridge to head further into North Shore to the Matakana region, which is known for its superb wineries and boutique vineyards set amidst rolling countryside apart from having a bustling Saturday Farmer's Market. You can call in at the cellar doors for a wine tasting or visit one of the vineyard restaurants for a leisurely lunch, but we decided to explore the village town and savoured on some locally made burgers at Matakana Market Kitchen. On another day we headed towards East of Auckland to the quaint little village of Clevedon which again had a fantastic Farmer's Market. With the local produces and food stalls in plenty, this market had pony rides, pet corner and musicians playing, and when he sang back-to-back Floyd tracks, I knew that my day has been made. The trip ended with a beautiful coastal drive of Maraetai Beach – another hidden gem around Auckland. The cherry on the cake of our Auckland stay was definitely the Roger Waters Show – 'Us & Them'. This was my second time after Manchester and very first time for Deenaz, to see the legend himself – Live in flesh.

> ### Tip
>
> *The day excursions from Auckland have plenty of options, especially towards the North and West side. Numerous 'coupon sites' offer excellent deals on the net and trips can be chosen based on preference. Plenty of Farmer's Markets and animal farms in the countryside and they are must visits to savour local delicacies and meet local people.*

New Zealand is also a food lover's paradise – its home to world-class chefs, food producers and winemakers, and we were going to find out about this fact during our tours of South Island and North Island in the coming days. It's easy to forget that New Zealand is the largest Polynesian land mass, and Auckland the largest Polynesian city in the world. Of course, the white settlers, still referred to as *'Pakeha'*, came with their cuisines of bread, meat and sugar, along with their own cooking techniques. All of that has now been integrated into indigenous cuisine. A word about New Zealand cuisine – that there are no words. An innocent looking question such as "What is New Zealand cuisine?" is likely to stump the average resident. Fascinatingly, the cuisine is not influenced from any one part of the world, but a mix of several world cuisines, and is mainly local and seasonal in nature. Necessity of getting familiar with local (Maori) words is an absolute must to understand most of the local eatables. Not only food, since the 1980s the country has been recognized as the source of some of the finest Sauvignon Blancs in the world. More recently, the award-winning Pinot Gris and rich, full Syrah have been sweeping wine-drinkers off their feet all across the globe.

## Other North Island Delights

North Island is all about food, wine and culture – all mixed up nicely to give you a splendid family holiday destination. So, while you can leave the 'adventure rush' to its Southern sibling, this part of New Zealand is about being culture vulture and exploring the never-ending countryside. There are farmlands in abundance and cattle & sheep clearly has the overwhelming strength over human population. All around North Island, it's hard to ignore the Maori influence in New Zealand, especially if you head out of the cities into the interiors of the country. You see this influence evident in the names of places, in the flashy facial tattoos, the intricate wood-carvings, and the bright-eyed smiling faces of one-seventh of the population. From a culture that was once repressed into near oblivion to one that is thriving, the Maori way has become the country's backbone. There are some cultural experiences around the world that are too touristy in the fact that they are just done for the tourists and to make money. But what I loved about the Maori experience is that it is more about sharing - sharing a culture, knowing that they had something of value to offer the world.

So while Rotorua is always steaming with excitement, because of the geothermal attractions, you have the Waitomo region to delve underground and admire the twinkling glow-worm caves. This part of NZ also has one of the 'windiest' cities of the world in Wellington, but go towards eastern side and you experience the stunning scenery in Hawke's Bay. The northernmost region has breathtakingly beautiful Cape Reinga and Bay of Islands which is a world class region for sailing and a collection of over 140 islands with a coastline sporting four villages. But with limited number of days and our focus mainly on the South Island road trip this time, we chose to cover the picturesque Coromandel Peninsula. This is a great route for a half-day drive, or a full day if you include some sightseeing along the way, and that's what we decided to do as we rented out a nice automatic sedan to hit State Highway 25. Only a few hours' drive from Auckland, the stunning Coromandel Peninsula is a wonderful road trip destination in New Zealand. With a mountainous spine running down the middle of the peninsula, a magnificent coast fringed with golden sand beaches, picturesque fishing villages and mining town, there's a lot to experience. And not only it's rich with a gorgeous nature, this region is off the beaten path - which means if you go during weekdays, you might find yourself alone on the road, with the most scenic views for yourself. The Coromandel is one of these places where you just want to drive, drive, drive and never stop. Of course, it all starts from the charming little town of Thames, where time seems to have stopped centuries ago. The town had its golden age during the great gold rush. Today, it's a quiet historic town lined with vintage boutiques. But instead of heading North on the conventional clockwise route, we decided to do this anti-clockwise and headed East on the Kopu-Hikuai Road.

We soon hit the east coast of Coromandel at the picturesque holiday town of Tairua which lies at the mouth of Tairua River and we could view the landmark twin peaks of Mount Paku guarding the harbour entrance. This small hamlet offers a superb setting beside the Pacific Ocean for exploring. As the Tairua – Whitianga road slowly started climbing up north, the scenery changed beautifully. We left the highway to take the Hot Water Beach road (You read the term correctly – they have a 'Hot Water' beach) to reach this thermal wonderland that no self-respecting tourist would miss out on. Hot Water Beach is named for its spring of thermal water at a low tide point in the middle of the beach. Careful pre-research on the internet gave us the correct timing to be there to witness this unbelievable phenomenon. Dig at the right spot on the right tide and you can create your own hot water pool, shaped to your liking. It's a great place to meet people from all over the world as they lie next to you in the pools of hot water – until the tide pushes in and hilariously sends everyone shrieking. But the craziness out there on the beach with hoards & hordes of tourists & locals flocking the space, led us away from it, and we diverted our car towards Hahei road. We were now headed to the biggest crowd-puller of this part called the Cathedral Cove, which is part of Te Whanganui-A-Hei Marine Reserve. This magic location is worldwide famous as the settings for the scene in which the Pevensie kids took their first steps back into Narnia...And it is a real wonderland indeed!!!

You can access the remote beach of Cathedral Cove by foot or by boat only, which limits the amount of people who visits the place at one time. Even though I'm not a big fan of touristy stuff, this time I chose to go for this locale, and that too by foot – with Arianna hopping on a piggy-back ride on me. The 45 min trek is tough & tricky at the same time, getting steep at times, but the views of stunning deserted beaches and gorgeous rock formations (Smiling Sphinx Rock & Sting Ray Beach are few of them) were worth every drop of sweat during the trek. We were in for a visual bonanza as we arrived at this heavenly beach. There was a gigantic arched cavern which was passing through a white rock headland to join two secluded coves. This cathedral-like arch gives the whole area an air of grandeur and of course, its name. The beach is sandy with shady Pohutukawa trees along the foreshore - a perfect place for a picnic and a swim. We selected a shaded area to rest our bums (I really needed it after carrying Arianna through the trek) and opened our little picnic bag with munchies & 'secret' water bottle). As Arianna got busy in playing in the amazingly transparent & turquoise blue water and making sand structures, we could see this large pinnacle of pumice breccia rock known as 'Te Hoho' right in front sitting off the beach. Over centuries this has been sculpted by wind and water - it now looks like the prow of a large ship steaming into the beach. It was a time well spent but the uphill trek now was the improbable task.

We moved out from Hahei Car Park with beautiful memories of the magical Cathedral Cove and also with empty hungry tummies. We did have the option of stopping over at the 'country-pub' Pour House in Hahei, but we decided to drive a bit more up north to coastal town of Whitianga for some fresh seafood. A little reference of Lonely Planet helped us in selecting the best option (both location & food wise) in Whitianga, and as we arrived at Stoked Restaurant, we exactly knew why it was recommended by LP. The philosophy at Stoked is simple – take some good old-fashioned hospitality, blend it with an outstanding food experience and add a stunning view to deliver an experience that delights all the senses. We soaked in this complete package offered by Stoked as we tasted some heavenly smoky flavoured dishes from their charcoal oven. Chargrilled Salmon is their signatory dish & a must-try, it's just exquisite and melts in your mouth, combine it with their freshly-brewed craft ale from the tap. After this sumptuous meal, we continued our road trip towards Coromandel town, but instead of taking the main highway we decided to rough it out on Road 309. It's a 22 kms narrow road going from East to West lined with gorgeous gems to discover, such as a great pine forest, beautiful streams and waterfalls, a lovely local honey shop (with delicious New Zealand Manuka honey), an impressive Kauri grove and an exquisite private garden. It will take you on a journey through dense nature with spectacular views. In Coromandel Town, we stopped off for a coffee and a bagel. This quaint little town will make you feel like in the Old West. Like most villages in the peninsula, its history is rooted in the gold that used to be mined outside of town. Nowadays, many artists and crafts people live in Coromandel Town. They have opened many creative shops and restaurants, creating a picturesque character to the place.

Not wasting too much time in the town, we excitingly hit what was the most beautiful part of the entire drive on the west coast of Coromandel Peninsula, also known as The Pohutukawa Coast (named on tree line enroute). The road hugs the coastline to the right with drops down to the rocky volcanic beach and views across the Firth of Thames. On the left were forest-covered hills. Pohutakawa trees line the route and hang across the road, looking stunning as they were in bloom at this time of season. It was a difficult stretch to drive on, not due to the fact that the coastal road becomes narrow at lot of places, but mainly because it was extremely difficult for me to concentrate on the road – with the kind of picturesque views all through the route, and even Arianna was enjoying from her car seat nicely raised to give her good view outside. The twisted roads in between were giving way to small fishing villages & their beach cafes, which gives the option of a roadside stopover for coffee or rolled ice cream (Beach café at Waiomu & Wharf Coffee House at Thames are noteworthy). Of course, there's the other option (which we took) of stopping over for own picnic bag & chilled beer at one of umpteen view-points. We arrived at Thames, a former gold mining boom town, late in the evening. Fortunately, the days are longer in NZ and we could drive through this 'crafty' town which is proud of its heritage and its connection to the natural environment. This lovely road trip culminated our North Island exploring and we were now looking forward to the South Island escapade.

> ### *Tip*
>
> *Renting and driving a car for Indian citizens is the best means of transport. Indian driving license is valid in New Zealand and right-hand drive on excellent roads makes it that much easier. Coromandel ideally should be covered in two days with a night halt, but a day trip is equally delightful if there's shortage of time.*

## South Island Road Trip

New Zealand's south island has so much to offer, see and do, that it's quite difficult to decide where to go, where to stay and where to spend longer time than the other place. Our trip was for about one week and we decided to skip the southernmost & northernmost parts of the island and to do a tour starting from Christchurch through the inland, all the way to the west coast, then up north till Nelson. This way we would see quite a lot of the island's diverse landscapes and have enough time to fully experience its stunning beauty. This part of the country was exciting for its promise of great outdoors, and offered us one treat after another. I have a nerdy list of things I'd like to do in this lifetime, and I was ticking off items almost at the rate of one a day.

We arrived at the fast-changing and funky Christchurch by air, which is South Island's largest city. Old English gardens contrast with pop-up bars and container-based shopping malls in this ever-changing city, which is rebuilding itself after a damaging earthquake in February 2011. Straight from the airport we headed to pick up our rented self-driven vehicle and also loaded it up with requisite travel info, road maps and stock of food & drinks for the way from New World. We zipped out of Christchurch in the comfortable Honda SUV, the radio playing old school rock much to our liking, and headed straight for the famed heritage area of Mt Cook National Park with its twin-wonders in form of Lake Pukaki & Lake Tekapo. The Southern Alps are the backbone of South Island, however we decided to remain on the foot hills of this spine hitting the picturesque Highway-8. As we drove past the Alpine Ski town of Fairlie, the gentle green carpet-like slopes were clearly visible on the right which transforms into a skiing paradise in winters, and our uninterrupted journey was suddenly halted by the almost impossibly turquoise jewel of Mackenzie Country, called Lake Tekapo. After a quick photo-stop right on the highway, we took a slight detour towards the lake to find two hidden photo opportunities in The Church of Good Shepherd and the sheepdog statue, both standing bang on the lake side.

This is where I tried my first hand on driving in southern New Zealand, as I took over the wheels of the smooth, but robust, Honda SUV. Very soon another picturesque delight was awaiting us in form of Lake Pukaki. Not only was it as strikingly blue in colour, Lake Pukaki one-upped Tekapo with its magnificent background of the mighty Mount Cook and surrounding snow-capped peaks. The opaque turquoise colour of this lake and others in the area is caused by fine, glacier-ground rock particles held in suspension. As we drove ahead, we passed first of many powder-blue hydropower canals running through the landscape which was a mixture of high country tussock, farmland and snow-capped mountains. Further, the broad braided river channels are a spectacular sight, back dropped by the Ben Ohau Range which remained in view all along the road post Lake Pukaki through Twizel, all the way to Omarama, where we were welcomed by the giant merino sheep statue. This area's unique geography has made it a magnet for gliding enthusiasts, but we kept our feet on the ground and continued our journey further south. The stretch going over Lindis Pass offered us breath-taking views of mountains on both sides. We skipped the turn towards Lake Wanaka and continued on the route via Cornwell to get our first glimpses of Lake Wakatipu & Queenstown.

## Twin Lake Towns of Queenstown & Wanaka

Sitting on the shore of Lake Wakatipu, Queenstown is post card pretty and comes with a tag of 'Adventure Capital of the World'. Jet-boating, rafting, body surfing hold sway under a skyline forever dotted with para gliders, and that near-death experience of the bungee jump is always just a bridge away. On top of all that, throw in some flying foxes and giant swings over death-defining valleys & gorges, along with life-changing experience of skydiving, and you got the perfect place to have rightfully earned the title of adventure hub of the world. As we drove through the city, we realized how beautiful this city is - located beside Lake Wakatipu and just in front of the incredible Remarkables, with a cosy city centre and lot of shops, cafés, bars and restaurants. We straight away drove to what was going to be our first Youth Hostel stays out of many – YHA Queenstown Lakefront. And it did live up to its name of being situated bang on Lake Wakatipu with our exclusive 'suite' room on the upper floor having splendid views of the lake & mountains. It was late evening by the time we checked in and we moved out immediately to explore the city centre which was just 5 mins walk along the lake. Being a weekend, the city was buzzing with tourists and activities on the streets including musicians, bagpipers, and all other sorts of street artists. Arianna was having time of her life savouring the delicious Move n Pick ice cream cone and enjoying the live performances on the street.

We retired after a long day of drive with a strange kind of enthusiasm of looking forward to an exciting day of activities the next morning. As we chatted with the Youth Hostel people, we found out to our delight that Queenstown has always something going on, so you never have to think about how to stay entertained. There's a daily roster of activities to choose from, and plenty to do independently too, and the options appeal to all kinds of age group. You'll find all operators of activities and adventurous stuff in the city centre, and most of them are located on Shotover Street. We stuck to taking things in our own hands with some assistance & guidance from YHA, of course (That's the best part of staying in a Youth Hostel – you get the best of information about all that's happening in the city). But as soon as we moved out, we found ourselves slipping into full-blown tourist mode (a mode that is almost impossible to avoid in the most touristic town in New Zealand). Our first stop was a trip up the gondola to the Skyline Queenstown. We were in the adrenaline mecca of the country, so of course I couldn't leave without doing something to get my blood pumping. We started by taking on the "Luge" challenge, which even little Arianna loved doing with me – so much so – that she went on a repeat ride with my BIL. And for changes, this time we could convince my sister also to do something 'adventurous', as she whizzed down the twists & turns at great speed. The 'open' chairlift ride up the hill to reach the luge starting point, in itself is quite dramatic (and scary !!!).

---

### Tip

*The stretch between Christchurch and Queenstown is extremely picturesque and can be broken into two days, if time is at hand. This region is also ski-hub of New Zealand during the winters.*

---

Standing atop Bob's Peak, getting unbelievably spectacular views of Queenstown & Lake Wakatipu and watching Arianna going Ga-Ga over the para gliders, I soon realized that there is no other city that offers such great views no matter where you stand. There's so much to do here that it definitely makes Queenstown one of the best cities for me. Here you can do things you've always dreamt about, the 'Zindagi Na Milegi Dobara' kinds, and then brag about it – of course, leaving out the bit where you may scream like a little kid.

While in Queenstown, you must give your lungs some exercise on one of many platforms set by AJ Hackett. And that's exactly where we headed next – where it all started some 30 years back when the very first commercial bungee jump originated at Kawarau Bungee Jump in 1986. I wanted my first experience of Bungee Jump to be something special and I was doing it what they call as *'Mecca of Bungy'*. As I ran up and swan-dived 43 meters off the Kawarau Gorge Suspension Bridge, not only did I get the adrenaline rush of a lifetime, I also got to enjoy the most picture-perfect views over the gorge and touched the bluish-green waters of the river on my way down. It was an experience I can clearly define as 'Once in Lifetime' kinds, and I was glad that I could further instigate both my BIL (who dared the Bungee jump) and Deenaz (who took the Zip-Line with me) also to indulge in little adventure. Of course, Arianna & Reshma were happy & content with their Luge experience only.

Once our tourist activities were complete, we started exploring a little out of Queenstown, and drove out of Queenstown to the access road up to the Remarkables. Here, you can find the ultimate picnic spots with literal 360 degree views over Queenstown and its surroundings. Dramatic mountain ranges and rolling hills on one side, snaking aqua rivers and glistening lakes on the other- this place is quite something. Another hidden gem slightly north-west is the charming historic town of Arrowtown - a town of some 2500 people with a pretty quay along the stream running through the town, a central market area & main street straight out of 1950s Western classic and no fewer than six 'self-professed' monuments to the town's credit. Once a gold-rush settlement, today it's a perfectly preserved piece of the past. We took the slightly longer, but potentially more scenic route, which took us over the historic Shotover Bridge and through Arthur's Point. After the excitement of Queenstown, Arrowtown was beautifully quaint and calm. On our way back we found a lovely spot overlooking the lower limb of Lake Wakatipu at this (in)famous location called "Devil's Staircase". We sat here for some time, drinking wine, feasting on cheese and crackers and soaking in the beauty of the sun setting beneath the horizon. Queenstown is also known for its Fergburger – a delicacy called lovingly as Ferg's, it's an iconic joint now in all of New Zealand for its heavenly burgers. Each of their 20 variants is amazing and super delicious, and they all come with a super yummy aioli and tomato relish. We reached Fergburger to find expectantly a long queue in from of the small restaurant which is the case during peak hours, and most of the 21-hour business time for Fergburger is peak time. But even if you have to wait, it is more than worth it and a visit to Queenstown is no actual visit if you haven't been to Fergburger !!!

A day in South Island has to be dedicated to visit the Fiordland, which is dotted with many scenic lakes with finger-like fiords that lead out to the many 'sounds' of this uniquely fissured coastline. The geology of it all is a little complex explanation involving the Ice Age, tectonic plate shifts and some lost continent. My knowledge to all this restricts to some fading memory of our Geology professor Mr Bhutani in CME and the series of Ice Age flicks. Even the sound of *'sounds'* was little confusing, but that's what they call it here. Tramping and Kayaking are the ideal ways to explore the sounds, while cruises are more family-friendly, and with a three year old kiddo involved, we predictably opted for a cruise to Milford Sound. I can easily rate the 120 km drive towards Milford Sound as South Island's most scenic. Mirror lakes, vast grasslands, grand mountains, quaint creeks, rivers and lush green valleys eat up the miles in quick succession while the steep mountainous roads and tunnels speak volumes for Kiwi engineering. Milford itself is brooding and wild, with Mitre peak looming large over the misty sound. Mists hung mysteriously around the mountains while we were at the mouth of the fiord and disappeared as bafflingly when we entered the sound. The cruise through the sound was surrounded by a mesmerizing rainforest – moss covered rocks, studded with tall tree ferns so dense you would need a machete to walk through it. The cruise liner was a sort of Santa Monica kind of vessel which you find in Goa and the biggest annoyance is the noisy engines which never really let you appreciate the famed silence, but the noise do tend to fade away gradually under the influence of mesmerizing surroundings of towering rocky mountains, thundering waterfalls almost looking as if milk is being poured by the heavens on the steep rock faces and sparkling waters underneath your vessel. The jaw-dropping scene looks straight out of one of the many Hollywood blockbusters, and you could almost believe to catch a glimpse of King Kong peeking out of his skull-cave from one of the mountains.

We opted for the top deck with winds almost sweeping you from your feet, but the views were just not to be missed. Saturated with natural beauty, we made our way to the cruise-café as the fresh air had whipped up colossal appetites in us. As we dug in fresh & juicy fish & chips, we could actually feel the freshness of the crayfish melting in our mouths. We made our way up to the deck again after our scrumptious meal, and we were up for a delightful surprise as we saw a bunch of fur seals frolicking on a nearby rock nicely sun-bathing in the serene blue environ of the fiord meeting the sea at the end. The sound is reportedly so deep that a Star Cruise luxury liner could sail all the way in, and the waters are so still that even Captain Cook was afraid of entering for fear of being becalmed. The weather in this part of the world is one of the wettest, but fortunately during our cruise, it shifted from being cloudy and sunny too in between. The fog and dark clouds seemed to set the atmosphere, making it feel like something akin to Jurassic Park, and with sun out, we could sit outside on the cruise and fully embrace the beauty of the place. It was quite late in the evening by the time we reached back our Youth Hostel in Queenstown, and did some cooking of our own which is one of the highlights I look forward to while staying in YH.

> ## Tip
>
> *Queenstown has so much to offer that sometimes it's hard to decide what has to be done in this Adventure Capital of the world. Look for some fantastic deals on Groupon or similar coupon websites for good deals. Youth Hostels also have discounts for residents. A fiord cruise in one of the 'Sounds' is a must and couple of adventure activities can be experienced (though expensive).*

We started the next day towards the second of the lake towns on our itinerary – Wanaka. We decided to take the lesser known of the two routes from Queenstown, this road over the range, known as Crown Range Road, is the highest main road in New Zealand. The road zigzags up to the Crown Terrace and from there you can look down to Arrowtown in the Arrow Valley, and across to the Remarkables Range. This particular drive was more exciting because of the tight bends and curves that came along. Also, the views were a lot greener than what we saw while going over Lindis Pass. We arrived in Wanaka by the afternoon and straight away fell in love with the place. We had again booked the Purple Cow Youth Hostel here and stayed for two nights there. This hostel is one of the best stay options here in Wanaka, having a mini-auditorium, activity area and a lovely sit-out for the evenings. The town has a small yet very vibrant and cosy centre and is beautifully located just at Lake Wanaka, offering amazing views on the lake and the surrounding mountains. Situated on the foot hills of Mount Aspiring National Park, the long-stretched out Lake Wanaka is locally known as the prettiest of New Zealand many lakes, and our lake view Youth Hostel was perfect for a few days of exploring in this quaint little lake town. Taking a stroll on the beautiful lake front all the way to 'That Wanaka Tree' (No idea why they call it by this term) was obviously first on our priority list, for some amazing photos of the Lake and neighbouring Southern Alps. The crispy fish & chips at Erik's along with its unique deep fried kiwi fruit is a must try whenever you are in this part of world. While walking back to the hostel, we noticed Patagonia Chocolates store which is a famous dessert store and we had to try this as well, finding several novelties for Arianna's likings.

New Zealand is also famous for its local wines with large parts of land – both in North and South Island, dedicated to wineries, and almost every meal is paired with local wine. Of course, I didn't want to be left behind in this tradition – after all being known to follow the concept of 'Do as Locals Do' in all my travel trips. So, the supermarkets of NZ such as New World became my hunting grounds for all deals and to pick up local wines. Most of these wines don't carry labels easily recognized in the wider world, or even easily available. To my absolute delight, the nearby Countdown store in Wanaka had fantastic deals on huge array of local NZ wines (few as low as 5 NZD) and I picked up few to go with the yummy platter being cooked in YH kitchen by Reshma & Deenaz, and we had the perfect dinner setting out at the patio under beautiful starlit night. We were up early next morning and wanting to make the most of the bright day, headed out for some kayaking on the sparkling blue waters of Wanaka Lake. We took two 'Double Kayaks' and I could even convince an otherwise baffled looking kayak rental guy, to take little Arianna, for what was her very first kayaking experience of her life. I agree that it was not a very safe thing to do – out in the middle of this massive lake on our own, and with two 'non-swimmers' – I had a challenge at hand, but the risk was worth it as all five of us had super fun exploring the lovely Lake Wanaka with some spectacular views of the mountains all around. The rest of the afternoon was spent picnicking on the shores of lake with snacks, fresh ice cream and chilled beer. The occasional swim in the water was the only activity apart from absorbing tantalizing views of Lake Wanaka framed as some kind of picture calendar. Arianna was alternating between going in the water with me to play with 'friendly' ducks and feeding the 'over-friendly' seagulls that were literally eating out of our hands. Later we went for a drive around the town and even checked out the quirkiness of Puzzling World and its 'Leaning Tower' which was almost falling over our heads.

---

**Tip**

*The Youth Hostels of both Queenstown and Wanaka are the best stay options in my opinion, offering excellent locations and amazing views, with very friendly staff and chance to interact with people from all across the world.*

---

## Wild West Coast of South Island

Next morning we left for what's known as Wild West of South Island, and within a few minutes of leaving Wanaka, we were driving on a hilly winding road along Lake Hawea, which was a stunning drive. There were mountains on one side, a distinct blue colour of Hawea, and green patches of grass on the other side, the road being a notch higher than the lake resulting in beautiful views. In between were small plots of land, with sheep and deer on them. They looked curiously at us as we took pictures. We managed to stop at a couple of lookout points and got some stunning images of the scenery. The scenery started to change slowly as we drove into lush green forest of the Makarora Valley. Somewhere along the way, we come across a farm on which about 40 deer were running together in a pack, it was such an incredible sight. Approximately one hour after Wanaka we found the sign to our first stopover - Blue Pools. As the name suggests, these are amazingly blue-coloured pools and you should definitely stop here. There is a clearly marked pathway that leads to a swing bridge (about 20 mins walk) where the actual pool is. Both me & Deenaz were wearing t-shirt & shorts that day, and people coming back from the track were giving us weird looks, almost as if they were hinting something at us. Later, we understood why this was the case. The Blue Pools and Haast pass area in general is filled with "Sandflies". They will just swarm all over and bite, so you need to cover whatever skin you can or apply insect repellent before you go to this place.

But the sandflies were soon forgotten as soon as we arrived at the swing bridge over the Blue Pools, the colour of the water was just unbelievable. It was a greenish-blue colour, which we had not seen anywhere else on South Island trip. For us, New Zealand was becoming a colour fest, it was all about the wonderful different shades of blue at various locations, be it Tekapo, Pukaki, Te Anau, Wanaka, Hawea or Blue Pools now. The reason for these unique colours is the different mineral contents in the glacial salts present in the water. We took a few pictures while dodging the sandflies. As a tradition, visitors at the Blue Pools often make piles of stones, apparently as a mark of their visit. So, we spent some time by the river flowing by the side, gorging on fresh cherries and making stone piles. We drove ahead to climb further into Mount Aspirin National Park after going through the narrow saddle corridor between Lakes Wanaka and Hawea on towards Haast Pass, and the rolling pastures gave way to towering rocky mountains of Southern Alps and the road began an anticipatory corkscrew. Suddenly we were winding along a coastal road tunnelling through cliffs, with the pale aquamarine waters of Pacific on one side and mighty wall of Southern Alps on the other, giving the image of mountains leaping straight out of shore at places – an unforgettable sight. The west coast really is one of the most astonishingly beautiful landscapes in the country, but its biggest attraction lies hidden in the waters of the ocean – an undersea world of creatures and structures. We stopped for a well-deserved coffee break, as also to witness the awesome sight of the angry Southern Ocean crashing against the shore.

Taking on this scenic route over New Zealand's highest motorable road, we headed further up north along the coast to the Westland National Park where the Franz Joseph and Fox Glaciers is a big draw. We followed the historic treks of these glaciers through the tough trail of broken pebbled path amongst dense forested areas and innumerable streams. With the limited time at our hand, we had to choose one of the two glacier-treks (which are pretty similar in nature), and I was glad that we decided on to Franz Joseph over Fox Glacier. This was about an hour & a half return trek and Arianna was once again having fun riding her favourite 'Horsie' on piggy-back throughout the trek. She did try her hand a little at rock-climbing as well, apart from playing her favourite game of throwing pebbles in the stream. The moderately difficult trail was worth the effort due to spectacular views of the glacier and a very different kind of landscape here. The road further is an amazing feat of engineering and sheer hard labour, it twists & turns, revealing spectacular new vistas at each bend, as it passes through charming little towns such as Ross and Hokitika before arriving at coastal town of Greymouth. The famous scenic Highway-73 route over Arthur's Pass also bifurcates from Kumara just short of Greymouth. You need to take a night halt either in Hokitika or Greymouth and we had selected the latter. We checked in for the night at this elevated villa, converted into a charming timbery boutique Bed & Breakfast which was an old-school kind of homestay with the complete house of fully-furnished living room & kitchen on one floor and three lovely bedrooms tastefully decorated on the other floor, all this with a private wooden patio overlooking the picturesque coastal town of

Greymouth (Not to forget mentioning that we got it at a 'steal-deal' on AirBnB). We had just the adequate time to go for a short walk along what they call as 'Great Wall of Greymouth' – a flood wall along Grey river (That's how the town got its name...Duh !!!) which has number of memorials, sculptures and similar history attached to it. Visit to this historic town couldn't be complete without a peek into Monteith's Brewery - New Zealand's most iconic craft brewery for its strong tasting, full-bodied ales, rich and silky stouts, and continual innovation with all the classic brews. The freshly brewed craft beer didn't disappoint at all, they even dish out delicious eats from their kitchen – smoked salmon spread & coast fried chicken were perfectly cooked and Brewer's Baby Back Ribs were melting in mouth. Whichever beer or cider we couldn't lay our hands on sitting there, we carried it along in their 'Taster Trays'.

We carried on past Cobden Bridge over Grey River the next morning along a stretch of the road known as Paparoa National Park, famous for its dramatic rock formations rising from the ocean, sculpted by the erosive force of waves and wind. As we arrived in Punakaiki town, famous for its Pancake Rocks, which are quite funny looking stone formations known to be almost 30 million year old. Accessible from Dolomite Point via a well-maintained walkway that loops from the main road, the area is home to giant cliffs and boulders amongst a turbulent and roiling coastline that is highly active – particularly at high tide. The most prominent features are the Pancake Rocks, which are exactly what their name suggests; large stacks of limestone formed gradually by the wind and water over the years resembling a stack of pancakes. Further along, the walk is made all the more dramatic by its blowholes of salt water from the Tasman Sea that surges up a narrow channel then spouts high into the air, spraying their voluminous contents dozens of metres above sea level. But this phenomenon is a bit over-rated, notwithstanding, I found the walk spectacular in its own right and a photographer's paradise. You can also go for a short walk on the Truman Track which passes another amazing stone formation looking like a huge wave breaking just in front of you. The Highway-6 follows the amazing coastline for some distance beyond Punakaki before turning east at Charleston and enters the 'Gorge Region'. We headed east, through the narrow Buller gorge with wind-crafted mountain ranges on both sides. It's impossible to dash across this scenic country, and our frequent stops to soak in the scenery were sure enough to stretch this four hour drive. But no worries, because the delay was all worth it, as we glanced across New Zealand's longest swing bridge, crossing the beautiful Buller River.

At the Kawatiri junction we turned left to head north and immediately spun into a landscape of gently sloping hills and rolling pastures, as the other road was heading eastwards towards the east coast town of Blenheim in what's known as Marlborough region. In sharp contrast to the wild, rugged beauty of the Ocean road, this is gentle pastoral country with low rolling hills, herds of woolly sheep, grazing cows, and impeccably manicured vineyards. After speeding through this picture-book countryside for a while, we pulled over to get out and savour the surreal surroundings of grassy slopes on either side of highway undulating into infinity. There was no traffic and no other soul in sight, but we were not alone. Across the grasslands stretched more sheep than you could ever hope to count. Not a flock, not a herd, more like a galaxy... And it struck me as the actual equivalent of the 'Milky Way' - pun intended !!! We arrived at the city of Nelson which is home to a fascinating community of beach, bush and art lovers. It is also famous for its wineries which we could see in plenty on our way approaching the city in suburbs of Hope & Richmond. Our accommodation in Nelson was memorable not because of the standard of quality or level of customer service, but instead for the well-maintained B & B and tudor cottage design. Our two-bedroom, self-contained cottage was extraordinarily decorative, and the host lady had taken efforts to make it as comfortable as possible. Arianna was delighted to find company of their two very friendly house-cats, for whom we had instructions to take care as well.

> ## *Tip*
>
> *The West Coast drive of South Island offers breath-taking views and has few stop-overs offering unique experiences. A trip on a boat to explore marine life can also be undertaken, but requires a night stay in one of the many coastal towns.*

In the next day & a half in Nelson, which is one of the oldest cities in New Zealand and the gateway to stunning Abel Tasman National Park, Golden Bay and the Marlborough region, we tried to make the most of the limited time. The good part was that most of the tourist attractions such as Christ Church, Montgomery Square and Queens Garden are all within walking distance from the city centre of Trafalgar Street. Christ Church Cathedral contains impressive stained glass windows which date back to the late nineteen hundreds when the original church of the diocese was redesigned and rebuilt. We found both the interiors and exteriors of this majestic church equally stunning and the view from back of the church looks out to buzzing Nelson city centre. We also explored the Branford Reserve and its dense forested area within the city, also home to Centre of New Zealand – an elevated spot used for central survey in the 1800s. The hike up to the top is bit steep but the stunning views over Nelson & beyond, makes the walk well worth it. We picked up some Thai food from one of many choices of eateries here in Nelson and headed back to our beautiful cottage BnB, but not before we made a small stopover at PIC's Peanut Butter Factory where you could see the peanut butter making process from start to end, as also taste their divine peanut butter ice cream.

Next early morning was our last day of the South Island trip and I was up before the rest and realized that it was a Wednesday, the day for Nelson's famous Farmer's Market at Maitai Boulevard. So I checked up from my sister if she's interested in accompanying which she readily agreed. Enroute on the beach road, we crossed the Nelson postcard photo of Boat Shed Café, which is cantilevered out over the water and is home to fresh seafood. We kept it pending for another day and arrived where the buzz was by the lovely timber bridge over Maitai River in Rutherford Park. The Wednesday Nelson Farmers market is based on supporting local, fresh and seasonal produce and products 'Made by Locals for Locals' (and everyone else!). They had eggs, oils, sweet treats, jams & sauces, breads & other bakery products, fruits & veggies of all kinds, but obviously, I went for the 'meat'. The Bacon Station was dishing out fresh crispy bacon buns and I couldn't resist that. The rest of the day was rightfully spent at Tahununi Beach which is the main beach, right in the centre of Nelson. It's a lovely beach with lots of activities especially for the kids, and Arianna found all the right kind of entertainment including few 'furry' friends of hers, while we sat on the seaside with light bites from the beach café and zesty Marlborough Sauvignon Blanc. Suddenly, I had a crisis of faith within myself, I thought of home and life in real world – why couldn't it all be a paradise of hills and sea and wine and fish ???

---

**Tip**

*A self-driven road trip is the most ideal way of exploring South Island of New Zealand, giving you plenty of flexibility to do things as per convenience. The option of picking up the car from one city and dropping in another is very much there at no extra cost. Charming options of Bed & Breakfast are available all over South island.*

---

## The End State

There's a reason why islands do so well, as wholesome getaways, though I am not quite sure which of the charms come out tops. Is it the relaxation that settles over you as you give in to the island's rhythms, or is it the sheer beauty of the setting, which refuses to let anything spoil your party? Or perhaps it's that feeling of having found your space under the sun, a spot isolated from the rest of the world to call your own. There truly is something about being surrounded by the blue pristine sheet of water and being with people close to your heart. Bungee jumping, jet boating, fjord sailing, hobbit visiting – now these are the prime reasons tourists go down under, but when we discovered that food & wine can also be one of the many reasons, it was a pleasant surprise. New Zealand's culinary delights are full of good eats & drinks, that you'll be glad to go on one of its many walking & cycling trails to burn some of it off. And when you've walked through every orchard and vineyard there is, it will throw up more for you to do.

New Zealand for me was something of a rightful mix of an amazingly beautiful foreign locale along with a 'homely' feeling. Maybe the main reason behind this is the fact that there is nobody you can call 'New Zealanders' in true sense. While there are the original Islanders from the ancient Maori tribe, but they cannot be called as conventional 'locals', the way you have British, French,

Italian, Americans or even Africans. This is the most soothing thing about this lovely country, it's filled with immigrants (Chinese & Indians being quite a majority), and that's what gives it a global & cosmopolitan feel where you won't get the 'foreigner' treatment. Apart from this, it's a holiday destination anybody & everybody would fall in love with – it's got so much of variety to offer, and activities in plenty that won't leave time to even catch a breath. The picturesque island-country is like a roller coaster ride, never a dull moment and a complete family package. So, come fall in love with one of the best countries I have visited till now.

# **Refer Page - 173 for Photographs of Travelogue - 13**

# Conclusion

*"Travelling – it leaves you speechless, then turns you into a storyteller"*

Ibn Battuta has rightly stated the above statement about travelling. Well, that's exactly what happens to me during and after each of my travel escapades – I am generally speechless during the entire trip (much to the discomfort of my fellow travellers), and then suddenly I get these images and statements and stories about my travel, which I try to convert to words in each of my Travelogue. I travel not to go anywhere, but to just go. I travel for the sake of travelling. The great thing is to keep moving...and going...somewhere.

So, the story of this travel bug of mine began way back as I travelled as a very young child with my father during his umpteen tours in Rajasthan, followed it with more of family travel trips with parents, sister & later with bro-in-law (The way we still do it – Refer Travelogue – 6 on Canada). I guess that's where the 'Travel Bug' was planted into me, which came alive again when I joined the Forces (Refer Travelogue – 1 on the Mountaineering Expedition as the first of the experiences in Forces). The bug kept on increasing as I discovered a new me during my Solo Travels, it opened my mind so much by seeing and living in a new culture, I got addicted to that feeling. Then came the golden period of this entire journey – travelling with friends, fellow-minded equally-crazy travel companions who re-defined the concept of travelling into these once in a lifetime Backpacking trips on Shoestring budgets (Refer Travelogue - 3 on Europe Backpacking Trip). Finally, I was united with my bestest Travel Buddy – my wife, one who taught me that travel is not only fun, crazy and maddening but it's also to learn, to love, to spend the best of times, because the more you travel the more you learn to adapt and understand to just go with the flow. It took me a little while to mould her into my way of travelling (Refer Travelogue - 4 on South East Asia), but then we both started enjoying this 'Do-it-Yourself' budget travelling.

Finally, our newest 'Travel Companion' joined us in our continued quest of more travel and accepted this family tradition of mine with open arms. My young daughter who broke all family records of already having visited more than ten countries in her first three years, overcame all our apprehensions of being a totally hassle-free travel companion, even with my style of travelling (Refer Travelogues – 10 & 12 on Backpacking with a Baby in Europe & Himachal). She also started loving this concept of being Travellers, and not Tourists. This brings me to the classical debate between being a traveller or a tourist. I read couple of very relevant lines to settle this debate - tourists don't know where they have been...and travellers don't know where they are going. The traveller sees what he sees, while the tourist sees what he has come to see. So, please be a traveller, not a tourist. Try new things, meet new people, and look beyond what's right in front of you. Those are the keys to understanding this amazing world we live in. I will leave you with few beautiful lines by Claire Fontaine that has quite a deep meaning. I hope you enjoyed reading my travelogues as much as I enjoyed penning them down for you all.

*"Travel empties out everything you've*

*into the box called Life,*

*All the things you accumulate*

*to tell you who you are"*

# Travelogue – 1

## Kedardome - A Thrilling Experience

# Travelogue – 2
## Kinnaur – God's Own Land

# Travelogue – 3

## Bachelor Backpacking Europe Trip on Shoe-String Budget

# Travelogue – 4

## South-East Asia : Indian Traveller's Backyard

# Travelogue – 5
## Ladakh – Heaven on Earth

# Travelogue – 6

## Canada : A Complete Vacation Destination

159

# Travelogue – 7

## The N-W Road Trip : From 'Vada-Pav' to 'Sarson Da Saag'

# Travelogue – 8

## A Backpacking UK Trip : Summer in British Style

# Travelogue – 9

## Bhutan : Land of "Happy" Thunder Dragon

# Travelogue – 10

## Backpacking with a Baby in Europe & Scandinavia

# Travelogue – 11
## North Thailand Ride : A Superbiker's Dream

## Travelogue – 12
## Trekking & Camping Sojourn in Parvati Valley

# Travelogue – 13

## New Zealand : The Southern Heaven

*"In the end, I would like to state that the credit behind this Travel Book goes completely to my Parents who have been the reason for this 'Passion for Travel' being imbibed in me.*

*My Father & Mother have been my inspiration in Living Life to the Fullest, and I hope their spirit of travelling remains alive for many more years.*

*This book is a humble attempt from me to pass on the 'Travel Bug' I received from my Parents, to the rest of the World"*

**–Author**

Made in the USA
Middletown, DE
02 February 2020

84080780R00116